Luke let out a soft wolf whistle.

"Dang, girl! Why do you keep that handsome mane bundled up like an old-maid schoolmarm?"

Katie tried to gather her hair back into some order and finally settled for pulling it to hang through the back of the cap.

"My husband didn't like me to wear it loose," she replied. "Too casual, he said. He wanted me to cut it to look more polished." Reflexively she rubbed the third finger on her left hand.

"Your husband sounds like a damn fool. Sorry, but that's how it looks to me. I'm glad you stood your ground."

"Me, too, not that it matters now."

"Sure it does—it matters to you." He studied her. "So...you ran away from home?"

Dear Reader,

Thanks for joining me and the Cameron family for the third novel in the Cameron's Pride series. *Luke's Ride* digs deep into the dangers cowboy bullfighters face every time the chute gate swings open and explores the true meaning of "cowboy up" both in and outside the bull-riding arena. I hope you'll enjoy becoming better acquainted with Luke Cameron and Katie Garrison, cheering them on through their challenges and triumphs. I'd love to hear from you with comments or questions: helen@helendeprima.com.

Enjoy the ride!

Helen DePrima

HEARTWARMING

Luke's Ride

———

Helen DePrima

HARLEQUIN® HEARTWARMING™

Recycling programs
for this product may
not exist in your area.

ISBN-13: 978-0-373-36833-4

Luke's Ride

Copyright © 2017 by Helen DePrima

All rights reserved. Except for use in any review, the reproduction or utilization of this work in whole or in part in any form by any electronic, mechanical or other means, now known or hereinafter invented, including xerography, photocopying and recording, or in any information storage or retrieval system, is forbidden without the written permission of the publisher, Harlequin Enterprises Limited, 225 Duncan Mill Road, Don Mills, Ontario M3B 3K9, Canada.

This is a work of fiction. Names, characters, places and incidents are either the product of the author's imagination or are used fictitiously, and any resemblance to actual persons, living or dead, business establishments, events or locales is entirely coincidental.

This edition published by arrangement with Harlequin Books S.A.

For questions and comments about the quality of this book, please contact us at CustomerService@Harlequin.com.

® and TM are trademarks of Harlequin Enterprises Limited or its corporate affiliates. Trademarks indicated with ® are registered in the United States Patent and Trademark Office, the Canadian Intellectual Property Office and in other countries.

Printed in U.S.A.

Helen DePrima grew up on horseback on her grandfather's farm near Louisville, Kentucky. After spending a week on a dude ranch in Colorado when she was twelve, Helen fell in love with all things Western.

She spent wonderful weeks on the same ranch during her high school summers. After graduation she headed for the University of Colorado to meet the cowboy of her dreams and live happily ever after in a home on the range. Instead she fell in love with a Jersey boy bound for vet school. She earned her degree in nursing and spent four years as a visiting nurse in northern Colorado while her husband attended Colorado State University.

After her husband graduated, they settled in New Hampshire, where Helen worked first in nursing and then rehabilitating injured and orphaned wildlife. After retirement, she turned again to earlier passions: writing and the West, particularly professional bull riding.

Books by Helen DePrima

Harlequin Heartwarming

Into the Storm
The Bull Rider

Visit the Author Profile page
at Harlequin.com for more titles.

To my husband, for his advice and support.

Acknowledgments

To my endlessly patient and supportive agent Stephany Evans who endures my megrims with good grace.

To Melissa Maupin, my valued First Reader for her encouragement and excellent suggestions.

To Earlene Fowler for her kindness and prayer.

Love you all!

CHAPTER ONE

A HAND TOUCHED his shoulder, a gentle shake at first, then rougher. "Luke, you're dreaming— wake up!"

He gave a last shuddering gasp and opened his eyes, still seeing the great bulk of the bull hurtling toward him, the dirt slamming up toward his face. He rubbed his eyes with both hands, trying to erase the images.

"Okay," he said. "I'm awake."

The hand shifted from his shoulder to his wrist as Betsy Fulton, his favorite night nurse at Hill Country Rehab, stepped from behind him to the side of his bed. Smart gal—he'd been known to strike out in the nightmare's grip, and from the hips up he was still quick and strong as a mountain lion.

Nights were always bad. All his life, Luke Cameron had worked hard and played harder, able to sleep like a healthy animal. Now he dreaded the hours after the bustle died down in the unit and he dawdled over dessert and

coffee—decaf only after 4:00 p.m.—as long
as anyone would hang around to gab. Eventually the night staff would chase him to his
room, citing the benefits of a normal sleep-
wake cycle. Alone in his bed, he fought off
sleep with its dreams of running and leaping,
laughing with his fellow bullfighters in the
face of danger, only to wake pinned to his bed
by the weight of his useless legs.

"Damn sirens," he said, wiping the sweat
of terror from his face with a shaking hand.
They didn't freak him out in the daytime, but
the banshee wail of any emergency vehicle
grabbed him by the throat in his sleep.

He'd been transported by ambulance twice
before during his career as a rodeo bullfighter, but he'd been out cold both times,
coming to in the ER or the recovery room
following surgery. This go-round, he'd been
awake and aware every second—the gritti-
ness of arena dirt between his teeth and the
explosion of pain in his lower spine, trying
to drag himself to safety using his elbows
and then Doc Barnett's voice asking if he
could move his legs. Followed by the howl
of the siren as the ambulance rushed him to
the nearest trauma center.

Betsy sponged his face with a cool cloth.

"I thought you might need company—a fire truck just went by. I guess you won't be hearing sirens much when you get home."

"Not hardly," he said. "We're the last spread on a dead-end road. Somebody gets hurt, we load 'em up and haul them to meet the paramedics. My dad had a heart attack a while back with a blizzard blowing in. My stepmom drove him an hour to the hospital with the roads closing down behind her. He probably wouldn't have made it if she'd waited for help to reach them."

Betsy flipped his pillow and filled his cup with ice water from the carafe on his nightstand. "I bet you'll be glad to get back to the wide-open spaces."

"You're right about that, darlin'." He could have gone from the hospital in Oklahoma City to a rehab facility closer to his family, but the trip from Oklahoma halfway across Texas to Austin, still immobilized in a body cast, had been grueling enough. Hill Country Rehab was Doc Barnett's home base. Every athlete involved in professional bull riding, cowboy or bullfighter, trusted Doc to deliver the best possible result.

Luke wasn't at all sure he was ready to leave. Here was security and a hand to hold in the night when the nightmares struck. He would hate showing that kind of weakness to his family except maybe to his father's wife, Shelby, who rarely put a foot wrong dealing with emotions. But he'd wanted to adjust to his new reality away from his family's well-meaning concern. He'd healed as much as he was going to, had mastered all the skills the therapists could teach him. Doc had told him bluntly his odds of walking again were slim at best even with the bone fragments teased from his spinal cord and rods stabilizing his lower back. Maybe Doc was right, but Luke had never been one to take much stock in the voice of authority.

IN SPITE OF his interrupted sleep, Luke was in the solarium at dawn watching, for the last time, as the sun came up across the Texas hills. Tomorrow morning he'd be somewhere in New Mexico and then in Colorado by nightfall the next day. He'd gone home beat up more than once, but always before he'd had a decent expectation of complete recovery.

Betsy's reflection appeared in the window behind his. "I was all set to bring you breakfast in bed your last morning with us, but you sneaked out again," she said. "Trying to make me look bad?"

From the time he was six or seven he'd groused about rolling out of bed before daybreak on the ranch; now he took a perverse pleasure in getting himself up and dressed before anyone came to help him.

"Gotta do as much for myself as I can," he said. "I won't have you around to baby me after today."

"I'm sure your folks will take good care of you. Will you be staying with them?"

He shrugged. "For now, till I get my feet on the ground." He gave a short laugh. "So to speak."

"Did you have your own place before the accident?"

"Darlin', it's a family ranch—we don't commute to work. I live at the main house, and my brother built a cabin half a mile up the creek when he got married. Maybe that's what I'll do once I figure out what kind of modifications I'll need."

He dreaded being dependent on his folks. Even more, he hated the thought of being useless—dead weight, like his legs.

He pivoted his wheelchair and headed toward the door. "You can help me pack. If I know Dad, he'll be ready to roll as soon as I get my final briefing from Doc Barnett." He propelled his chair down the hall with Betsy following but offering no help.

Sure enough, Jake Cameron, Shelby and Dr. Barnett were waiting for him when he returned from breakfast.

"Vacation's over," Doc said, peering at Luke over his gold-rimmed half-glasses. "I'm kicking you out."

Luke snorted. "Some vacation—I trained harder here than I ever did for dodging bulls." Images flashed through his mind of himself and his fellow bullfighters performing their split-second choreography to lure away a ton and a half of bucking bull from the cowboy rolling in the dirt. Even with a couple serious injuries, he'd stayed ahead of the game almost fifteen years until the odds finally caught up with him.

"Any last-minute instructions?" Jake asked. "Anything we shouldn't let him do?"

"He can do whatever he wants," Doc said. "He'll take some falls, but he knows how to take care of himself. The bull stepped on his back, not on his head."

He turned to Luke. "I've faxed outpatient orders to the PT department in Durango—

you can set up appointments once you get home."

"A visiting nurse came out to the ranch," Jake said. "She said Luke should be fine with the changes we made downstairs for Tom that time the bull fell with him."

Dr. Barnet nodded. "I figured you folks would be able to manage." He turned to Luke. "I'm sending your records to the University of Colorado School of Medicine. I know Denver's a haul from your corner of the state, but they're doing some great research on spinal injuries—I hope you'll get in touch with them." He handed him a card. "Here's the contact number."

"Maybe." Luke stuffed the card in his shirt pocket. Or maybe not. He'd had all privacy stripped from him in the hospital; he didn't much feel like becoming a case number in a research study.

As if he could read minds, Doc said, "I can't promise you'd get any personal benefit, but you could add to their data, maybe help other patients in the future."

Luke flushed. "Sure, I get that."

He switched gears. "Okay if I ride?" If he could get a horse between his knees, he could be of some use on the ranch. After all the years he'd complained about mending fences and clearing irrigation ditches, now he'd give up years of his life to stand knee-deep in icy snowmelt.

"Okay with me—riding would be good for your balance and core strength. But can you?" Doc shrugged. "You'll have to figure that out for yourself."

Luke couldn't imagine hanging on to his own cutting horse. Jigsaw had great cow sense but was so quick he'd left Luke sitting in the dirt more than once. Old Sadie, maybe, but she stood over sixteen hands and had gaits like a truck with square wheels.

"We're on it," Shelby said.

Count on Shelby to put him on horseback. She'd find him the right mount and train the crap out of it.

"Sure you don't want to go home by plane?" Jake asked. "It'll be two long days on the road. I can fly with you and let Shelby drive the van home."

"I can't," Luke said. He'd flown all over the US and Canada, to Australia and Brazil as well for bull-riding events, but the thought of being wheeled through the airport made his throat close up in near panic. Even worse would be the ordeal of security screening. Old ladies and kids in wheelchairs got hassled—they'd take a guy his age apart from his bones out. He'd never backed down from a challenge, but he wasn't ready for this one.

"I'll be fine," he said.

"I'll miss you," Betsy said and planted a kiss on his mouth, something he'd been angling for ever since he landed here three months ago.

"You could come with me," he said, wrapping his arm around her waist.

"I am so tempted, but my husband wouldn't care for the idea." She shook hands with Jake and Shelby. "Take care of this boy—he's one of the good ones."

Luke grabbed his gear bag off the floor and settled it on his lap. "Let's hit the trail."

CHAPTER TWO

KATHRYN GARRISON SHIVERED, chilled to the bone in her navy wool suit, the only outfit in her closet appropriate for a funeral. The calendar might say spring, but the March wind off Long Island Sound still held the bite of winter. She leaned closer to her husband, wishing Brad might think to put his arm around her shoulders, but he was staring toward the mourners amassed on the far side of her mother's grave.

She dragged her attention back to Reverend Blackstone's words—*no more suffering, gone to a better place, together again someday*—breathing past the hollow ache in her chest. She didn't begrudge a single moment of caring for her mother, but her release from twenty-four-hour nursing duties left her unsteady, as if she had entered a sudden calm after trudging forever against a pitiless gale.

Maybe some sense of normalcy would return tonight when she slept in her own bed instead of napping on the foldout sofa in her mother's room. She had stayed in her mother's house two extra nights caring for Blondie, Mama's old spaniel. Brad didn't like dogs and Blondie didn't like Brad, growling every time she saw him. After the funeral Blondie would live out her days with Aunt Joan, who had given Mama the puppy twelve years ago.

Another cold gust buffeted the canopy over the grave. A few more hours and Kathryn could return to her own home where a long, hot soak in the jetted tub would drive the chill from her bones. Maybe Brad would join her and they would lie together in each other's arms for the first time in months. Tomorrow she would start gathering the threads of her life as it had been before her mother's diagnosis of advanced ovarian cancer only four months ago.

Brad nudged her and she realized Reverend Blackburn had stopped speaking.

Kathryn stood and took the first yellow rose from the florist's box to lay on her mother's casket. After the rest of the roses had been placed by the other mourners, she was free to return to the limousine with its soft seats and comforting warmth.

Later, she would come back alone to bid

farewell, although she and Mama had said their goodbyes over the past months. Elizabeth Gabriel had endured the roller coaster of crisis and remission with lupus for nearly twenty years before the cancer had taken her down quickly. Kathryn had loved her mother dearly, but she was glad the ordeal was over for both of them.

One more trial: the obligatory post-funeral luncheon. Brad's old secretary, recently retired, would have booked a room at a local restaurant, but Brad's personal assistant had arranged the event at the country club. All Kathryn had to do was nod and smile as friends and relatives shared their memories of her mother.

The limousine pulled up at the canopied entrance of the Tudor-style mansion built by a Connecticut Valley tobacco baron, now home to the Rolling Hills Golf and Tennis Club. Kathryn followed Brad through the carved doors, half expecting to be stopped and ejected as an intruder. She was hopeless at tennis, and if she wanted to hike across rolling hills, she would rather carry binoculars and a camera than trundle a bag of golf clubs behind her. She understood Brad's explanations that big contracts could be landed on the links and afterward in the bar, but every function she was obliged to attend was an ordeal.

She followed him to a private dining room overlooking the golf course, still drab in its winter brown. A willowy blonde wearing a black pencil skirt with an ivory silk blouse looked up from a clipboard and hurried over to meet them.

"Mrs. Garrison, I'm Britt Cavendish, Mr. Garrison's personal assistant. Please accept my condolences—Mr. Garrison has told me what a wonderful woman your mother was and how devoted you've been, caring for her."

Kathryn had never met Britt, although she'd spoken to her on the phone a few times.

"Thank you for taking care of the luncheon arrangements, Britt," she said. They exchanged a few more pleasantries and then Britt excused herself to tell the headwaiter the hot dishes could be brought out to the buffet table.

Kathryn turned to Brad, but he had drifted away and stood in conversation with a couple she recognized from club dinners, although she wasn't sure of their names—*Vera and Charles something*, she thought.

At last, it was over. Tomorrow or the next day she would return to her mother's house to restore the parlor from sickroom to its original function, but tonight she wanted only peace and pampering and uninterrupted sleep.

She was nearly stumbling with fatigue by the time they left the country club. Brad pulled his Mercedes into the garage and unlocked the door leading to the kitchen. All was in perfect order, with gleaming surfaces and quietly purring appliances. Kathryn always kept the house up with no outside help, but Brad had gotten a weekly cleaning service during the months she had been caring for her mother. She had made quick trips home—forty miles each way—to pick up clothes or books she wanted to read during the long nights. Now she stood in the middle of the room as if she were a visitor.

"I guess I'll have a cup of tea," she said, mostly to break the silence.

"I'll make it for you," Brad said, slipping off his suit jacket and loosening his tie. "You can pour me a Scotch."

She watched him move around the kitchen with assurance, putting the kettle on the eight-burner Viking range, taking a mug and tea bags from the cabinet. He'd learned to do more for himself while she'd been gone, although she suspected he'd eaten most of his meals out. He looked like he'd spent more hours at the gym, as well. He'd never been soft, but he appeared leaner and more muscular—younger, somehow. Apparently her absence had done him no harm.

She opened the liquor cabinet and found his favorite Scotch behind bottles of cordials and brandies she didn't remember seeing before, probably gifts from sales reps at Christmas. His phone chimed while she was dropping ice cubes into a glass. He pulled it from his pocket and frowned before answering.

"No," he said after listening. "I can't make it tonight. Tell them I'll meet them tomorrow. It'll have to wait till then."

She touched his arm. "Brad, go if you need to—I know the funeral arrangements have taken up a lot of your time the past few days."

"Hold on," he said into the phone and turned to her. "You're sure? This deal has been simmering for weeks. These guys came up from the city with no warning—"

"It's okay. I don't mind. I need some time to decompress anyway. You won't be late, will you?"

"I promise I won't. I'll pick up Chinese on the way home."

He spoke into the phone again. "Tell them I can be at the office in half an hour—we can talk there or maybe go out for drinks, but I promised my wife I'd be home early."

He picked up his jacket. "You're sure you're okay? I can call them back—"

She waved him toward the door. "Just go and take care of business. We can both relax better if your mind isn't on work."

He kissed her cheek and left.

The kettle began to whistle. She poured boiling water into a squat iron teapot and added two Earl Grey teabags, leaving it to steep while she made her way through the spacious downstairs rooms. She and Brad had occupied this house only a few years, and like the country club, she wasn't at ease in the elegant open-concept rooms.

She did like the big soaker tub in the master bathroom. She also loved the kitchen, with its high-end appliances and acres of marble counter space, but would have enjoyed it more if she'd had a big family to cook for. An only child, she had hoped for sons and daughters with Brad's blond, college-boy good looks or her own chestnut hair and freckles, but it hadn't happened. Maybe it was time to find out why or why not. And there was always adoption. Thirty-four wasn't too old to start a family.

She returned to the kitchen and set dishes and candles on the breakfast table before carrying her steaming mug upstairs to place on the edge of the tub. The tensions of the long day dissolved while she sipped her tea and relaxed in the swirling, lavender-scented water.

She had set the timer on the tub jets for twenty minutes so she wouldn't miss the sound of the garage door opening if Brad returned early. She wanted to greet him in the kitchen, ready to pour his drink. When the bubbles died down, she climbed out and padded to her closet, taking out a silky robe the bronzy green of new willow leaves. Brad had bought it for her two birthdays ago, calling her his Celtic princess. She brushed her hair until it shone and returned to the kitchen just as she heard his car door slam.

When he walked through the door carrying a takeout bag from the China Dragon, she wrapped her arms around his waist under his jacket and gave him the kiss she'd been saving for months.

"Hey!" he said with a laugh when the kiss ended. "Maybe I should have stayed away longer."

"Not a minute longer." She set the bag on the counter and peeled his jacket off his shoulders.

She sniffed and frowned. "I must have sprayed you with my cologne while I was dressing for the funeral." She couldn't recall using it but couldn't say she hadn't. Most perfumes were too heavy and gave her a headache, but she ordered this light, woodsy fragrance from a cottage boutique on Cape Cod.

"I'll take your suit to the cleaner's tomorrow," she said and hung the jacket over a chair.

They ate by candlelight almost without speaking, he nursing his Scotch and she sipping a glass of wine, before they climbed to the bedroom with their arms wrapped around each other. Kathryn laid her robe across the cedar chest at the foot of the bed and slipped between the sheets. When he joined her, she slept at last in his arms, cherished and utterly at peace.

CHAPTER THREE

LUKE REVELED IN the first few hours on the road home, almost like returning to his life before his injury. He'd taken this route dozens of times driving to and from bull-riding events, mostly with his brother at the wheel and then alone after Tom retired from competition five years ago.

After a career traveling every weekend to a different city and working on the ranch during the week, almost three months of confinement had been first cousin to a prison sentence. With his wheelchair stowed in the back of the van his dad had rented for the trip, he could lean back in the front seat and enjoy the passing scenery. The Austin suburbs gave way to countryside with armies of white wind turbines marching to the horizon. Farms petered out to rangeland; the terrain became more broken the farther west they drove. Buttes rose in the distance like tables for an extinct race of giants.

Jake was describing this spring's relatively trouble-free calving season when the muscle spasm hit Luke. He doubled in his seat with a grunt of agony.

Jake swerved the van onto a gravelly ranch road and swiveled in alarm. "What's happening? What can we do?"

"Gotta straighten my legs," Luke said through gritted teeth as the agonizing cramp brought tears to his eyes. He got his door open and released his seat belt.

Shelby was beside him in an instant, helping him turn sideways and extending his legs to brace his heels on the door's armrest. "Tell me where to rub," she said.

"Back of my thighs." He fumbled a medicine vial from his shirt pocket and reached a hand behind him. "Water bottle, Pop."

Jake slapped the bottle in his hand, and Luke swallowed a capsule with one long gulp. Shelby's strong hands had already begun to loosen the muscles. The medication to relieve the spasm would do the rest once it kicked in.

Jake patted Luke's shoulder. "This happen often?" His voice shook.

Luke swallowed to steady his voice. "More than I like. My nerve pathways are all screwed up. Sometimes it feels like knives or broken bones, mostly when I don't move around enough."

"Would you like to lie down for a while?" Shelby kept rubbing. "I brought along an air mattress—I can fold down one of the rear seats so you can stretch out."

Luke sighed. "Probably a good idea." The attacks exhausted him, and the pill would make him drowsy, as well. "Sorry to be a bother."

Jake's voice cracked like a whip. "That better be the last time I hear you talk that way. You're no more bother than your mother was with lupus."

Luke's chin dropped on his chest. "Sorry, Pop—it's still a lot to get used to."

Shelby settled Luke's feet on the van's running board. "I'll have you set up in a minute. Do you need the wheelchair?"

He had driven himself like a slave during physical therapy to maintain upper-body strength; now with Shelby to guide his legs, he managed to pivot himself into the rear of the van and lie down. Jake pulled back onto the road; soon the steady hum on the tires and the muted twang of country-and-western music on the radio lulled Luke to a drowsy half wakefulness.

Random thoughts rambled through his mind—uppermost was the yearning to be home. Here he was, thirty-six years old and totally screwed—no wife or kids, unsure of his future. Though he was the older son, he'd never shared the same passionate devotion to the ranch, to the whole family tradition, his dad and brother did. Now his heart reached toward Cameron's Pride like a wounded animal seeking refuge in its den. Maybe he'd walk again, maybe he wouldn't, but he understood for the first time how generations of Camerons had endured by drawing strength from the green valleys and red-rock ravines.

The van slowed, breaking into his reverie, and gravel grated under the tires. He jacked himself up on his elbows as Jake pulled into the parking lot of a low adobe-front building with a simple sign above the door: Ana's Kitchen. He knew the place; he and Tom had stopped here for meals.

The side door of the van slid open. "We checked this out on our way to Austin," Shelby said. "Good food and a wheelchair-accessible restroom."

Luke's heart dropped like a shot bird, jerking him to the reality he'd now be planning his life around his disability. He settled his black Stetson on his head and eased into his wheelchair, rolling into the dim interior of the restaurant while his dad held the door open.

A round-faced hostess with black hair in a sleek braid showed them to a table that would accommodate his chair. They all ordered coffee and studied the menu. The food at the rehab center hadn't been bad, but Luke's mouth watered at the prospect of good Southwest food with plenty of beef and beans, cheese and green chili. And real fresh-made tortillas—he could see a skinny kid in the kitchen slapping out dough into thin circles.

Luke was trying to decide between pork enchiladas and carne asada when he became aware of a little boy, maybe six, standing beside his chair. He turned with a smile. He liked kids, had been thinking lately about having his own, especially with his younger brother's two always underfoot at the home ranch. Fat chance of that now. Doc Barnett had said there was no physical reason he couldn't father a child, but who would want him like this, a broken man?

"Hey, pard," he said. "What's your name?"

"I'm Danny, sir." The child held out a tiny paw. "My daddy's got a chair like yours because he's a soldier and he got blown up in the war. Did you get blown up, too?"

"No, I got stepped on by a bull," Luke said, shaking the boy's hand. "I'm a cowboy."

Danny's eyes got big. "A real cowboy?"

"Pretty real." At least he used to be—who knew what he'd be in the future?

A young blonde woman appeared from the direction of the restrooms and hurried over to the table. "I'm so sorry Danny's been bothering you," she said.

"He's no bother," Luke said. "Danny, your daddy's a hero—he's lucky to have you for his top hand." He touched his hat brim. "Thank your husband for his service, ma'am, and thank you, too."

She nodded, tears in her eyes, and led her son to their table.

Jake and Shelby sat in silence during the exchange. Now Jake surprised Luke by reaching across the table to shake his hand. "I reckon you made that little guy's day."

Luke shrugged. "Little enough I could say.

A lot of veterans have it lots worse than me—
it's just my legs that don't work."

He'd tried to keep his relative good fortune
in mind through the drudgery of learning new
ways to manage daily activities, functions
he'd never given a thought to in the past. At
least he had full control of his body except
for his legs, and he planned to keep fighting
against all logic to walk again even if his
chances were slim.

By LATE AFTERNOON the next day, Luke regret-
ted his decision not to fly. Jake and Shelby
had done everything in their power to make
the trip comfortable for him, but the hours
in the van and the effort of personal care in
the motel's impersonal setting exhausted him
more than his rigorous exercises at the rehab
center.

"We have to make a quick stop to pick
Lucy up," Jake said as they approached Durango. "She's going to drive the van back tomorrow."

"Lucy's in Colorado? I thought she was acting in a play on Broadway."

"Off Broadway," Shelby said. "And the play
folded. She's going to do summer stock in New
Hampshire starting in June, but right now she's

home managing the Silver Queen. Marge had double knee replacements last month."

"Ouch," Luke said. "Not fun." He'd had both knees rebuilt after tendon injuries. And Marge Bowman was no spring chicken, although she always seemed ageless. "Lucy's running the whole show?"

"Pretty much," Shelby said. "Marge decided they would do just breakfast and lunch, so Lucy moved into the apartment upstairs and opens in the morning. Jo and I have been pitching in for breakfast until the regular waitress shows up to work lunch."

Jake double-parked across the street from the Victorian storefront with Silver Queen Saloon and Dance Emporium in ornate gold letters across the wide window. He honked the horn; a few minutes later a slim young woman wearing jeans and a leather jacket came out carrying an insulated bag.

Lucy Cameron climbed into the back seat beside Shelby and leaned forward to kiss Luke's cheek. "Hey, big bro—good to have you back."

He reached over his shoulder to ruffle her ruddy curls. "Good to see you, too, Red."

She slapped his hand away, a ritual performed many times. "Don't call me Red." She settled in and latched her seat belt. "I brought chicken fricassee and biscuits plus a peach pie, enough for a small army."

Shelby tapped Jake's shoulder. "Home, driver."

Half an hour later they rolled under the Cameron's Pride ranch sign, and Luke sighed with relief. He would have kissed the ground if he'd been able to get up off his face afterwards.

He noticed at once that modifications had been made for his benefit. A blacktop parking pad had replaced the graveled area by the back door and a ramp sloped up along the side of the house. He swung himself into his chair and wheeled up the ramp and into the spacious kitchen.

By the time Lucy had unpacked the food, Luke heard his brother Tom's voice outside, answered by his wife, Joanna. The kitchen door slammed and running footsteps clattered on the wood floor. Luke locked the wheels on his chair just as a small red-haired whirlwind flung herself at him.

"Uncle Luke, you're home! I missed you! I lost a tooth, see?" His seven-year-old niece, Missy, stretched her mouth in a monkey's grin to demonstrate. "Can I ride in your chair with you?"

"Sure you can, Shortcake." He pulled her more securely into his lap as her four-year-old brother, JJ, pounded into the kitchen and scrambled up to join her.

Dang, it was good to be home!

CHAPTER FOUR

A HOWLING MARCH wind woke Kathryn during the night. She shivered and snuggled closer to Brad to sleep again.

The morning's first light revealed at least six inches of fresh snow covering grass that had begun to show hints of green. Flakes still swirled, almost hiding the woods behind the house. Judging from the low hum of the standby generator, power lines must be down.

Brad strode into the kitchen dressed in the clothes he wore to construction sites and pulled boots and a heavy coat from the closet. "No time for breakfast," he said. "I need to get to the office. We've got projects in trouble from Stamford to Providence." He slammed through the door to the garage and Kathryn heard the roar of the snowblower.

She watched from the front window while he blasted a path down the driveway and then returned to gun his Mercedes out onto the unplowed street.

She sighed and returned to the kitchen. She had scarcely filled her mug with coffee when she heard the garage door opening again. Brad stamped in, running his hand through his hair so that it stood in stiff spikes like an angry cat's fur.

"There's a big pine down across the end of the street," he said. "No telling when the town will get around to moving it."

"The downside of a secluded country setting," she said, hoping to defuse his anger and frustration. Theirs was one of only six houses on a cul-de-sac bordering a conservation area. Although Kathryn wasn't fond of the house, she loved the easy access to the woods and swamp just out their back door.

"At least you'll have time now for a decent breakfast," she said. "Pancakes or waffles? And I still have some of that good bacon we got from Vermont."

He scowled but then took a deep breath. "Waffles, I guess."

"Waffles coming up." She took his coat from him, pausing to pat his shoulder as she carried it to the closet. "Being marooned could be kind of fun."

The scowl returned, with interest. "You have no idea what you're talking about."

"I used to know, when I was working for you and your dad," she said, stung by his curt reply. Since Brad's father had retired and an architect had joined the firm, she didn't feel welcome in the new glossy chrome-and-glass offices. "Now I'm not so sure."

He stared at her for a long moment before turning away.

She prepared breakfast in silence. He caught her wrist as she set the plate before him. "Look, I'm sorry I snapped at you. This snow has hit at the worst possible time. We'll have to wait till the ground dries out before we can start excavating or the heavy equipment will bog down. We'll be behind before the season even gets underway."

The spring construction start-up was always stressful, but a mini break like this would be welcome. Kathryn had been working hard to ready her mother's house for its next occupants. She couldn't bring herself to put it on the market. Instead she had offered it for the cost of upkeep to her cousin Greg Gabriel, newly out of the Marines—little enough to thank him for his service.

She bent and kissed Brad's cheek. "We've both been under a strain," she said. "Enjoy your waffles while they're hot. We'll hope the snow lets up and they get the road cleared soon."

The snow persisted most of the day, and they heard no chain saws working on the downed tree. Brad paced laps around the kitchen island, barking instructions into his phone and muttering curses at the end of each call.

Kathryn cooked Brad's favorite dinner, pot roast from his mother's recipe. She held him close in the night but lay awake sad and frustrated when she wasn't able to penetrate his angry preoccupation.

When the town plow finally ground its way up their street late the next day, she was glad to see Brad roar out of the driveway. Once he resolved all the construction crises, maybe she could talk him into a brief getaway, a few days on Cape Cod or at an inn on the Maine coast. She laughed at her fantasy—she wouldn't be able to pry him loose until construction wound down in late fall.

She saw little of Brad during the next week. He left the house early and returned late, usually eating dinner somewhere between job sites and falling into bed with only a few words to her.

She filled her days with sorting through

the contents of her mother's house. The work might seem a sad occupation, but she rediscovered forgotten memories, taking comfort that her mother's suffering was over.

Kathryn's last chore was rearranging the top floor of her grandparents' Victorian to accommodate any furniture Greg and his wife Allie might want to store there to make room for their own possessions. The attic had always been a magical place for her. When she was very small, she had played with her dolls under the south-facing window while her mother hung bundles of herbs to dry under the rafters. On Kathryn's sixth birthday, her mother had placed an old bridge lamp and a bookcase beside a shabby wing chair to create a private reading nook. From her aerie, Kathryn could look out into the top of the copper beech in the backyard. Now in early spring the budding branches framed a view of the old carriage house still holding her mother's gardening tools and where her father had restored a succession of antique autos and refinished secondhand furniture.

She began sorting through the trunks and boxes shoved under the eaves. In a camelback trunk she found a white tin bread box decorated with red and yellow tulip decals.

Inside were letters tied in bundles with the
gardener's twine from long-ago herb swags.
Arranged in chronological order beginning
nearly twenty years earlier, each bore the letterhead Cameron's Pride, Hesperus, Colorado
and were signed by Annie Cameron.

Kathryn began reading the earliest one.

Dear Elizabeth,
Too bad we met under such sorry cir-
cumstances, but I'm glad you felt well
enough to travel to the Grand Canyon.
Like you, I'm always grateful when the
Red Wolf lets me do something I've
looked forward to. Thanks for letting me
know what a great time you and your
husband had the rest of your trip.

She laid the letter down. Her parents had
taken a driving trip to the Southwest her
freshman year in college. Her mother's lupus
had flared up, landing her in the hospital in
Albuquerque, but a simple adjustment in
medication had solved the problem. She must
have met Annie Cameron there. Her mother
often spoke of her struggle with lupus erythe-
matosus as "fighting off the Red Wolf." Had

she thought up the expression or adopted it from Annie?

The afternoon sunlight was beginning to fade, so Kathryn switched on the old lamp and continued reading. Annie's letters carried her into a foreign world of cattle and horses, mountains and desert, introducing her husband, Jake, their young daughter, Lucy, and their sons, Luke and Tom, both involved with the sport of bull riding. Annie hadn't written much about her illness except in one of the last letters, telling Kathryn's mother the disease had damaged her kidneys to the point she needed a transplant.

My sons are mad at me because I won't accept a kidney from either of them. I don't know whose job is more dangerous, Tom riding bulls or Luke fighting them, but I can't leave either of them with only one kidney in case they get injured. Luckily my Jake is a good match, so he draws the short straw—he would move heaven and earth to help me.

The sun had almost set by the time Kathryn unfolded the last letter, dated more than ten years ago. Jake Cameron had written a brief note saying his wife had died from complications following the kidney transplant. Tears filled Kathryn's eyes for Annie, for her own mother's long decline and for the suffering both women had endured.

Kathryn wondered if Annie's family would like to have these letters, this wonderful chronicle of their lives, but she didn't recall seeing the name Cameron in her mother's address book. Then she remembered she had given her mother a new book five Christmases ago; inactive addresses wouldn't have been transferred. Maybe she could call the post office in Hesperus, Colorado, for an exact mailing address or check online. She carried the letters downstairs, thinking to show them to Brad.

The attic had been warm enough as heat rose from the lower floors, but the kitchen seemed unnaturally chilly. She turned up the thermostat and heard no answering hum from the cellar. Frowning, she peered down the stairs. She'd had the furnace serviced in the fall, but it was almost twenty years old. A quick inspection showed no flicker of flame from the boiler.

She sighed and dialed the heating contractor's number.

"Not till tomorrow morning?" she said after describing the problem. "I guess that's no big deal—the temperature won't drop enough for the pipes to freeze."

Next she called Brad. "The furnace just quit," she said. "Someone's coming over first thing in the morning. I don't know how early that might be, so I guess I'll sleep here. I'm sorry—I had a nice dinner planned."

"Don't worry about it. Looks like we might have a thunderstorm, and I know you don't like to drive in the rain. I'll grab something to eat and put in a couple more hours at work. You sure you'll be warm enough?"

"I'll be fine. I bought an electric heater for Mom's room." She'd always felt cold. "I'll see you tomorrow evening."

"I may be late," he said. "The Springfield project has turned into a hairball. I'll be there all day, maybe into the evening."

"Just don't drive too tired," she said. "I'll have supper waiting."

She ended the call and took a can of chili from the pantry. While it heated, she finished the list she'd been compiling for her cousin—whom to call for plumbing and electrical problems, who delivered oil and repaired the furnace, how to jiggle the light switch beside the front door to turn on the porch light. Greg could call her with questions, of course, but she wanted to make his occupancy go as smoothly as possible.

She finished her meal and was peering into the freezer in search of ice cream when a knock sounded at the back door. She switched on the porch light and recognized Frank Dutton, who had serviced the furnace ever since its installation.

"I saw Gabriel on my work order for tomorrow," he said. "I figured I'd stop on my way home and see if this might be an easy fix—I didn't want to leave you ladies in the cold overnight."

"Bless you, Frank," Kathryn said. "Although there's just me here—Mom died a few weeks ago."

His face screwed up in distress. "Say, I didn't hear about that. I'm sure sorry—she was a nice lady, always sent me off with a piece of her applesauce cake."

He hefted his tool bag. "Let's take a look at that furnace. It's got some years on it, but you've always kept it serviced—should be good for a while longer."

He clumped down the stairs, and soon Kathryn heard clanking and banging. A short time later the whoosh of the burner floated up the stairs. Frank emerged from the cellar wiping his hands on a square of red cloth.

"Good as new," he said. "It was just a clogged valve. You selling the house?"

"Not any time soon," Kathryn said. "My cousin just got out of the Marines, so he and his wife are moving in to take care of it. Maybe they'll want to buy it sometime down the road."

"Good for you. I'm a Navy man myself, but the jarheads deserve all the perks they can get. Just tell him to ask for me if the furnace gives him any trouble."

The house was deathly quiet after Frank's service van rolled down the driveway. Kathryn shivered. She wasn't afraid to stay in the house alone, but announcing her mother's death again had brought home its reality, the utter finality, as nothing had done before. She couldn't bear to be alone tonight. She needed the warmth and comfort of her husband's arms.

Only eight o'clock—she could be home in less than an hour. She locked the back door and set the box containing Annie Cameron's letters on the front seat of her Volvo. The air was heavy with the threat of rain, but the first drops held off until she pulled into her own driveway.

A dim light shone through the front window from the kitchen and another from their bedroom—Brad was probably already upstairs, watching TV or getting ready for bed. If she didn't open the garage door, she could slip in quietly and surprise him.

She stepped out of her shoes in the entryway and padded barefoot into the kitchen. A soft rumble overhead told her the tub jets were running. Brad must be relaxing after a hard day, although he seldom used the big soaker tub without her.

She decided to carry two glasses of wine upstairs and join him. She crossed to the wine keeper and picked up the cork already lying on the counter; he must have taken a bottle up with him. When she reached toward the overhead rack, she saw two glasses were missing. Puzzled, she looked around for the missing glass, and then her heart stopped before beginning again in slow painful rhythm. A woman's jacket hung on a chair in the breakfast nook. A purse and scarf lay on the table.

She set the cork down like an unexploded bomb precisely where she had found it and lifted the scarf. A whiff of her own cologne struck her like a slap in the face. The name on the cards she found in the purse came almost as an anticlimax: Britt Cavendish.

Moving without conscious volition, she drifted to the stairs. She froze with a foot on the first step when she heard Brad's laugh answered by a woman's giggle. The grumble of the tub jets ceased.

Kathryn fled through the kitchen as if pursued by demons; she would never be able to live with the sight awaiting her at the top of the stairs. Into her shoes, out through the rain to her car. She had enough presence of mind to put the gear into Neutral, letting the vehicle roll down to the street before starting the engine.

The downpour lashed at the windshield all the way to her mother's house while lightning streaked from heaven to earth. Some benevolent angel guided her safely—in her present state, she didn't care if she lived or died.

She sat in the driveway while raindrops ran down the car windows like endless weeping. Thunder boomed and lightning illuminated the black sky in strobe-like bursts while she sat dry-eyed, wounded too deep for tears.

Brad had been her first and only lover—she had never considered settling for a cheap thrill outside marriage. She might have understood if he'd said he'd been lonely with her gone so much, that he'd fallen to temptation in a single lapse that would never be repeated. Instead his betrayal was deliberate, calculated and ongoing. As the ultimate insult, he had ordered her special perfume for another woman—maybe for many women— to divert suspicion.

By the time the storm moved on, her course was set, her resolve hard as the rocky New England shoreline. She laid her hand on the box containing Annie Cameron's letters, a testament to faithfulness and courage, before entering her mother's house. That night she slept as if she hadn't a care in the world.

CHAPTER FIVE

A HORSE'S NEIGH and the slam of a car door woke Luke before dawn. The bedside clock read five thirty, the usual beginning of a workday on the ranch. Great—now his dad would be on his case for goofing off when he should be halfway to the barn or at least sitting down to breakfast.

He started to swing his legs out of bed before reality flooded back in a bitter wave. He flopped down and considered his options: hole up and feel sorry for himself or get dressed and try to make himself useful.

He pulled on jeans and socks before propping himself up on the edge of the bed, waiting to make sure of his balance before reaching for a shirt. He had just transferred to his wheelchair when he heard a soft knock at his door.

"You up, Luke?" Shelby asked. "Ready for some French toast?"

"Five minutes," he said and dragged on his boots before heading into the bathroom.

He wheeled into place at the kitchen table and accepted the mug of strong New Orleans coffee Shelby poured for him.

"Man, I've missed this," he said. "Makes other coffee taste kind of sad."

"I told your dad to stop ordering that for me when the blizzard almost wiped us out," she said, "but he bought it anyway."

"You deserve it, lady—you kept us all going through that trouble."

She waved his words aside. "You feel like working today?"

"You need me to peel potatoes?"

"Later, maybe. You know Cinnamon, that roan filly I started last fall? Something about her trot feels off to me. I'd like you to ride behind me and tell me what you see. You've got the best eye in the family."

Luke snorted. "I doubt I can keep up in my wheelchair."

"I don't expect you to. You ready to meet your new legs?"

He plowed through his breakfast in record time and drained his coffee before donning his hat and denim jacket.

"Lead on," he said. "Time for me to get back in the saddle."

Out the back door he discovered a narrow blacktop walk now led to the barn. The dirt floor inside had been raked smooth and rolled flat; he could propel his chair almost as easily as on the paved surface. Later he might fret over the extra trouble everyone had taken for his benefit, but now his eagerness to be active overrode all other thoughts.

Getting on a horse would go a long way toward making him feel like more than half a man.

He followed Shelby to the side door opening to the horse pasture and halted beside her as she gave a piercing whistle. Several horses paused in their grazing, but one lifted its head and started toward the barn.

"Whoa! That's my ride?" A flashy Appaloosa gelding, dark chestnut with dramatic white markings on his rump, halted in front of Shelby and dropping his muzzle into her hand.

"I knew you'd fix me up," Luke said, "maybe with a nice old bombproof mare, but I didn't expect anything like this."

"I got him from a rescue in Utah," Shelby said. "His owner died and left them a chunk of money if they'd take special care placing his horse. He's been used for hunting, so he's not likely to blow up with you."

"This guy have a name?"

"Luke, meet Duke. Duke, here's your new person."

"Duke and Luke—that's kind of much. How about Dude? He sure is one handsome dude."

The gelding dipped his head into Luke's lap, inviting a scratch under his mane.

"Give him this." Shelby handed Luke a piece of hard candy. "He's a sucker for butterscotch."

"Whatever you say, stepmama. Just tell me what to do." Luke fed Dude the candy and was rewarded with a gentle nudge.

"I'll tack him up for you this time, but you'll be able to do it yourself with a little practice."

She walked into the barn with the horse following like a well-trained dog. He stood in the passageway without hitching while she curried dust and loose grass from his still winter-shaggy coat.

"Here's how you'll do it," she said, and tapped Dude's foreleg. The horse slowly collapsed, folding all four legs beneath him. She lifted a saddle from a tack chest beside the wall and set it in place, steadying it while Dude stood again to let her fasten the cinch. He ducked his head into the hackamore she held out.

"Dude's trained to go bridleless," she said, "but you'll probably feel more secure with reins until you guys get to know each other." She tapped the foreleg and the horse lay down again.

"Think you can get aboard?"

"I can sure as heck try," Luke said, eagerness running through his veins for the first time since his wreck. He pivoted his chair parallel to Dude's side and locked the wheels. The saddle was almost level with his seat, allowing him to slide on sidesaddle and drag his right leg across the horn.

Dude lay still as a statue except for turning his head to watch.

"Well, all right!" Luke knew he was grinning like a fool, excited as a teenager with his driver's license. "Where's his gas pedal?"

"A couple things first," Shelby said. "I wasn't sure how steady you'd be, so I've added seat belts for your legs." She pulled straps with Velcro tabs from under the saddle skirts and snugged them across Luke's thighs. "I doubt you'll need these once your balance improves, but I don't want you landing on your head in the meanwhile."

She fitted his feet into the stirrups and secured them with wide elastic bands. "Now you can tell him, 'Dude, up.'"

Luke grabbed the saddle horn with both hands to hide their shaking. "Dude, up."

The horse snorted and scrambled to his feet.

Luke laughed in sheer pleasure: he was riding, actually riding, even if he did have to be tied to his saddle. For the first time since his injury, he felt close to normal.

"Take him out into the pasture while I saddle Cinnamon," Shelby said, and turned away to lead a strawberry roan filly from a box stall.

Luke guided Dude out the side door, grateful for Shelby's matter-of-fact lack of hovering. He reined the horse in easy circles, pleased to discover he felt steady in the saddle with no hint of vertigo. He could work—he could ride fence lines, he could check mineral tubs and help move cattle between pastures.

Shelby came out of the barn a few minutes later mounted on the roan filly and they rode side by side to a level track cutting across the pasture.

"I'll jog ahead so you can watch her gait and see if you can spot any problem. Dude has gaits like glass—he should be an easy ride for you."

"Shelby, I'd marry you if you weren't already married to Dad."

She laughed. "Just help me figure out Cinnamon's problem." She rode ahead of him at a slow trot.

Dude followed in a smooth gait no harder to sit than a walk. Luke reveled in the freedom of movement for a moment before concentrating on Shelby's mount.

"She's going a little short on the off hind leg," he called to her.

Shelby reined in to let him catch up. "I knew it was a hind leg," she said, "but I couldn't tell right or left. Let me ride past you—maybe you can pinpoint exactly what's happening."

Luke halted Dude to the side of the track and watched while Shelby jogged by. "Got it," he said. "She's going stiff on the pastern. Just a little, but that's what you're feeling."

Shelby rejoined him. "You just earned your

keep for today. We'll take it easy on the way back."

Luke's heart dropped at the prospect of returning to the bondage of his wheelchair. "What's Dad doing? Maybe we could swing by where he's working."

"He rode over to the Bucks' this morning to help Oscar enlarge his corral."

"Say, I could ride over and say hi to Auntie Rose." Not exactly his aunt, but the matriarch of the Ute branch of the Cameron clan. "I've sure missed her fry bread."

"An hour's ride each way. You think that's a good idea first time out?"

He sighed. "I guess not. Maybe I could stop by to see Jo and the kids on the way home." Pretty silly, but he longed to share his progress.

"Jo's in Durango helping Lucy at the Queen today," Shelby said. "How about we check the new calves here in the lower pasture before we head back? I don't think Cinnamon will take any harm from a little exercise."

Luke got the message. Shelby wasn't going to lecture him, but she wasn't going to let him do anything stupid, either. They continued at a leisurely pace through the cow-calf herd to the far edge of the lower pasture.

By the time they turned back toward the barn, he had to admit, at least to himself, maybe he'd overdone it just a little. The muscles in his back and shoulders ached from the simple act of staying in the saddle, something he had done reflexively longer than he could remember. What sensation he had in his lower back registered the presence of titanium rods in his spine; he was hard put not to brace both hands on the horn to ease the ache. The barn, partially hidden by the willows along the creek, looked to be at least a mile distant, and his wheelchair beckoned with its promise of comfort.

He was so focused on surviving his first outing he didn't notice the yellow pickup parked by the barn until Shelby said, "Looks like we've got company."

Great—earlier he had craved an audience, but now he just wanted to get off Dude with some shred of dignity. At least he wouldn't have to perform in front of a stranger. The lanky blond cowboy sprawled on the tack trunk was an old friend, practically kin.

"Well, look at you. One day back and already working," Mike Farley said. "What do you think of your horse?"

"I think Shelby's done me proud. Have you seen his trick?"

"Just heard about it from Lucy," Mike said.

"Line him up with your chair," Shelby said, and handed Luke a light crop. "Just tap his left knee."

At the signal, Dude folded his legs as he had done earlier and turned his head toward Luke.

"Let me guess—he wants his treat, right?" Luke took the butterscotch from Shelby and fed it to the horse, who snorted with pleasure.

"Think you can get to your chair without help?" she asked.

Luke swallowed. He'd made it into the saddle pretty easily, but now the distance between the horse and the wheelchair looked like the Grand Canyon. He squared his shoulders and grabbed his right jeans cuff to swing his leg over Dude's withers.

The spasm struck without warning; he doubled up and fell forward. Only Mike's quick leap kept him from pitching facedown in the dirt. He found himself seated in his chair with Mike steadying his shoulders while Shelby massaged his legs until the cramp eased.

He straightened and took a deep breath.

"Thanks, guys," he said, embarrassed that his voice shook.

Mike squatted on his heels beside the chair. "Man, you scared me—you all right now?"

Luke managed a crooked grin. "Better than a few minutes ago. You looking for Lucy? She's in Durango."

"Yeah, I've been washing dishes for her at the Queen." He held up his hands. "Much more of that and I'll have to build up new calluses. No, I came to see you. I need a favor."

"Like what?" Luke couldn't imagine what he could do for Mike. He'd be no use at the Farley ranch five miles up the road, and he knew nothing useful about Mike's second career as an accountant and sports agent for a handful of bull riders.

"You guys go to the house," Shelby said. "I'll take care of Cinnamon and Dude."

Luke made no objection when Mike pushed his wheelchair. The muscle spasm, which added to his exhaustion, had left him limp as an old rope. Mike wheeled him into the kitchen and set about making coffee, the universal remedy. Once Luke sucked down a full mug and eaten one of Shelby's homemade beignets, he revived enough to ask what Mike had in mind.

Mike leaned forward with his hands wrapped around his mug. "It's my busy time with tax prep, and I'm trying to carry my share with calving at our ranch, too."

"And help Lucy at the Queen," Luke said. "You treat her way better than she deserves. You want me to smack some sense into her?"

"No way! It'll all even out someday—I gotta keep believing that. Here's my problem. The gal who helps me with the preliminary prep is having a rough pregnancy. Her doc says she has to stay flat on her back till she delivers or she'll lose the baby. One big job she does for me is sorting through expense receipts for allowable deductions. You think you could handle that?"

"I could screw things up royally," Luke said. "I don't know squat about tax deductions."

"Sure you do. You've been sending me your receipts for five years—you know what's legit and what's not. Just a few clients, all bull riders—kids who've never earned more than gas money mowing lawns or bagging groceries. Now they're getting big checks and have to keep track of all their deductible expenses."

Luke shook his head. "I don't know—I

could try, I guess. If you really think I could help."

"Just take a look, okay?" Mike stood. "I've got the files in my rig." He left the kitchen without waiting for an answer and returned carrying a cardboard fruit box containing a dozen or so fat manila envelopes.

Luke pulled one from the box and spilled its contents on the table, a whole year's worth of hotel statements, airline tickets, car rentals and receipts from gas stations, restaurants and convenience stores.

"Just do your best—help me save these guys some money. Tag anything that doesn't look kosher and make notes if you think important stuff is missing. Riders' expenses only, not wives and kids."

Mike's plea stirred Luke's interest. He could probably figure this out—he could be of use to someone.

"I'll give it my best shot," he said.

CHAPTER SIX

KATHRYN MOVED THROUGH the last day of her old life like a perfectly programmed robot. She had gone to sleep with a list of must-dos firm in her mind and wrote down the sequence over her morning coffee. First she visited the bank and raided a money market account, withdrawing no more than she figured she deserved for fifteen years of faithful service. Next she stopped at her mother's bank where she deposited it in a new checking account with a debit card.

At the mall she bought a new cell phone with a prepaid plan and new number before going to the AAA office to pick up maps. She would have GPS, of course, but she had no address to enter other than Hesperus, Colorado. Paper maps would help her choose what route she might decide to follow.

At times the memory of Brad's laughter and Britt's answering giggle pushed into her consciousness, but she silenced it with ruthless determination. Time enough for tears when she had accomplished all she needed to do.

In the office of Robert Foster, her mother's lawyer, she signed numerous documents.

"You're sure you want to do this, Kathryn?" His kind old face furrowed with distress. "After one incident?"

"Once that I caught him," she said. "This was too slick to be the first time. All those evenings working late, and the last-minute overnight business trips... I was too dumb to catch on before, but I'm a quick study." She shoved the papers across his desk. "Hold on to these—I'll be in touch."

Brad handed her an unexpected gift midway through the day, a text saying he needed to stay overnight in Springfield. She texted back with appropriate concern, grateful he hadn't called—she couldn't have borne the sound of his voice.

On impulse, she called his office. Disguising her voice—she hoped—with a handkerchief over the phone, she asked for Britt.

"Sorry," the receptionist said with no hint of recognition, "she's out of the office today."

Kathryn's mouth twisted—imagine that. She steeled herself for her last stop and drove to her own home, reasonably sure she wouldn't be disturbed. Just in case, she backed up the driveway and opened the trunk before entering the house.

First she went to the small wall safe in Brad's study, removing the title to her car and a jewelry box. She didn't care for the showy dinner rings, the diamond earrings and tennis bracelet Brad had given her, but she'd be damned if she would leave them for another woman to enjoy. They were hers, she'd earned them and they were good pieces she'd have no trouble turning into cash.

She started up the stairs and then turned back to the kitchen, looking in the fridge without finding what she sought. The recycling bin held an empty Chablis bottle with a few drops left in the bottom. She grasped it like a trophy and collected a pair of shears from a drawer before continuing upstairs.

Not looking at the bed, she stripped her closet and drawers of all the clothes she cared to take, filling her own luggage and plus a storage bin. The tennis clothes and cocktail dresses she wore for country club functions she left behind—she'd never have to wear them again.

She carried the first load down to her car,

peering down the street for any sign of Brad's Mercedes, and then ran back to the bedroom. Finally, she turned to the bed she had shared with Brad, where she had known such delight in his arms.

She took the silky green robe from the closet, the robe she had worn in innocence to welcome him home when he'd gone to his mistress after her mother's funeral. With great deliberation, she slashed it to shreds and dropped her cell phone on the mutilated garment along with the wine bottle. Last she poured a nearly full flask of her special cologne on the heap like a sacrificial libation.

Gathering the rest of her possessions, including her laptop, she descended the stairs with her head high, dumped the last load into the trunk and drove away without a backward glance.

After a fast-food supper, she checked into a small motel a few miles from her mother's house, not sure when Brad might return and find her parting display. Propped against the faux-Colonial headboard in her room, she called her favorite aunt who had taken her mother's dog.

"Aunt Joan," she said without preamble,

"I'm leaving Brad. I wanted to let you know because he might call looking for me."

"Good riddance," her aunt said. "I've always thought he's too pretty to be wholesome. Would you like to come here? You're welcome to stay as long as you want."

"Thanks, but I'll be traveling. I won't tell you where so you don't have to lie for me, but I'll check in with you. Give Blondie a hug for me."

The next morning, Kathryn drove her year-old Volvo sedan to a high school classmate's used car dealership and transferred her possessions to a low-mileage Ford SUV with tinted windows. Cloaked with her new anonymity, she left house keys for her cousin with her mother's neighbor. She gave her childhood home, sitting quiet and a little aloof in the spring sunshine, one last glance, then steered her new car toward I-84, heading west.

TEN DAYS LATER she took the exit from I-25 onto Route 160 in southern Colorado. She had zigzagged southwest through New York and Pennsylvania in easy stages, dropping into West Virginia to turn west through the Kentucky Bluegrass, as idyllic as she'd always pictured it. She'd paused in Louisville for a couple days, relishing her first taste of the South and selling her jewelry at an elegant, old-fashioned store with mahogany-framed display cases. Then she drove west to St. Louis and beyond, leaving the shelter of shade trees for the daunting vistas of the Great Plains, where the vault of the sky made her feel insignificant as a bug crawling across a windowpane.

She'd never been on an extended road trip; vacations with her parents had been one-day drives to a family resort in the Adirondacks or visits to relatives in New Jersey. Twice she had gone to the West Coast with Brad and once to Florida for conferences, but his idea of travel was airport to airport. She'd seen no more of strange cities than the taxi rides to and from their hotel.

She reveled in her flight from her past, even with the threat of snow crossing the Alleghenies and a horrendous thunderstorm in southern Illinois that left her driving blind. She didn't think about her destination except for the box of Annie Cameron's letters riding beside her like a benevolent familiar and managed to stay one jump ahead of her emotions by focusing on regional accents and changing landscapes, stopping at local inns and dining at small-town cafés.

Brad didn't have her new cell phone number, but he did email her. At first he expressed remorse and concern, then impatience—"How long before you get over your snit?"—and finally anger. She read the first few messages with detachment, almost with amusement, as if her pain nerves had been severed. When the repetition grew boring, she blocked his emails.

One day short of her goal, Kathryn began to feel a little silly. What a fool's errand, to drive more than two thousand miles to deliver a box of old letters. Maybe the Camerons wouldn't even be interested, but remembering Annie's tales of family closeness, Kathryn was sure the letters and their bearer would be welcome.

At first driving the state highway west from the interstate was a relief. All the way from Connecticut, big trucks had been her nemesis. Giant tractor-trailers just plain scared her, muscling their way along the highways as if lesser vehicles were invisible. She would have left the interstates to escape their bullying but didn't trust her navigation skills enough to abandon the well-marked routes.

Now on the two-lane road, she found herself stuck behind a hay truck, unable to see around its towering load to pass. The road began to climb between steep canyon walls, and the truck slowed even more. Its right turn signal flickered just as Kathryn resigned herself to following the behemoth all the way to Durango, the nearest town of any size to the Camerons' ranch. The big rig lurched onto a narrow side road with groaning gears and black exhaust dirtying the mountain air.

Kathryn had been so absorbed in fuming at the delay she hadn't noticed the morning's bright sunshine had dimmed. The sky overhead, what she could see between towering cliffs, had turned gray, and inky clouds hid the peaks ahead.

She glanced at her watch. The drive from Walsenburg, where she had spent the night, should have taken only four hours or so, but following the hay truck had delayed her considerably. Still, she should be able to reach Durango by early afternoon.

She passed a sign welcoming her to the San Juan National Forest and then a couple of campgrounds with chains across the entrances. A few desultory snowflakes drifted down.

She slowed as she rounded a steep climbing curve and drove with no warning into a com-

plete whiteout. Mountains, canyon, the road
itself disappeared. She hit the brakes reflexively and her car skidded for endless sicken-
ing seconds before rocking to a halt against
a snowbank. She sat clinging to the wheel,
numb with fear, enveloped in a snowy shroud.

Turning back would be impossible; going
forward was too terrifying to contemplate.

Gradually she became aware of a grunting
sound, a grumble that grew into a roar. An
avalanche? She'd passed a sign saying Slide
Area. Before she could panic even more,
flashing red lights appeared in her rearview
mirror. A huge dump truck ground past her,
spewing sand behind it, its wide wing plow
missing her vehicle by inches. Acting purely
on instinct, she gunned her car into its wake
and crept through the storm behind the fan-
shaped spray of grit covering the icy road.

Twenty minutes later the snow lightened,
the mountainsides reappeared, and the road-
way turned from packed snow to wet blacktop. The plow truck pulled aside into a wide
parking area to turn and head back up the
mountain. Below, a broad valley lay in bright
sunshine, untouched by the snowstorm still
raging over the peaks.

Kathryn made the rest of the descent as if

still on ice. The pavement was dry, but the
road clung to the mountainside in tortuous
curves above a deep canyon. Her hands ached
from clutching the steering wheel and sweat
soaked the back of her shirt by the time she
reached the valley floor. Stopping for lunch
in Pagosa Springs just ahead was tempting,
but she knew once she got out of her car she
wouldn't want to drive any farther. Durango
lay only another hour to the west—better to
keep going and then settle in at that night's
destination.

When Kathryn reached the outskirts of
Durango, she had recovered enough compo-
sure to be awed by the grandeur of the snowy
peaks rearing their heads north of the town.
Driving down the main street, she passed the
Silver Queen Saloon and Dance Emporium,
its Victorian storefront like a set from a classic Western movie. She had checked her Colorado guidebook this morning at breakfast;
the Silver Queen was rated four stars for classic regional fare. She glanced at her watch—a
few minutes before three o'clock. With luck,
they would still be serving lunch.

She had her hand on the ornate brass door-
knob when someone inside turned the Open
sign hanging in the window to Closed. The

distress on her face must have been apparent, because the door opened.

A young woman with red-gold curls gathered on top of her head, wearing a white chef's apron, beckoned her inside. "I was just closing," she said, "but you look like you needed feeding at least an hour ago. Would soup or a sandwich work for you? I've already shut off the grill."

"That sounds like manna from heaven," Kathryn said. "I'm starving—I haven't eaten since I left Walsenburg this morning. I thought I'd get here earlier, but I got stuck behind a hay truck and then it started to snow—"

"You just came across Wolf Creek Pass? Brave lady. I'm surprised the road wasn't closed—the forecast this morning said heavy snow above eight thousand feet."

"I wasn't brave," Kathryn said, "I was clueless." She shuddered, reliving the moments of terror in the whiteout. "Luckily I got in behind a snowplow or I'd still be sitting on top of the mountain waiting for spring."

"You might have had quite a wait," her savior said. "I've seen it snow on that pass in June. What can I get you? I have chicken noodle soup or chili. And coffee? Or tea?"

"Chili sounds wonderful. And coffee, please."

"Green chili or red with beans?"

"I've never heard of green chili," Kathryn said.

"So you're not from around here—better stick with red. A bowl of old-fashioned diner chili will hold you till supper time."

She disappeared into the kitchen. Kathryn heard her tell someone to bring out a cup of coffee. A few moments later a little girl, possibly six, with the same ruddy hair and wearing her own miniature apron, appeared. She carried a mug in one hand and a cream pitcher in the other, setting them on the table with a sigh of relief.

"Your chili will be right out," she said.

"Thank you," Kathryn said. "You're doing a great job helping your mom."

"That's not my mom, that's Aunt Lucy," the little girl said. She returned to the kitchen, switching on overhead lights that had probably been dimmed for closing.

Kathryn dosed her coffee with cream and sugar, gulping a few swallows before the waitress set the chili and a small salad on her table.

"That should keep body and soul together

until you land for the night," the waitress said. "Do you have much farther to drive?"

"I plan to stay in Durango for the night and then drive on to Hesperus tomorrow."

"Not much to see in Hesperus. You have family there?"

"Not exactly—it's a long story."

"I love a good story. You mind if I join you? I'm ready for my afternoon coffee." The waitress returned to the kitchen and came back with her own mug and two slices of pie. She slid into the booth opposite Kathryn.

Kathryn took her first good look at her rescuer. "I've never been out West before, but I could swear I've seen you somewhere."

"I've been spending a lot of time on the East Coast. Where do you live?"

"A little town near Hartford," Kathryn said.

"Do you ever attend local theater?"

"That's where I saw you, at the Seven Angels Theater in Waterbury. You're Lucinda Cameron, right? Someone gave my husband tickets for *The Seagull*." Could this possibly be Annie Cameron's daughter, Lucy, who she had described so lovingly?

"Just plain Lucy on my home range. Did you enjoy the play?"

"I hated it," Kathryn said. "I felt like going

home and putting my head in the oven. But you were wonderful."

"Chekhov can be pretty heavy," Lucy said with a laugh. "But he wrote great female roles."

"And now you're running a restaurant?"

"Temporarily. I started working at the Queen when I was fourteen, right after my mom died. The owner is one of my dearest friends—I'm keeping the doors open while she recuperates from knee surgery." Lucy added cream to her coffee and leaned back. "So tell me your story."

Kathryn hadn't yet rehearsed a coherent narrative. "Actually, I came to see you," she said. "Your family, that is. My mother had lupus. She met your mother in the hospital in Albuquerque almost twenty years ago and they corresponded right up to the time your mother died. Mom kept all her letters—I thought your family might like to have them."

Lucy's eyes widened. "I know who you are. I've read all of your mother's letters. Her name was Elizabeth, and you're Katie."

A lump lodged in Kathryn's throat. "I used to be Katie, but no one's called me that for years." Brad had decided Katie sounded childish; eventually even her mother began calling her Kathryn.

"Surely you didn't drive all the way from the East Coast to bring the letters."

"Surely I did. The only address I had was the letterhead—Cameron's Pride, Hesperus, Colorado. I could have gotten a mailing address by calling the post office there…" Kathryn flushed. "I know it sounds crazy, but I decided to deliver them in person."

She started to rise. "I've got the box in my car—"

"No, no! You have to bring them to the ranch. We've all read those letters. Your mom was so proud of you—she wrote all about you, she sent pictures."

Lucy whipped her cell phone out of her pocket and hesitated with her finger poised. "You will come, won't you?"

"If you're sure it's no imposition." In truth, Kathryn had hoped to visit the family and the ranch Annie Cameron had described in such glowing detail.

"Are you kidding? We'll be insulted if you don't let us welcome you."

Lucy touched the screen. "Dad," she said after a brief wait, "you remember all those letters the lady back East wrote to Mom? You'll never believe who's sitting here in the

Queen—Elizabeth Gabriel's daughter, Katie, all the way from Connecticut."

She listened with a big grin. "Of course I'm bringing her home with me."

CHAPTER SEVEN

MIKE FARLEY CLOSED the last folder and sat back with a long whistle.

"That bad, huh?" Luke said. "I told you I'd probably mess up."

"Are you kidding? You've done twice the job on these receipts anyone has before—you've saved me major time and trouble." He took a printed sheet from one of the folders. "Plus a list of what's missing." He flipped one sheet with his finger. "According to this, Joel Baker never eats while he's on the road. He'll have to come up with a reasonable dining history so I can claim deductions for meals."

Luke breathed in relief. "I separated out the receipts that didn't seem allowable for each rider—you'll know if those should be added back in. To tell the truth, I kind of enjoyed it."

Mike gave him a sharp glance. "You've

been hiding some smarts behind all your horsing around."

Luke shrugged. "Tom got the brains in the family."

"You got your share. How many hours did this take you?"

Luke pondered. "About an hour each, more or less. And then I went back to check out inconsistencies and make notes. So maybe fifteen hours."

"I'll send you a check—"

"You don't have to pay me—I was glad to help. Like I said, it was fun. A challenge."

"Don't be a jerk," Mike said. "You deserve to be paid. You did a great job because you know bull riding. I'll be able to get these tax returns in on time, but I've had to apply for extensions on some others. You interested in doing some more grunt work for me?"

Mike's praise made Luke sit a little straighter. "Sure, if you really think I can help." His disability insurance kept him from being a financial drain on his family, but he needed to work, to feel useful.

He'd practiced with Dude the past ten days so he could saddle without asking for help and ride out alone. He could move cattle and check fence lines, but he couldn't dismount to mend broken wire or doctor a sick cow. It galled him he still fell short of doing a man's share on the ranch.

A confusion of voices erupted outside the back door. He heard his dad say, "They'll be here pretty soon. Get in there, woman, and start cooking."

"Calm down, Jake," Shelby said. "There's extra stew in the freezer—"

And then JJ's piping voice said, "Will we have ice cream and cake?"

Luke frowned. Meeting new people still set him on edge—the pity in their eyes, the questions they were too polite to ask. Maybe he should print up cards like deaf people sometimes handed out to explain their disability: *I can't walk because a bull stomped on my back. I don't know if I'll ever walk again.*

Mike gathered the folders into their box. "I'd better get going if you guys are expecting company."

Luke wanted him to stay as a buffer against the unknown, but he knew he needed to cowboy up. He wheeled himself into the kitchen, where Shelby was taking the makings for salad from the fridge for JJ to carry to the table.

"Who's coming?"

"You remember all those letters your mom got from that lady back East?" Jake said. "Her daughter, Katie, found them after her mom died recently and came all the way from Connecticut to bring them."

The unexpected thoughtfulness of the gesture sparked his interest. Driving two-thirds of the way across the country took planning and spunk; he wouldn't mind meeting a woman who would do that. At the same time, the prospect rattled his nerves. He hadn't spoken with any women not involved with his rehab since his wreck, a special sadness to him. His greatest pleasure, along with pitting his quickness against the bulls, had been the company of the female fans who swarmed bull-riding events.

Luke liked women, genuinely liked them— all ages, shapes and sizes, both in and out of bed. Strong, smart women like Shelby didn't scare him—neither did sassy, willful ones like his sister. He'd been in and out of love a dozen times but had dodged marriage until finally— probably because he saw his younger brother heading down the bridal path—he'd gotten hitched on impulse in Las Vegas five years ago.

Cherie hadn't been a bad kid, but she'd

bailed after two weeks of wedded bliss when a bull had sent him to the hospital with a broken neck and ruptured spleen. Maybe she would have hung in if they'd had more time to build a relationship. Instead she'd disappeared from his life while he was still on the operating table.

He should have started looking for a real wife the minute the divorce was final, but after Cherie he'd been gun-shy. He'd figured there'd always be plenty of time to find the right girl. Uh-huh.

"You mind putting the salad together?" Shelby asked. "I want to whip up some biscuits to go with the stew."

"You got it." He set to work tearing lettuce and slicing cucumbers the way his mom had taught him when she was too ill to cook. He finished chopping the green peppers as he heard one vehicle and then a second rattle across the cattle guard and pull up behind the house. Jitters struck again, but he could always plead fatigue and excuse himself right after dinner.

Doors slammed and a woman's voice, soft and low, answered his sister's bright chatter.

Curiosity overcame caution; he wheeled to the big window to check out the newcomer.

He couldn't see her face, but he admired her trim figure in pants and a sweater the color of aspen leaves in autumn. Her glossy russet hair in a neat bun reminded him of his tenth-grade English teacher, on whom he'd had a hopeless crush.

He turned away. The doubts and fears constantly hovering since his injury swooped down like vultures. He saw himself ten, twenty years in the future, a burden first to his dad and Shelby, and later to Tom and Jo.

He spun his chair and headed toward his room, but Missy burst through the door and flung herself into his lap.

"Uncle Luke, I helped Aunt Lucy serve lunch," she said, hugging him hard. "And Katie said I did a good job."

"Of course you did, Shortcake. You'll be working the grill before you know it." He heard footsteps behind him and pivoted toward the door.

"Dad, Shelby, this is Katie Gabriel," Lucy said. "Katie, this is my brother Luke."

With reluctance Luke took the hand Katie extended.

"This is a first for me," she said. Her gray eyes met his with no hint of pity. "I never met a bullfighter before."

"Ex-bullfighter," he said, unable to keep the bitterness out of his voice.

JJ erupted from under the table, his favorite place to stash his toys. "We're having a party, with ice cream and cake."

"No, with ice cream and peach pie," Lucy said, setting a pastry box on the counter.

JJ's face fell.

"I may have some cake in the freezer," Shelby said, and his face brightened again.

Luke turned loose of Katie's hand and returned to making the salad.

"I'm going back to Durango after supper," Lucy said, "but I thought Katie could stay here. She came over Wolf Creek Pass today in that snow squall—she should be done driving for the day. And maybe someone can show her around the ranch tomorrow."

Like who? Luke wondered. In the past, he'd enjoyed giving visitors, especially female guests, the guided tour, but now he felt self-conscious about the restrictions his injury laid on him. Still, Katie Gabriel might be okay—she had greeted him as if she saw a man, not a man in a wheelchair.

"If you're sure it's no imposition," Katie said, picking up the box she had set on a chair to shake hands with Luke. "Here's what I came to bring you."

Lucy took it as if it were a holy relic. "This means so much to us. Mom died when I was just fourteen." Tears filled her eyes. "I missed her so much I made myself and everyone else miserable."

"You were entitled, Red." Jake entered the kitchen. "I wasn't much help to you back then."

"You did the best you could, Dad." She rolled her eyes. "And don't call me Red."

He held out his hand to Katie. "Jake Cameron, and mighty glad to meet you. We feel like we know you from your mom's letters."

"I don't suppose…"

"Of course we saved them. I reckon you'll be happy to have them, just losing her so recent. She sounded like a special lady."

"She was," Katie said. "We were more like best friends, especially after my dad died."

Missy set the table with great concentration while Shelby pulled a pan of biscuits from the oven. Lucy took an enameled pot of beef stew from the stove to put on a trivet made of horseshoes. They all took their seats around the big oak table.

Shelby waited until everyone was settled

before bowing her head. "Lord," she said, "our family's been through some rough times, but we've always come through together. We thank You for Your help and for bringing Katie to join us tonight. Amen."

"Can I have a biscuit with honey?" JJ said.

"*May* I have a biscuit," Lucy said.

"Sure," JJ said with a giggle, "you can have one, too."

Missy gave an exasperated big-sister sigh.

Luke ladled stew into JJ's bowl and cut the meat into smaller pieces. He loved both his brother's kids, but he felt a special bond with his nephew. He saw a lot of himself in JJ and wished his brother and sister-in-law luck when JJ hit his teens—they would need it.

He kept mostly silent during dinner, speaking only enough not to seem surly, listening to Katie's account of her solo trip across country. He liked the way she laughed at herself for mistaking a state road number for an interstate in Missouri, driving ten miles behind a manure spreader, and silently applauded her quick thinking in following the snowplow over Wolf Creek Pass. Pretty dang good for a green Eastern driver.

"So where do you go from here?" Jake

asked Katie while Shelby served the peach pie à la mode, with chocolate cake for Missy and JJ. "Once we let you go, that is."

"I really hadn't thought beyond bringing you the letters," she said. "I'm kind of at loose ends right now."

"Back to Connecticut?" Lucy asked.

"No, not there. I'll have to return eventually to take care of some business, but not soon." She massaged the faint ridges on her ring finger. "Right now I'm looking for a job."

"What kind of job?" Shelby asked, cutting a second sliver of cake for JJ.

"I know a little about bookkeeping—I worked for a construction firm for a while." She flushed. "And I love to cook. I don't have any formal training, but I did some catering while I was in college."

Lucy sat straighter. "Did you really?"

Luke could read his sister's mind.

"Hold on, Luce," Jake said. "The poor girl just landed—don't try to draft her before she has time to take a deep breath."

Lucy closed her mouth, but Luke knew she wouldn't be able to hold her tongue for long.

Jake looked at his watch. "You'd better

head to town if you're going to open the Queen for the breakfast crowd." He stood. "I'll bring Katie's bag in."

CHAPTER EIGHT

KATHRYN HAD AWAKENED in so many different rooms since leaving Connecticut she needed a few seconds to orient herself. As driven as she'd been to flee from her husband's betrayal, she still missed his warmth in the night, the many intimate details of living as a married woman. Longing to return to the comfort of the familiar tugged at her for a moment; she banished it with the memory of Brad's and Britt Cavendish's mingled laughter polluting her own private space.

Last night she'd been shown to Luke's bedroom upstairs, since he now occupied the main floor guest room. Too tired then to notice much beyond the single bed covered with a bright Indian blanket, she now saw the framed museum-quality prints on the walls—Gauguin's Tahitian women, Van Gogh's sailboats drawn up on a beach, El Greco's stormy skies over Toledo. Interesting decor for a cowboy bullfighter.

And here she was—Cameron's Pride at last. The ranch and the Cameron family had assumed almost mythic qualities in her mind, but she had schooled herself not to expect too much. Finding the setting as idyllic as she had pictured, being welcomed like long-lost kin seemed too good to be real.

Lucy had brought her swiftly up to date before leading her out to the ranch: her father's remarriage two years after Annie's death, her brother Tom's marriage and retirement from bull riding with a new career as a high school history teacher, and Luke's crippling mishap only a few months ago.

Her thoughts stalled when they reached Luke Cameron, his brown hair and deep tan resembling his stepmother's Indian-dark skin and black hair more than his father's and sister's redhead coloring. Her hand tingled as she recalled an instant of connection when their hands met, quickly broken when she mentioned his career as a bullfighter. Stupid of her—who could blame him for being bitter about his injury?

She lay for a few minutes longer, enjoying the luxury of not facing another day on the road. Later today she would take her leave with the proper thanks for the hospitality and carrying the precious box with her mother's letters.

Her mind turned to Jake's question: Where to from here? Her mission to reach Cameron's Pride had absorbed her until now, but she needed to make plans for her future. Although she'd been frugal with her spending, her reserves wouldn't last forever. At some point she would finalize the divorce proceedings she had set in motion. She should demand a hefty settlement from Brad, but she wanted nothing from him. For her own sense of self-worth, she needed to prove she could support herself by her own wits.

She could look for work near her mother's relatives in New Jersey, but she'd never cared for the urban sprawl of the East Coast megalopolis. She might look for work in Maine— she had worked as a nanny on an island one summer in college and loved the open vastness of the ocean. Maybe she would just keep driving until she came to a town that took her fancy, someplace like Durango...

Loud whispers outside her door brought her back to the present.

"Hush, you'll wake Katie." The bossy big sister. "Uncle Luke's gonna be mad."

Kathryn smiled—apparently Missy and JJ

were back. Tom's wife, Jo, returned from a field trip to an archaeological site with Tom's high school students, had arrived to pick the kids up after supper the night before. She had dropped her husband off first at their home because he had aggravated an old back injury helping to carry a student who had sprained her ankle.

And Kathryn had been changed back into Katie. Well, why not? Kathryn was Brad's wife. She was done with him and with the name.

"Katie," she said, savoring the name on her tongue. A new life, a fresh identify, one truer to her roots.

A pony-like thunder of small boots on the stairs followed the growl of a man's voice from below. Katie looked at her watch—almost nine. She had slept like the dead for nearly ten hours. A chilly breath crept in from a window she had opened a crack the night before, so she added her UConn sweatshirt over her jeans and polo shirt. She brushed the tangles from her shoulder-length hair, wound it into a bun and descended to the kitchen.

Missy sat at the table under Luke's stern eye. He turned to Katie with an apologetic grin. "Sorry about the brats disturbing you—

they've figured out I can't chase them up the stairs. Jo's in town helping Lucy with the breakfast rush—she'll be by to pick them up in about an hour."

"It's okay—I'm usually up much earlier. Is this a school vacation week?"

"We don't get weeks off," Missy said. "We're homeschooled." She held up a map she was coloring. "I'm studying geography."

"What can I get you for breakfast?" Luke asked. "Shelby left a French toast casserole in the oven, and we've got eggs, bacon…"

"I can make scrambled eggs," Missy said. "Grandma Shelby showed me how."

"I'll bet you can," Katie said, "but I think I'll try the French toast." She noticed Luke's mug was nearly empty. "Can I get you more coffee?"

He handed it to her; when their eyes met, she felt a hint of yesterday's warmth. "Cream, two sugars," he said. "Mugs are above the urn."

She turned away, busying herself with the coffee while he pulled a Pyrex dish from the oven and served a generous portion onto her plate.

He pushed a pitcher toward her. "No maple syrup," he said, "but we have chokecherry.

My mom and grandmother used to put it up—now Jo and Shelby pick the berries and make the syrup."

"I help pick, too," Missy said.

Luke looked around the kitchen. "Where's JJ?"

"He's on the couch," Missy said. "His tummy hurts."

"Dang, I should have known when he didn't ask for more French toast." Luke wheeled around the big leather sofa facing the fireplace and reached down. "Yup, he's got a little fever." He spread a crocheted throw over the child. "Your mom will be here pretty soon, buddy."

He returned to the table. "This kind of screws up our plans for today," he said. "Jo was going to give you the six-bit tour of the ranch, but she'll want to take JJ home." He gave her a sidewise glance. "Or you could go with me."

"If I won't be in your way." He must have a vehicle with hand controls.

"I'd be pleased for the company. Have you ridden much?"

"Horses?" She tried to hide her astonishment. "Not since summer camp when I was twelve, but I really enjoyed it."

"Great. But we'll have to find you some boots—you can't ride in sneakers. Missy, get the boot box out of the front closet, will you, darlin'?"

Missy laid down her colored pencil and left the room, coming back dragging a packing box almost as tall as she.

"What size?" she asked.

"Eight, I guess," Katie said.

Missy dived headfirst into the box and tugged out a pair of boots with pointed toes and stacked heels, tied together with a tag. She handed them to Katie. "Size eight."

Katie laughed. "Your own shoe store."

"We never throw away anything that still has some use in it," Luke said. He peered at the boots. "Looks like an old pair of my mom's—Lucy and Shelby both have smaller feet. See if they fit."

Katie pulled on the boots and stamped her feet. "I feel like a cowgirl already."

The cattle guard at the front gate rumbled and a car pulled up behind the house. Jo hurried into the kitchen. "Sorry I'm late," she said. "This has been such an education— waitresses deserve hazardous-duty pay." She smiled at Katie. "Let me sit for five minutes and we'll hit the trail."

"Afraid not," Luke said. "JJ has a bellyache—best you take him home. I planned to check the south fence line today. Katie can ride along—we'll stop at the cabin for lunch."

Jo frowned with concern and exasperation. "He got up early and pigged out on chips we brought home from the field trip. Honestly, he's worse than a pony in the feed room."

"Could you saddle Rooster for Katie before you go?" Luke said.

"Will do. Missy, pack up your lessons and get JJ's things, too."

The door closed behind her, and Luke opened the fridge. "Roast beef sandwich or tuna salad? Snag some bread from the bread-box, will you?"

"Roast beef is fine," Katie said and found a loaf of whole wheat—home baked, from the look of it—in the lithographed tin box labeled Bread and Cakes. Before Brad had gone up-scale with his business and his lifestyle, she'd made his lunch every day to eat perched on a sawhorse or on the seat of an excavator. She had loved that chapter of their life, had even enjoyed washing his grimy work clothes.

She sighed. Taking his Armani suits to the cleaners didn't give her the same satisfaction as laying out fresh shirts and dungarees each morning.

Luke set mayo and mustard on the table and assembled sandwiches with a practiced hand, adding a couple of apples and oatmeal cookies studded with raisins. By the time Jo returned, he had the lunches packed in saddlebags Katie brought him from a peg in the mud room.

"Rooster's hitched in the barn," Jo said, "and I saddled Dude, too." She scooped up her son from the couch. "You guys have a good ride."

Luke hung the saddlebags over the back of his chair and collected his hat and a denim jacket from a hook beside the door. He held the door for Katie, letting her precede him down the ramp. She followed him along the walkway, still wondering how a man in a wheelchair could mount a horse. When they reached the barn, she saw a sturdy brown horse hitched to the ladder leading to the hayloft.

"Katie, meet Rooster. He's steady as they come—JJ rides him." He held the horse's reins while she climbed into the saddle, hoping she didn't look as clumsy as she felt.

"That little tyke rides a big horse like this? I'd think a pony would be more his size."

"Ponies can be tricky rascals," Luke said. "Too smart for their own good sometimes. A well-broke horse is safer. JJ shinnies into the saddle like a monkey."

He adjusted her stirrup length. "Knot the ends of your reins together so you won't lose them if they slip out of your hands. And wait here while I get my horse." He rolled his chair to the side door and gave a shrill whistle.

Katie laughed as the horse, already saddled, ambled into the barn. "What happened to him? He looks like someone dumped a bucket of paint on his rump."

"Dude is an Appaloosa, greenhorn—a breed developed by the Nez Perce tribe in Idaho. Shelby got him from a rescue in Utah. Smartest horse she ever trained, she said."

Luke set the brakes on his chair, and to Katie's surprise, the horse sank to the ground at a tap on the foreleg. Luke tied the saddlebags in place, transferred to the saddle with a single supple twist of his body and secured Velcro straps around his thighs. He settled his boots in the stirrups and said, "Dude, up." The horse scrambled to his feet and turned his head to take a treat from his rider's hand.

"That's amazing," Katie said. "Was he hard to train?"

"Shelby said not—she had him all ready for me when I got home from rehab in Austin. Not much she can't get a horse to do, especially one as smart as Dude."

Katie gestured toward the horse's head. "Did you forget his bridle?"

"Don't need one." He touched the loose loop of rope lying around Dude's shoulders. "This is my steering rig, and Shelby taught him to answer to voice commands since I can't cue him with my legs. Let's move out." He leaned a little forward in the saddle. "Dude, walk."

He led the way out the side door of the barn and slid it shut before turning his horse's head to ride along the creek bordering the pasture.

Seeing him in his proper element, in his cowboy hat and snug jeans, mounted on the spectacular horse, increased her awareness of him as an attractive man.

"Do we have far to ride?" she asked to mask her confusion.

"Maybe an hour if we step up our pace a little. You know how to neck-rein?" he asked.

"I've heard of it, but I've never ridden Western." She'd been holding one rein in each hand as she'd been taught at her long-ago summer camp.

Luke rode close, his knee touching hers, and put his hand over hers. "Both reins in one hand—you steer by laying a rein against your horse's neck, like you're pushing the direction you want to go. Try it."

She almost snatched her hand away, but not because she found his touch unpleasant. The light pressure from his calloused fingers sent a wave of heat through her body she hadn't experienced since her first date with Brad. A confusion of emotions rampaged through her mind: first shock and shame that she should react so avidly to a man other than her husband, and then hope glowing like a fitful coal beneath the rubble. She could feel again, she could respond, maybe even learn to love and trust someday.

She broke the contact by moving her hand holding the reins to the right, and Rooster shifted smoothly away from the pressure. "That's a lot easier than the way I learned," she said, hoping her voice didn't betray her inner turmoil.

"Mostly we're on horseback for work, not recreation," he said. "Neck-reining keeps one hand free for roping or leading another horse or opening gates."

"And what do you do for recreation?"

Luke laughed. "Go for a ride."

"Well, I'm having fun right now, even if this is a working trip," she said.

"So let's move along. Rooster's gaits are smooth as silk—Missy started on him before she graduated to a real cow pony. Dude, jog," he said, and his horse moved into a slow trot. Rooster followed suit.

Katie found she could sit the quicker gait without bouncing around like a marionette with its strings cut. She tried to concentrate on her reins and ignore the breadth of Luke's shoulders, his easy seat in the saddle just ahead of her. She had never looked twice at another man after she first met Brad in college; she'd be a fool to rush into any new relationship now. No law against admiring the scenery, though.

Luke glanced over his shoulder. "How are you doing, cowgirl?"

She felt her face flush. "Okay, I think. Maybe you should ask Rooster."

He looked at her more closely. "I think you're getting too much sun—it's stronger at this elevation than you're used to." He dug in one saddlebag and pulled out a purple ball cap. "Lucy keeps these stashed everywhere. Her coloring, she has to cover up to keep from frying like a strip of bacon." He handed the cap to Katie.

She set it on her head, fumbling with one hand to fit it over her hair tucked up in its bun.

"Just hook your reins over the saddle horn," Luke said. "He won't bolt with you."

She did as he said, using both hands, but she had dislodged the clip holding her bun so her hair tumbled down over her shoulders.

Luke stared. "Dang, girl. Why do you keep that handsome mane bundled up like a schoolmarm?"

Katie tried to gather her hair into some order and finally settled for pulling it through the back of the cap.

"My husband didn't like me to wear it loose," she said. "Too casual, he thought. He wanted me to cut it to look more polished." Again she rubbed the third finger on her left hand.

"Your husband sounds like a sure-enough fool. Sorry, but that's how it looks to me. I'm glad you stood your ground."

"Me, too. Not that it matters now."

"Sure it does—it matters to you."

Dude turned at some invisible signal and resumed his gentle jog. Rooster fell in beside him, and they rode stirrup to stirrup without speaking. Katie hadn't known how tightly she'd been wound on her flight from Connecticut, but the soft clop of the horses' hooves, the sun warm on her shoulders and a playful breeze laced with some scent like incense lulled her into almost boneless relaxation.

Luke's soft "Whoa," jerked her out of her trance. They had halted at the crest of a long ridge overlooking a wide valley showing hints of new grass in the winter brown. Brighter green and trees just coming into leaf marked a stream's winding course in the middle distance. The vista stretched away in shades of tan and terra cotta to fade against the horizon.

"We always stop to breathe the horses at the top," he said. "You can get a good lay of our land from here. The Ute Reservation starts beyond that fence yonder." He pointed to a glint of wire in the middle distance. "A little higher and you'd be able to see clear down to the Navajo rez in New Mexico."

He spoke to Dude, and the horses descended the gentle slope at a jog. After they'd ridden some minutes in silence, he said, "Maybe I should keep my mouth shut, but I'd hate to have Lucy pounce without giving you warning. I'm pretty sure she wants to recruit you for the Queen. If you're really looking for work, you could take a big load off Shelby and Jo. Durango is a pretty nice place to hang out for a while."

"I don't know… I hadn't considered…" But she had. Maybe because Durango had appeared as a haven after her harrowing trip over Wolf Creek Pass, maybe because of the Camerons' warm welcome, but she already felt an unreasoning sense of homecoming.

"Here's the deal," Luke said. "Lucy has a commitment with some summer theater company in New Hampshire starting in June. No place I ever heard of, but she says it's a real career builder. She's not sure Marge Bowman will be fit enough by then to take the reins at the Queen."

"Would that be the Peterborough Players? That's professional-grade theater—sometimes they get reviewed in New York papers."

"Yeah, that's the place. So it's the real deal?"

"It is—Lucy should grab it. I've seen her perform. She has real talent."

"We think she's good, but what do we

know—we're family," Luke said. "Just don't say I gave you the heads-up. I don't want her going all redheaded on me. Shelby says she's like a microburst—spins you around before you know what hit you."

He looked up at the sun. "Still an hour shy of noon—let's take a look at the east fence line before we break for lunch." He led the way down the slope and across a roistering creek as deep as the horses' knees.

Katie clung without shame to the saddle horn as Rooster picked his way over the rocky bottom and scrambled up the far bank. She noticed with envy that Luke sat his horse as casually as if rocking in a porch swing. Another fifteen minutes jogging beyond the creek brought them to a barb-wire fence broken by a heavy steel gate.

"This is the edge of Cameron's Pride," Luke said. "Other side is the Buck ranch on the Ute Reservation. We're kin with the Bucks going back to Jacob Cameron, who came west from Virginia after the Civil War. He was headed for California, but this is as far as he got."

"What stopped him?"

"A grizzly bear and a pretty Ute girl. My dad tells the story best—it's like holy scripture to him. To all of us, I guess. I didn't value it like I should till I spent three months away in rehab."

He touched the side of his horse's neck, and Dude turned to the left. "We'll ride up to the top of that next ridge—we can check a couple miles from there. Dad plans to move the cow and calf pairs to this range as soon as calving is done, so the fence needs to be in good shape. Just lean forward and let Rooster take care of you."

Rooster followed Dude up the steep trail, and Luke halted Dude at the top. He pulled a pair of binoculars from his saddlebag and began scanning the fence line with a slow sweep of the glasses. Suddenly he halted in his survey. "Dang it."

"What's wrong?" Katie squinted into the distance but could see only rocks, bushes and a single brown-and-white cow.

"It's my cousin's—" His mouth clamped shut, editing his comments, she suspected. "His pet bull's busted out again." He jerked his cell phone from its belt holster and punched in a number with angry jabs. He waited, running his hand over his face, and then said, "Oscar, Buckshot's on our side of the fence again. I can cut the fence and shove him back, but I can't mend the break."

Frustration spoke in every line of his face and body as he listened. "Yeah, I've got somebody with me, but you better come get him before I turn him into all-beef patties. Half a mile south of the gate, right by that little draw where he likes to sneak in."

He stuck his phone into place without saying goodbye and turned to Katie. "I could use some help, if you feel like playing cowgirl."

He had to be crazy; her consternation must have shown on her face.

"No rough stuff. Buckshot's tame as a pet goat—he's just got no respect for boundaries."

She swallowed. "Tell me what to do."

"Good girl. First we ride up to him real easy, a slow-speed chase. Rooster knows the drill—he was quite a cow pony in his day."

"Does this happen often?"

"Too often. Buckshot's a retired bucking bull. Nobody wanted him because supposedly he was sterile from an infection, so Oscar adopted him. Turns out he's still got what it takes. Trouble is, he's so big that any cow he covers has trouble calving. Oscar doesn't have the heart to castrate him, so Buckshot has turned into the neighborhood pest."

They rode toward the bull. As they got closer, he grew to the size of a brontosaurus in Katie's eyes. Neither Dude nor Rooster appeared intimidated.

"Here's what we do," Luke said. "I'm going to cut the wire near him and then we'll send him back where he belongs and stay in the gap till Oscar shows up to collect him."

Sure. Of course. "Okay," Katie said, chagrined that her voice emerged as a squeak.

"Just stay put." Luke pulled wire cutters from his saddlebag. He reached down and snipped the strands so they sprang away from the post. Then he rode in a wide circle to position himself to one side as he shook out his rope. Buckshot watched with no sign of alarm.

"Okay," Luke said. "Walk Rooster toward him at a forty-five-degree angle, but stop when I tell you."

Katie's mouth was too dry to answer, but she did as he directed.

"Stop," Luke said as Buckshot pivoted to face Rooster. "Don't worry—he won't charge you. Okay, now five steps closer."

Rooster seemed to be enjoying the game; his ears pricked sharply toward the bull. He stopped on his own after a few steps.

Buckshot snorted—in disgust, Katie thought—and ambled through the gap in the fence. Luke rode down to join her, coiling his rope. Together they blocked the bull's return to Cameron's Pride.

"Good work," he said. "Lucy couldn't have done any better."

She ducked her head to hide her pleasure at his praise. "Why did the bull give up so easily? He could have rushed right past me."

"That bull's a smart old guy—he's been worked dozens of times. Rooster was giving him the evil eye, moving in on his territory but not invading it. Buckshot decided to retreat with honor. He also saw I had my rope ready."

"So you could have just roped him and dragged him through the opening?"

"I'd just as soon not try—he's half again Dude's weight. Better if he thinks it was his idea to go home."

"How did he get in?"

"The fence line crosses a little ravine with about three feet clearance under the wire. His size, you wouldn't think it's possible, but he crawls under—I've backtracked him. But drive him back? Good luck with that. Oscar dumped some logs to block the gap last fall, but the spring runoff must have washed them out."

A few minutes later the mutter of an engine broke the quiet, and a battered green pickup lumbered over the rise to brake beside the damaged fence. A broad-shouldered man with a single long braid, his skin a few shades darker than Luke's, climbed out.

He frowned. "Look what you did to my wire, you sorry-assed cowpoke. And you better hope my bull's all right." He walked over to Buckshot. "You okay, baby?"

The bull twitched one long ear and kept grazing.

"Mind your manners, Oscar—there's a lady present. Katie, this is my cousin Oscar Buck."

Katie rode forward to shake his hand. "We didn't lay a glove on Buckshot, I promise."

Oscar whipped off his well-worn straw cowboy hat. "You must be visiting Cameron's Pride from away, Katie. I know all the pretty girls in these parts."

"All the way from Connecticut," Luke said. "Mom and her mother were pen pals for years."

"What's with you Camerons? You keep importing women from back East—Shelby's from Louisiana, Jo's from New York…"

"Katie came to bring us a box of Mom's letters. We're hoping she'll decide to hang around."

"How come you're strapped in today?" Oscar asked. "I thought you didn't need the safety rig anymore."

"I didn't want to fall off in front of Katie and look like a fool," Luke said.

"Still showing off for the ladies," Oscar said and dropped the tailgate on his truck to reveal an open bag labeled Cattle Chow. Buckshot stuck his nose in the feed while his owner spliced new wire into the break.

Oscar dusted his hand on the seat of his jeans after he finished the repair and offered it to Katie again. "I'd apologize for Buckshot, but if he'd stayed home I wouldn't have gotten a chance to say howdy. Enjoy your stay, and don't believe half of what this cowboy tells you."

He climbed in his truck and drove away at a crawl with the bull following, his nose still in the bag of feed.

CHAPTER NINE

"DO YOU FALL off very often?" Katie asked as they continued along the fence line.

"Not so much anymore, and Dude waits for me when I do. I didn't want to take a chance today and scare you, flopping around on the ground like a fish on the riverbank."

He leaned toward her and gave her a light punch on the shoulder. "I wasn't kidding—you handled old Buckshot like a pro. I knew he isn't dangerous, but he must have looked like a four-legged mountain to you." Pretty gritty considering she'd likely never faced down anything bigger than a raccoon in the trash.

"I concentrated on following your directions," she said. "Cowboy up, right?"

They rode in silence while Luke did some hard thinking. He would have handled Buckshot the same way if Shelby or Jo had been with him; neither of them was much of a roper. If Tom or his dad had been along, maybe he would have been the one to ride down on the bull as Katie had done.

If he had the nerve. He hadn't been eyeball to eyeball with a bucking bull since that night in Oklahoma City.

"Is this as far as we go?"

Luke had been sunk so deep in thought that Katie's question startled him. They had come to a corner where the fence turned at a sharp angle.

"Yep, this fence just separates two of our pastures. Not the end of the world if some cows drift over, but we try hard to keep the boundary fences tight so we aren't chasing stock halfway across the Ute Reservation. Or kicking Buckshot out."

He turned Dude toward a high ridge. "We'll take a shortcut to the cabin and have lunch before we check in the other direction. Just lean forward and give Rooster plenty of rein—he'll take you up safely."

He rode behind Katie in case she faltered, but she took the steep trail without hesitation. The downgrade on the far side was an easy slope; in less than an hour they were back at the creek crossing.

"The cabin is just around that bluff," Luke

said. "We can water the horses and get out of
the saddle while we have lunch."

She wondered how he would manage that
maneuver but didn't ask. They rounded the
bold sandstone outcropping and splashed
through the creek again, stopping to let the
horses drink.

"There it is, the Cameron shrine, the original homestead," Luke said, pointing ahead.
"Don't be surprised when you go inside—
Shelby's turned it into a museum. She lived
here a few weeks when she first came to the
ranch, hiding out from a guy who'd been
stalking her long-distance for years."

"I don't know Shelby that well," Katie said,
"but I can't picture her hiding from anything."

"She says Dad and this spot gave her the
courage to fight back. They spent their honeymoon here."

Luke eyed the cabin for any damage from
the winter, but no windows were broken.
The roof and the corral looked to be in good
shape, although some shingles might need to
be replaced.

"You can turn Rooster loose inside the
gate," he said and rode Dude alongside the
porch stretching across the front of the little
house. The horse lay down on cue and Luke

eased from the saddle onto the stoop. He had lunch spread on the boards by the time Katie finished shutting Rooster in the corral.

"There's spring water to drink, but you'll have to fetch it," he said. "You can grab a jug from inside and then follow the path out back—you'll see where to fill it."

"Is the door locked?"

"Wouldn't do any good if someone wanted to break in. Nobody comes this way except the Bucks, and they're welcome if they need shelter from the weather."

Katie went inside, coming out several minutes later with a plastic jug. "I could spend an hour looking around in there," she said. "It's like stepping back in time."

"Yeah, Shelby has fun finding that old stuff while she's on horse-training trips."

Katie disappeared around the corner of the cabin and returned with the full jug. "And there's a spa. I wanted to jump right in."

"Feel free—a hundred and five degrees winter and summer." He'd taken girls skinny-dipping in the hot spring when he was in high school, but he'd never brought a woman here since he'd started working as a bullfighter. Now he might never be able to climb the path again and relax in the warm water. Another piece of his life taken from him.

They sat with their legs hanging off the porch and ate lunch washed down with icy water in agate-ware mugs Katie had found inside. Dude left his grazing by the creek and wandered over to beg chunks of cookie from Luke's lunch.

"I think I could live here forever," Katie said. "Why did your family leave this location?"

"Probably the womenfolk wanted to be closer to the road when it came through between Durango and Cortez farther west," Luke said. "And it was easier to drive the cattle to the railhead back then and truck them out nowadays. We've always used the cabin for hunting and keeping an eye on the herd in their summer pasture, so it never fell apart like a lot of old buildings like this."

He broke the last cookie in two and handed half to her. "You're not ready to go back to your husband? He must be missing you considerably."

"I doubt it." She couldn't keep the bitterness out of her voice. "Why do you ask?"

"My line of work, you have to read body language. How likely a rider is to buck off before the buzzer. Or if a bull plans to trot out with no bother or try to nail someone. I noticed you were fine till I mentioned your pretty hair, then you started rubbing your ring finger. I'm guessing you have a lot of unfinished business back East."

"I do, but I'm not ready to deal with it. Not yet."

A shadow flashed across the sun accompanied by a high keening cry.

Katie jumped. "What was that?"

"One of our eagles—a pair nests up behind the cabin."

"You have your own eagles? I feel like I've stumbled into some kind of fairy tale."

"Not really," he said. "Bad stuff happens here, just like anywhere else."

Katie's lips trembled. "I know. Bad stuff happens everywhere." Tears overflowed as she let the whole story spill out—the long months nursing her mother, meeting Britt Cavendish at the funeral luncheon, the whiff of perfume on Brad's jacket after he left her alone that evening, the shattering discovery in her own home, in her own bed. And her parting display left for him at the site of his betrayal.

Luke wished he could comfort her but was

afraid to interrupt. He sat running his fingers through Dude's forelock until she fell silent at last and then handed her his bandana.

"I was so stupid," she said, mopping her face. "I never suspected a thing, but now I'm sure she wasn't the first. The perfume trick was too clever. I'd read about that stunt in a novel, but I never dreamed it would happen to me. You must think I'm a real coward for running away. I'd have done things differently if we'd had children, but since we don't..."

"I don't think you're any kind of coward. It took real grit to break loose like you did. And you really put the spurs to him before you left."

She sniffled a last time and folded his bandana. "I'll wash this when we get back. And thanks for not patting me on the head and saying 'there, there.'"

"Never occurred to me. I was admiring your gumption—we Camerons set great store by gumption."

He stuffed debris from their lunch into the bag. "Time to hit the trail. Mount up in the corral and I'll get the gate for you."

He transferred to his saddle and slid back the heavy bar on the corral gate for Katie to ride out. They retraced their path to the gate between Cameron's Pride and the Bucks' spread, checking the rest of the fence line before heading to the home ranch.

He shot a sidewise glance at Katie, wondering how she was holding up. It had been a long day, especially for someone not used to riding. She caught his look and gave him a thumbs-up. Good girl—grittier than he'd expected of a gal raised in the East. He had prolonged their day simply for the pleasure of her company.

Following the bull-riding circuit, he'd talked with dozens of people every day—his buddies, the riders and the bull contractors, announcers, fans, and, of course, the buckle bunnies. Now his only contacts outside his family were the physical therapists in Durango. He'd be sorry to see Katie go.

"Luke," she said as they descended the long slope toward the ranch house, "do you really think staying in Durango to work at the Queen would be a good idea? If that's what Lucy has in mind, I mean. I need to be useful while I'm sorting things out."

"I can't see anything wrong with you pitching in at the Queen," he said, surprised by the burst of pleasure her question triggered. "Shelby's a great cook, but not being on the ranch with Dad makes her crazy. He had a heart attack about six, seven years ago, and she still frets something will happen while she's not here to keep an eye on him. Jo's a good worker, but she can't shortchange Missy and JJ, especially since she's homeschooling. Neither of them has any restaurant experience."

"And Lucy's anxious to get to New Hampshire," Katie said. "How long before she has to leave?"

"Sometime in June—I don't know just when." He pulled off his hat and ran his hand through his hair in frustration before clapping it down over his brows.

"I hate dragging you into our little drama, but our family kind of adopted Marge Bowman more than twenty years ago. Dad even cosigned for a loan so she could buy the Queen. She's good people. Any emergency, a fire or a flood, Marge is right there with food and hot coffee. And she's never turned away anyone who doesn't have the price of a meal."

"If Lucy has to be in New Hampshire the beginning of June, that would give me at least a month to learn the ropes. You think the owner would go for that?"

"I guess you'd have to ask her," Luke said.

"I guess that's what I'll do," she said with a smile.

At the barn Luke showed her how to un-saddle Rooster and brush him down before turning him out with the other horses. He pulled his own saddle off Dude, who oblig-ingly turned first one side and then the other to be groomed before joining Rooster in the pasture.

"You can go along to the house if you want," Luke said. "Something I need to do out here for a few minutes."

"Anything I can do to help?" Katie asked as she slid Rooster's saddle onto its rack.

Luke flipped a mental coin—should he brush her off and share his fight with her? "I exercise at least once a day," he said. "More if I can manage it. Dad and Tom installed sort of a gym for me here in the barn. I don't mind if you stay."

He turned away for fear of seeing pity or dismissal on her face and wheeled toward the rear of the barn. He locked his chair below a steel bar mounted crossways in a tie stall and began to chin himself, counting under his breath—six, seven…

"Shoot." He'd lost count.

"That's nine," Katie said. "How many more?"

"Eleven," he said with a grunt.

She counted along with him up to twenty. "What's next?"

"Standing," he said. "The doctors say I don't have much chance of walking again. I plan to make liars out of them."

He flipped up his footrests and set his boots against two blocks nailed to the floor. Grasping two ends of a thick rope looped around the manger, he pulled himself forward, lifting off the seat of his chair a few inches and then lowering himself again. He had a little control over his legs, but he wobbled almost uncontrollably as soon as he got close to upright. After ten reps, he sat, panting and soaked with sweat.

"That's it for today," he said. "Tomorrow I'll go for fifteen."

"Sure you will," Katie said. "You're doing great."

The phone rang as they entered the kitchen. "Grab that, will you?" Luke said as he hung his hat and jacket on their hook. "Just say 'Cameron's Pride.'"

Katie answered as he directed and then said, "Hi, Jake. We just got back. Your cousin's bull was on the wrong side of the fence, so we had to herd him to where he belonged and wait for his owner to come get him and mend the fence. Let me get Luke—"

She listened, frowning a little, then her face cleared. "No, of course not. I'm sure we can manage. Enjoy your evening."

She set the phone on its charger. "Your dad and Shelby are in Durango for a dinner meeting—Cattlemen's Association, I think he said. Someone wants Shelby to check out their new horse in the morning. They'd like to stay overnight if everything's okay here. So I guess you get to sample my cooking tonight."

Luke had a good idea of his dad's side of the conversation: "You mind keeping an eye on Luke tonight?" He hated being watched and coddled like a child, but he was grateful his folks could enjoy an evening away.

"Fine by me," he said. "Show me what you can do."

CHAPTER TEN

"So what appeals to you for dinner?" Katie asked. "Anything you absolutely hate?"

"I'll eat whatever you feel like making," Luke said. "Or I can cook. Mom made sure we all learned how. My green chili rules."

"Lucy mentioned green chili, too—I'll have to try it sometime. But tonight I'm the chef. Okay if I explore the larder?"

He waved his hand. "Explore away. Check the freezer in the cellar, too. I don't know what Shelby has stashed down there."

Katie opened cabinets and poked her head into the walk-in pantry before descending to the cellar to return with a whole chicken.

"How about chicken pot pie?"

"Sounds great—we haven't had that here since Mom died. Shelby doesn't do piecrusts. I think Mom used a recipe your mom sent her."

"Okay then," Katie said. "I'll put the chicken in cold water and grab a shower while it thaws."

Half an hour later she came downstairs

with her hair hanging in damp waves. Luke's flattering comments had canceled out Brad's complaints that wearing her hair loose made her look like a schoolgirl or a hippie. His wolf whistle when she entered the kitchen reinforced her resolve never to cut her hair. Unless she felt like it.

She put him to work peeling and chopping carrots while she set the chicken to simmer and assembled the ingredients for a piecrust.

They worked together as if they'd been sharing kitchen chores for years, exchanging stories of growing up in such wildly different settings. Luke made her laugh as he described his scrapes with authority as a teen, graduating from high school only by the skin of his teeth.

"I wasn't dumb," he said, "but I spent my time in class thinking up new stunts to drive the teachers nuts. Once I started traveling between bull-riding events, I caught up on all the reading I'd skipped in school."

"I was just the opposite," Katie said. "I was the dull, plain girl who never blew off an exam and turned in my term papers two days ahead of schedule."

"You were never plain or dull, just not

flashy like the prom queens and cheerleaders. Look at you now."

She flushed with pleasure and turned away to check the flame on the big gas range. The chicken had cooked to falling-off-the-bone tenderness, so she assembled the filling and shaped the crust over the casserole dish.

"This has to bake about forty-five minutes," she said. "Any chores I can help with while we wait? Your dad said a neighbor would check the cows."

"That'll probably be Mike Farley, Lucy's fiancé," Luke said. "Or maybe his dad. They'll let us know if there's any problem. You can come along with me to visit the horses before dark if you like."

Katie laid aside the apron she'd found hanging in the pantry and followed Luke to the barn. He stopped by the feed room and scooped a handful of nuggets from a metal can before rolling back the side door.

"Dessert time, guys," he called, and a dozen or so horses, led by Dude, came at a trot. He distributed the treats, stroking each horse's head and scrutinizing their legs before turning each one away with a slap on the shoulder.

"All present and accounted for," he said. "One more stop."

He pulled a plastic baggie from his pocket and wheeled through the barn to a box stall opening out into a separate paddock. A gray horse with a delicately shaped head and dainty ears peered over the stall door. Even with her limited knowledge, Katie could see the difference between this face and those of the horses in the pasture.

"Meet Ghost—he's Shelby's horse. She gentled him when he was a young stud running wild and turned him into a top cutting horse. He sires the foals Shelby trains to sell as ranch horses—I guess you'd call them cow ponies."

"Is he an Arabian?"

"Part, maybe—nothing we can document. Probably a lot of Barb in him, a throwback to the horses the conquistadores brought from Spain." Luke handed Katie a bit of candy from the bag. "He loves licorice—give him a piece on the flat of your hand."

Katie held out the treat as Luke had directed her, surprised at the softness of the stallion's muzzle as he lipped the candy from her palm.

"You're so lucky growing up with animals," she said. "My dad was terribly allergic, so the only pets I could have were fish."

"Pretty hard to cuddle a fish, I guess." Luke scratched behind Ghost's ear. "My grandmother took in all kinds of injured birds and animals. We grew up with hawks and owls and baby squirrels and foxes around the house. But they were never pets—Gram made sure we understood they were passing through."

Katie looked at her watch. "The chicken pie should be about ready." She led the way through the barn and halted in wonder at the sunset light flooding the valley. To the west, the sky had turned a peachy pink; evening mist, like spun gold, floated over the creek. A few clouds hung above the western horizon, framed in pure light.

"This must be how heaven looks," she said.

"Could be," Luke said. "That's a real Tiepolo sky."

Katie's mouth fell open.

"I couldn't resist," he said with a grin. "I can't draw a straight line with a ruler, but I sure like looking at art. Every city on the tour, I'd find the art museum. Most of my downtime, I'd be sitting in front of a painting just sucking it in like a kid with an ice cream soda." He looked away. "And chasing girls after the event, I gotta be honest."

"Didn't you take ribbing about visiting museums?"

"Are you kidding? I never let on. Nobody knew except Tom—he saw the brochures I picked up and some prints I especially liked. You've probably noticed the ones in my room."

"You Camerons are full of surprises—your brother's a teacher, Lucy's an actress and you're an art connoisseur."

"Yeah, right." He wheeled past her toward the house. "Come on. That chicken pie is calling my name."

Luke set the table and put together a salad while Katie carried the casserole from the oven and made fresh coffee.

She spooned a small helping onto Luke's plate and waited while he tasted it.

"Katie Gabriel," he said, "this is a mouthful of heaven."

"My grandmother taught me how to make it. The secret ingredient is Bell's Poultry Seasoning—I found some in the pantry. I've made this recipe so many times I can practically do it with my eyes closed."

As if on cue, she yawned so widely her jaw cracked. "Sorry," she said. "It's been quite a day."

"You've worked hard, and you're not used to the elevation. Early to bed for both of us, I'd say. I've got to tell you, that was the longest I've been in the saddle since I got home. And the first time I've felt like I did a real day's work."

They finished the meal with coffee and slabs of gingerbread Katie found in the freezer.

"Anything you'd like to watch on TV?" he asked after they'd loaded the dishwasher.

"Not really—I'm more of a reader."

He hesitated, staring at nothing. "You want to see some old videos of Tom and me working? I haven't felt like watching before this, but if you wouldn't mind…"

How hard would this be for him, to watch his life as it had been before the accident?

"Sure," she said. "I'll join you."

She sat riveted by the action on the screen, the raw violence, the brute strength of the bulls and the absurd courage of the men attempting to ride them. And the three bull-fighters who repeatedly flung themselves in danger's way to save the riders from the bull's hooves and horns. Luke's hand crept toward hers, and they sat with their fingers intertwined.

After nearly an hour, he drew a deep breath and pulled his hand away. "That's enough," he said. "Thanks for sitting with me. I haven't wanted to watch before this, but tonight I was ready."

She yawned again. "I was glad to keep you company. Can I do anything for you before I turn in?"

"Nope, I take care of myself," he said with an edge to his voice. "Sleep well." He spun his chair away and propelled it toward his own room.

She watched him go, a little stung by his abrupt dismissal until she thought again how difficult the last hour must have been for him. The Luke she'd seen on the screen ran and leaped and spun like a gymnast. Watching must have been excruciating for him, confined to a wheelchair like a wild hawk in a cage.

She left a single light on in the kitchen in case she should need to come down during the night, and climbed the stairs. Once in bed, she read a book on local history she had found on a shelf in the living room. She left her door open in case Luke called out.

After a few minutes she closed her book and replayed Jake's words from their conversation on the phone: "We wouldn't think about staying in town if Luke was there alone. He has to take pills at night for muscle spasms, and I don't know how drowsy they make him. If there was a fire…"

Maybe she should have told Luke about his father's request, but instinct told her to keep it to herself. He was a proud man; seeing her as a babysitter would surely gall him.

And why had he chosen tonight to watch the videos? She was glad if she'd been of some use, but why with her rather than a trusted friend or even alone? Maybe the casual nature of their relationship made it safer, without personal investment.

She yawned again and closed her eyes.

WHAT HAD WAKENED HER? She lay still, listening. The sound came again, a wordless cry followed by a crash. She shot from her bed and flung her robe over her nightgown as she raced down the stairs.

No light shone from Luke's room. She hesitated—maybe the sound had come from outside. Then she heard a soft groan and ran barefoot to his door. In the dim light from the hall, she could see the empty bed and the wheelchair toppled on its side.

Luke lay facedown beside the bed. He wore only a pair of gym shorts, the waistband only partially hiding the fresh scar along his lower spine. Katie flew to his side and knelt beside him as he tried to turn over.

"Don't move. Is anything broken?"

"Just my pride," he said as he managed to roll onto his back. He touched his face. "Maybe my nose." Blood seeped from one nostril.

He levered himself to a sitting position against the bed and scrubbed at his eyes with both hands. "Damn dream again. Could you get me a washcloth?"

She fetched a cloth and wrung it out in cold water before returning to switch on the bedside lamp. She stifled a gasp as its light revealed older scars on Luke's abdomen, both knees and both shoulders.

"Lean your head back," she said and sponged the blood from his face before settling the cloth across his nose and eyes. "What happened?"

"Ol' Buckshot happened—first time I've been close to a bucking bull since my wreck. And then watching those videos. I dreamed the bull was coming at me in the arena and ended up on the floor. I had these nightmares during rehab when an ambulance went by, but not since I got home. Till tonight."

He lifted the makeshift compress and cocked an eye at her. "I know my dad drafted you for night duty. Sorry I put on such a show for you."

She felt her face coloring. "He was concerned about you being here alone," she said. "Are you ready to get into bed?"

"I should, I guess, but I really feel like a cup of coffee and another piece of gingerbread."

"Coffee at this hour?" She checked the clock beside the lamp. "It's past midnight."

"It won't bother me. I need a little time to chase that bull out of my head." He reached for the overturned wheelchair and righted it. "Now I've got to figure out how to mount up."

"I can help you."

"You?" He snorted. "I'm not that heavy, but more than you can lift."

She eyed him with speculation. "I'll bet you don't weigh more than one fifty—one fifty-five, tops."

"Good guess—one forty-eight at my fighting weight. Okay, smarty, how do we do this?"

She pulled the belt from her robe. "Prop

your knees up a little," she said. "I watched you trying to stand in the barn. I think this will work." When he had pulled his legs into a flexed position, she tied the soft sash loosely above his knees and set his chair close by.

She stood in front of him with her bare feet bracing his and held out her hands. "Okay, grab on tight."

They linked their hands and wrists like trapeze artists. She rocked back on her heels, pulling him upright with her own weight, and pivoted him into his chair.

She pushed her hair back with a triumphant grin. "Easy-peasy."

"Dang, girl. Where'd you learn that trick?"

"We lived with my grandparents. The visiting nurse taught us that technique after my grandfather had a stroke. He hated asking for help, so we had to get him up a lot when he fell.

She retrieved her sash from around his knees. "Coffee and gingerbread coming up."

CHAPTER ELEVEN

LUKE SAT AT the kitchen table long after Katie had finished her gingerbread and glass of milk and gone back to bed. The nightmare had been as terrifying as ever, and he'd likely have a good shiner from banging his face on his wheelchair.

He hated showing weakness, especially to a stranger who happened to be an attractive woman. But Katie had come to his aid without hesitation, showing no fear or disgust on finding him flat out in need of help.

He'd had a lot of time to think, lying in the body cast and later sitting in this chair. He was learning the hard way that putting off important stuff like finding a wife until "someday" was asking for trouble. He'd never lived anywhere but this valley, and finding the right woman in the sparse population would be a challenge.

He looked at the clock on the mantel—2:00 a.m. was a bad time to ponder his pros-

pects. Somehow tonight, even after the nightmare, the future scared him less than usual.

LUKE WAS UP and had coffee brewing by the
time Katie came downstairs. Today he wore
sneakers and sweatpants instead of boots and
Wranglers.

She stopped short when she saw his face.
"Oh, dear. I should have fixed you an ice
pack."

"No big deal," he said, touching his right
eye. "It looks worse than it feels."

"What's up for today?"

"I need a favor. Shelby called earlier—she
was supposed to drive me to a physical therapy appointment in Durango at eleven, but
their rig broke down north of town. Think
you could give me a ride?"

"Could we use your car? The back of mine
is stuffed to the roof with all my worldly possessions. I don't think I can make room for
your chair."

"Yeah, sure—my Explorer needs exercise."
He leaned forward with his elbows on the
table. "You could drop me off at the hospital
and drive over to the Queen. I'll be a couple
hours, so you could have a cup of coffee and

see how the place operates before Lucy starts hounding you."

Her eyes brightened. "I'd like that. I was so tired and hungry the first time I stopped there I can't remember much about it."

"All right, then." Maybe the lunch-hour chaos would turn her off, but better she got a realistic idea of what she was signing on for before Lucy started her pitch.

"You're sure you're okay after your fall? You took an awful whack."

"You're joking, right? You saw those videos."

She laughed. "Okay, you just stubbed your toe last night."

"I thank you for rescuing me—helluva thing to ask you to do for a stranger."

"You're not a—" A look of confusion flickered across her face. "I mean, I didn't mind. I'm just glad I knew what to do."

"The hardest thing for me to learn in rehab was asking for help—cowboys generally don't holler unless there's broken bone ends sticking out. Tom always acted like a bull beating him up was some kind of disgrace. Not me—I played bruises for all they were worth. Women love comforting a wounded hero." He gave her a droll glance. "Sneaky, huh? What can I get you for breakfast?"

Katie opted for scrambled eggs with bacon; Luke had eaten warmed-up chicken pie, leaving enough for Jake and Shelby to sample when they got home. He texted Shelby to let her know he had a ride into Durango and that Katie planned to visit the Queen.

They checked on the horses before leaving. Katie carried fresh water for Ghost and climbed to the loft to throw fresh hay into his manger.

"Poor Ghost," she said, stroking his neck. "Does he ever get out to play with the other kids?"

"Sure he does, but only with the mares. We separate the geldings out first. Mostly he tolerates them, but sometimes he decides they're rival males. Stallions are notional that way."

"Where are your cows?" Katie asked as they left the barn.

"Over the far side of the creek. We keep them close in till all the calves are on the ground. We work them up here—tagging and vaccinating before we move them to the range we visited yesterday."

He looked at his watch. "About time we head into town." He pulled keys from his jacket and tossed them to Katie as a familiar pickup turned in at the gate and pulled up beside them.

Mike Farley climbed out and pulled a cardboard file box from the back seat. "I checked your mamas and babies last evening," he said. "All looking good, although you've got a couple ready to drop their calves any minute now."

He touched the brim of his straw cowboy hat to Katie. "Is this the company you were expecting?"

"Mike, meet Katie Gabriel. She drove all the way from Connecticut to bring us a box of letters Mom wrote to her mother."

Mike whistled. "That's some delivery run. I hope you'll visit long enough to make the trip worth your while."

"I'm seriously considering it," Katie said.

He turned to Luke. "You said to let you know if I needed more help," Mike said. He shifted the box in his arms. "This is the same kind of sorting, only from ranches here in the valley. They don't mind you digging through their accounts. Everyone said pretty much the same thing—if you can't trust a Cameron, who can you trust?"

"I'll do my best," Luke said, "but right now Katie's driving me into Durango for PT. Just set the box in the living room and I'll jump right in when we get back."

Mike carried the box into the house and handed Luke a check when he returned. "Don't give me any crap about not being paid," he said. "Your notes all checked out perfectly— I'll be able to get those returns to the guys in time to pay their taxes on schedule."

Luke pocketed the check without looking at the numbers. "Maybe I'll set up in competition with you."

"Go for it—there's plenty to keep both of us busy." Mike touched his hat to Katie again and drove off.

"What kind of work are you doing for him?" Katie asked after familiarizing herself with Luke's vehicle.

He explained his first assignment for Mike and what he'd be looking for in the ranch records.

"You're a real renaissance man, Luke Cameron—cowboy, bullfighter, art critic. And now a budding accountant."

"I guess I could be that—gotta be something. I'm too young to sit around in a bar and tell tall tales about bullfighting. And I did enjoy putting order into the mess Mike handed me."

He directed her through Hesperus and east toward Durango to Mercy Regional Medical Center. "Give me your cell number," he said outside the hospital. "I'll call you when I'm done."

He wheeled himself inside, mentally crossing his fingers that Lucy could talk Katie into helping out at the Silver Queen. A goodly stint of working at something she enjoyed might go a long way toward healing the damage her husband, whom he labeled the Jerk, had done.

Doug Pruitt, his physical therapist, whistled when he saw Luke's shiner. "What's the other guy look like?"

"I had bulls chasing me in my sleep last night. I didn't get very far trying to run away. But say, I learned a new stunt. A gal who's visiting us got me up off the floor, slick as you please." Luke described the method Katie had used to lift him.

"Stabilized your knees and levered you up with her own counterweight—a great home-nursing technique." Doug led the way to the large open exercise area. "Get out of those pants. We're going to do something different today."

Luke squirmed out of the sweatpants down

to his gym shorts and transferred to the padded platform. Doug wheeled an electro stimulator unit to the table and attached patches to Luke's thighs and calves.

"Let me know if this gets too painful," Doug said.

Luke grimaced. "I'd welcome pain—I can't feel anything except when a spasm hits, then nothing again when it passes." He punched his own leg. "Just these damn useless things hanging off me. Creeps me out."

"I hear you. I had a shoulder repair a while back—they blocked the whole arm for twenty-four hours. A really freaky feeling." Doug turned the dial and made some notes on a clipboard while Luke tried to imagine how things were going at the Silver Queen.

A timer sounded and Doug advanced the dial. Maybe Lucy was overselling the idea of Katie working there. Maybe there would be some kitchen disaster that would be a real turnoff. Maybe—

Luke bolted upright. "Holy…" He looked over at a grandmotherly lady doing shoulder stretches. "I felt that! My leg jumped."

"Yup." Doug adjusted the dial. "I'll back off the current and let the muscle rest, then we'll try it again. You really felt it? Or just the leg moving?"

"No, I felt the shock." Luke turned his head to hide his emotion. "Do it again."

"Not for a few minutes—we won't get a true picture if I hit you again so soon. Patience, little grasshopper."

Patience—easy for Doug to say. He probably went hiking on weekends and skiing in winter. Luke lay on the table trying to round up his stampeding emotions. Had he felt the shock? His mind ricocheted between foolish optimism and bleak despair. In his darkest moments, he beat at his dead limbs with his fists in impotent fury, as if his legs were parasites draining his future of hope.

One thing he knew for sure: if he never walked again, it wouldn't be for lack of trying.

Luke started when Doug slapped him on the shoulder. "Once more, Luke. Tell me if you feel anything."

More fiddling with the dials and then Luke almost leaped from the table. "I felt it again, thigh and calf, both on the left side. Maybe a little on the right side, too."

He and Doug high-fived in elation. "No promises," Doug said, "but it's a good sign. Any time you're bored, try wiggling your toes." He pulled off the electrodes. "Enough goofing off—time to get on the bike."

Luke climbed into his chair and then onto the motorized exercise bike, reveling in movement even though he couldn't activate the nerves and muscles on his own. Sweat soaked his shirt by the time the bike's timer signaled the cooldown period; he was shaking as Doug helped him into his chair.

"I rarely have to tell patients to back off," Doug said, "but you're one of those knotheads who don't know when to quit. Falling on your face if you pass out won't help your cause."

"Moderation has never been my strong point," Luke said, wiping his face with the towel Doug offered. "I've got two speeds— full-out or dead in my tracks."

CHAPTER TWELVE

KATIE PUSHED BACK the strand of hair that had escaped from her bun and blew a loud breath of relief—four orders of green chili with tortillas to the quartet of tourists in the front booth and a BLT, no mayo, for the lady seated alone, reading a novel with the silhouette of a cowboy on the cover.

Katie grabbed the next order slip from the overhead carousel as Lucy blew by with mugs of coffee and slices of peach pie for two men in Blue Seal caps seated at the antique mahogany bar.

"More cream at table six," Lucy said. "And you're awesome."

Katie took a fresh cream pitcher to fill from the carton in the commercial refrigerator—no do-it-yourself minis at the Queen. No sugar packets, either—old-fashioned glass-and-chrome dispensers along with real salt and pepper shakers sat on each oilcloth-covered table. She glanced at the clock on the wall above the pass-through—almost one o'clock. She should be getting a call from Luke soon, but she hated leaving Lucy with orders still to be filled.

Roger, the grizzled busboy/dishwasher, elbowed his way through the swinging door carrying a tray stacked with dirty dishes. "Booth four is empty," he said. "Looks like they left a nice tip—you're doing fine, kid. I haven't had time to ask—which Cameron are you?"

"No kind of Cameron," Katie said, "just a family friend." Although she already felt like part of the clan. "But I'm sort of looking for work."

"Plenty of that here. And heads up—the boss lady just hobbled in."

"Lucy will have to take care of her." Katie squinted at the slip in her hands. "Who eats chicken-fried steak for lunch?"

"People who raise beef for a living, cookie. The coating mix for the steak is in the fridge—it's marked *chicken*, just to confuse you."

Katie pounded the seasoned cracker-crumb mixture into two slabs of chuck steak and slid them into an iron skillet on the eight-burner range before peering into the dining room.

Lucy stood beside a woman with a halo of white curls seated at a table for two; crutches lay on the floor beside her chair.

So that was Marge Bowman. On the drive into town, Luke had told her the story of the foolish bandit who had thought to rob an old lady of her day's receipts. The bad guy had ended up with a minor gunshot wound from Marge's nickel-plated .38 and his intended victim seated on his back until the police arrived.

Lucy spotted her peeking through the door and beckoned. Katie held up a finger and turned to flip the steaks before joining them.

"I guess you're Lucy's new patsy," Marge said, taking the hand Katie offered after wiping it on her apron. "She's drafted everyone in the Cameron family to help out."

"Marge, meet Katie Gabriel," Lucy said.

"Garrison, not Gabriel," Katie said, "although I'll be going back to my maiden name."

"My grandmother had a saying," Marge said. "'Change the name but not the letter, change for worse and not for better.' She was so right. My family name was Barlow before I married Charlie Bowman. He was a sweet man but a lousy provider."

"My husband was a great provider, but…" Katie didn't care to air the grubby details again. "You'll have to excuse me—I've got chicken-fried steak on the stove."

"Let Lucy take care of it. Sit down and talk to me. Lucy's explained the situation?"

"Just that you had knee surgery and everyone is trying to keep the restaurant open while you're recuperating."

"A little more than that to the story. Jake backed me when I opened the Queen more than twenty years ago, even though he couldn't have afforded to get stuck for the loan if I failed. Lucy came to work for me when she was just fourteen, right after her mother died. I'd like to think I helped her through a rough time then."

Lucy returned from the kitchen with a cup of coffee for Marge, who patted her hand.

"So the Camerons and I are tighter than fleas on an old dog. I don't think I'd even try to come back if they weren't pushing and pulling me up the hill."

"Everyone in the family so far has been wonderful, although I still haven't met Luke's brother."

"Poor Tom—a bull smashed him up pretty bad probably eight or nine years ago. His back still gives out from time to time if he's not careful. Mighty few cowboys walk away from bull riding without some lasting souvenir."

"Why do they do it?" The memory of Luke's scars rose in Katie's mind. She leaned forward with her arms on the table. "Luke showed me videos of him and his brother last night. I don't know how much prize money is involved or how much he got paid but it can't be enough to justify the risks they take."

"I can't tell you, girl. Raised on loco weed, I guess, but I love 'em. Especially Luke, bless his heart. How's he doing?"

"Why don't you ask me yourself, darlin'?" Luke wheeled through the door.

"Lover!" Marge leaned into Luke's hearty embrace. "Why haven't you been to see me?"

"Lucy's got everyone who can drive working here, and it's a long haul into town with just these two wheels." Luke kissed Marge's hand like a courtier, and she giggled. "And look at your hair—I thought some big-city celeb had stopped in for lunch."

Marge fluffed her short ringlets. "The beautician at the nursing home talked me into letting her chop it short—I've been skinning it back in a knot so long I forgot how it kinks up."

"You'd look beautiful to me bald as an egg,

but you're cute as a baby lamb with those curls."

"Seriously, Luke…"

"Seriously, I'm about to fade away from hunger. A big piece of your peach pie would fix that." He surveyed Katie's flour-dusted apron. "I'll bet your new help could rustle one up for me."

Katie beamed at him with her best perky-waitress smile. "Yes, sir, you bet, sir. Ice cream on your pie?"

He gave her a thumbs-up as she turned on her heel and headed to the kitchen.

Lucy handed her two plates with the steaks, mashed potatoes, peas and gravy. "Table five," she said. "I'll get Luke's pie—he won't leave till he has it."

The door finally closed behind the last luncheon customers, and Lucy flipped the Open sign to Closed. "Another disaster-free day in the book, thanks to Katie."

Luke yanked on Lucy's apron string as she passed. "So how did you talk Katie into working, Red?"

She slapped at his hand. "I didn't talk her into anything. Our regular lunch waitress is home with a sick kid today. When Katie saw how busy I was, she just pitched in. And don't call me Red."

Roger appeared from the kitchen with more coffee cups and a carafe. He poured for everyone and pulled up a chair. "The new kid did real good, boss. And she says she's looking for a job."

Marge gave Katie a beady-eyed stare. "Are you? You think you could work for a crabby old woman who's demanding as all hell and set in her ways?"

"It's your restaurant—you can be as demanding as you like. And your ways seem to be working, so why change them?"

Marge gave a bark of laughter. "She's a diplomat, too. Look, I can't pay you much, but you can live in the apartment over the Queen for free. It's a little cramped, but I know Lucy's kept it clean. And you'll appreciate the location when you have to set up for breakfast— we have regulars who come in around seven. Want to give it try?"

"I don't have any real experience working in a restaurant," Katie said.

"You do now," Lucy said. "You jumped in like a real pro today. I'll stay on long enough to make sure you know the routine."

"And I've been known to flip a burger or

two," Roger said. "We won't let you fall on your face."

Katie looked at their eager faces, her eyes stopping when they reached Luke.

"What do you think?" she asked him.

He shrugged. "I think you can do anything you set your mind to. You said you wanted a job cooking—here's your chance."

She smiled at him as if sealing a pact and turned to Marge. "I guess you've got yourself a cook, Mrs. Bowman."

"Who?" Marge made a great show of looking around the dining room. "Just Marge, honey—my mother-in-law was Mrs. Bowman, God rest her soul."

She reached for her crutches. "Lucy, I told my neighbor she didn't need to pick me up— you'd give me a ride. Time to drag these old bones home. And you—" she pointed a crutch at Katie "—I'll expect you to be moved in by tomorrow evening. I want Lucy to have a little time with her folks before she heads East again."

"That's okay," Lucy said as she held the door open for Marge. "They'll just put me to work if I'm out at the ranch full-time."

The big room seemed very quiet after Marge and Lucy departed. Roger gathered the cups. "I'll finish cleaning up, Katie. You take this cowboy home." He stuck out his hand. "Glad to see you back, Luke."

"Glad to be back." Luke shook his hand. "You take care of this lady, you hear?"

"Like a prize calf." Roger returned to the kitchen.

"I had a notion you might be kind of busy," Luke said, "so I bummed a ride with one of the nurses coming off duty. Now tell me the truth—how did you like it?"

"My feet are killing me—I'll need to buy some shoes with better support—I have a fierce headache from the noise of the exhaust fan and I burned my wrist reaching over a hot skillet." She held out the wounded hand for his inspection. "And I loved it. I really enjoyed myself."

"Sort of how we feel when we look at a pen full of calves all tagged and branded— beat-up and worn to a nub, but happy with a good day's work." He grasped her hand and dropped a light kiss on the burn. "To make it better, darlin'," he said.

He pivoted his chair. "We'd better get home before they send out a posse looking for us."

CHAPTER THIRTEEN

LUKE SAT MOSTLY in silence on the ride to the ranch while Katie chattered about her afternoon's adventures in food service. Of course he was pleased she would be working at the Queen, but he would miss her. She would be moving into Durango come morning—no more sitting at meals with the family or riding beside him across the ranch. In a short time, she had become family—more than family.

He gave himself a sharp mental slap. Katie needed running room, a chance to grow her identity, and he needed to concentrate all his energy on rebuilding and recovery. After all, Durango was only an hour away, and if she did end up getting a divorce...

"So how did your therapy go?"

He started to wave off her question with his usual breezy disclaimer, but he longed to share his elation, the simple joy of feeling pain in his useless limbs.

"It hurt," he said.

Katie veered his vehicle into a dusty side road and turned to face him. "It hurt? Your legs hurt? You felt—"

He nodded. "I get electric stimulation to keep the muscles from wasting, and I could feel it today. Twice, both legs." He swallowed hard. "First time I've been able to feel anything more than spasms since that bull stomped on my back."

She grabbed his left hand in both of hers. "Oh, Luke! I'm so glad for you. Does that mean—"

"It means I shouldn't get my hopes up, but it's a start." He laughed. "I've stumbled into an electric fence a time or two, but I never thought getting zapped would be something to celebrate."

When they reached Cameron's Pride, they found Shelby waiting outside the barn. "I know you're tired from your PT," she said, "but could you ride out to the cabin? Jake and Missy are checking the roof and I can't raise Jake on his cell phone—you know what the reception is like out there. Tell him Art Duffy is on his way to look at our yearlings. I can entertain Art when he arrives, but Jake will have to dicker with him."

"Sure," Luke said. "I'll go change into my boots while you saddle Dude for me."

"Mind if I come along?" Katie asked. "I may not get another chance to ride for a while."

"Be glad to have you," he said, happy for more time with her before she moved to Durango.

"Then I'll saddle Rooster, too," Shelby said over her shoulder.

Ten minutes later Luke rode out with Katie by his side. "Art Duffy pays top dollar for our yearlings," he said, "but price negotiations are always like a summit meeting. He won't deal with anyone but Dad, so we need to pick up the pace a little."

He leaned over and pulled the reins a little shorter in her hands. "We're not going to gallop full-out, just a nice easy lope to get there a little faster. Rooster's as easy as a rocking horse—just lean forward a little and move with him."

Katie nodded, tight-lipped, and tugged her cap down over her forehead.

Luke spoke to Dude, who flowed forward in so smooth a gait Luke could have carried a full glass without spilling a drop. He cast a glance at Katie, who had relaxed her death grip on her reins, rocking in the saddle as if she'd been riding for years. He didn't ask if she was enjoying herself. Her blissful smile spoke without words.

They kept up the pace through the lower pasture to the big metal gate closing off the open rangeland beyond. Luke slid the latch for Katie to ride through and then closed it behind them. They continued at a jog until they forded the creek and the cabin came into view.

Two horses stood in the corral. Jake and Missy sat on the porch roof with their legs dangling over the edge. A ladder lay on the ground.

Luke sat back in his saddle with a snicker. "I guess we know now why you're AWOL. You got your phone, Katie? We need a picture of this."

Jake scowled at them and turned to Missy. "Your uncle Luke's a mean man, honey. He'll sit there hee-hawing like a jackass till we starve up here."

"I can shinny down the post, Grandpa. Honest, I can."

"No need, Missy." Luke rode under the overhang and reached up a hand. "Just step down onto Dude, then you and Katie can put the ladder up for the old man."

Missy clambered onto Dude's back and then slid to the ground. Katie dismounted to help Missy prop the ladder up for Jake to descend.

"Thanks, I guess," Jake said. "What brings you out here?"

"You, Pop. Art Duffy's on his way to look at the yearlings. Shelby will keep him busy till you get there, but she was getting worried when you didn't answer your phone."

Jake sighed. "No help for that, I guess."

"Get moving. We'll close up here and get Missy home."

Jake caught Blackjack, his black gelding in the corral, mounted and splashed across the creek before lifting the horse into a fast lope.

"I'm afraid to ask," Luke said, "but what happened to the ladder?"

"I was helping Grandpa measure for new shingles," Missy said, "and then a bull elk came and rubbed his fanny on the ladder till it fell down." She pointed at tracks in the soft dust by the porch. "See? And I could have shinnied down the post, only Grandpa was afraid I'd fall."

"Sure you could have, but we'd better get

home before your mom gets worried. Check Babe's cinch before you mount up."

Missy nodded and caught her horse—a showy paint mare—swarming into the saddle nimble as a monkey.

Katie shook her head in disbelief. "She looks like she was born on horseback."

"Nope, she didn't get on her first horse till she was almost two."

Katie laughed. "Practically over the hill."

They rode three abreast while Missy entertained them with the misdeeds of Angus, her mother's Maine Coon cat. "Angus sneaked out and killed a prairie dog and left it in the hallway and Daddy stepped on it in the middle of the night and said a lot of bad words."

"I might have said a few myself," Luke said with a straight face.

"Let's race home," Missy said when they reached the lower pasture.

"You know better," Luke said. "We can lope a little, but no racing." He leaned forward and Dude broke into his rocking-horse gait; Rooster and Babe followed his lead.

They dropped Missy off at her home, a compact version of the main log ranch house with its own small stable and corral. Jo met them outside. Missy launched into an excited account to her mother of being stranded on the cabin roof. "The elk was as tall as the ladder and he kept trying to reach up and hook us!"

"Uh-huh," Jo said. "You've got your Aunt Lucy's sense of drama, for sure. Now go take care of your horse."

"Is Tom home?" Luke asked. "How's his back?"

Jo shook her head in exasperation. "He should be lying flat until it settles down, but of course he's at school. At least he's agreed to use a cane—that tells me how much it hurts. The girl he carried feels guilty, but he told her he could have thrown it out just as easily shoeing a horse or wrestling a calf."

"Missy's a pistol," Luke said as he and Katie rode on the home ranch. "Tom about broke his heart looking for her, but she's his kid, all right."

"Jo's not her mother?"

"Her mother took off pregnant before he could marry her. Traci was bound to try for a singing career in Nashville—she had no notion of being a ranch wife. Sad story—she got killed during a mugging when Missy was just a couple months old. Jo located Missy right before an adoption got finalized."

"I mistook her for Lucy's daughter when I first saw her," Katie said.

"Yeah, Lucy's baby pictures convinced the Tennessee authorities Missy was a Cameron. We spawn one real redhead in every generation, like Dad before he went gray."

"Missy and JJ are adorable," Katie said. "I've wanted children, but now I'm glad it didn't happen. I can walk away free and clear."

"Tom's two are a hoot," he said. "I could use a couple or three myself." With his extended family, he wasn't worried about raising kids, even confined to a wheelchair. Grandparents and aunts and uncles would always be available to lend a hand, but the thought of never being more than Uncle Luke to Tom's or someday Lucy's kids saddened him.

They arrived at the home ranch in time to see Jake shake hands with Art Duffy, a bulky man with a snowy handlebar mustache, a silver belt buckle the size of a cow pie and ostrich-skin boots. He spotted Luke and reached through the barnyard gate to shake his hand.

"Dang, Luke—you're looking good. I saw that wreck in OKC on TV. Guess it looked worse than it was—here you are riding high on a handsome horse." He touched the brim of his cream-colored Stetson. "And with a fine-looking lady. Howdy, ma'am."

Luke introduced Katie as a friend from Connecticut.

"You ever been out West before, Miss Katie? No? Well, you couldn't pick a prettier ranch to visit anywhere in Colorado. Of course, I could show you some spreads in Texas…"

"Don't get started on Texas, Art," Luke said. "We'll be sitting here till midnight."

"Durn if you're not right. I need to get on down the road." He tipped his hat again to Katie and climbed into his arterial-red King Ranch F-150. His horn sounded a farewell—"The Yellow Rose of Texas"—as his truck rattled across the cattle guard.

Luke turned to Katie. "I'm right proud of you, Miss Katie—you kept a straight face."

She burst into laughter. "Is he for real? The next thing I expected out of his mouth was 'little lady.'"

"As real as can be, considering he's from New Jersey. He made a pile of money in real estate, retired and moved to El Paso to start a new career as a cattle buyer. Now he has fun playing Texan for all he's worth, which is considerable."

DINNER TURNED INTO a celebration; Art had agreed to buy all the yearlings Jake cared to sell.

"And how would you have gotten down off that roof if Luke and Katie hadn't come looking for you?" Shelby asked.

"I'd have let Missy climb down and ride over to the Bucks' for help," Jake told her. "Stop fretting, woman—I wasn't planning to jump and break my neck."

She stroked his back as she refilled his coffee mug. "Don't mind me, Jake. I can't spare you just yet."

Luke watched their fond sparring, recalling his father's patience in courting Shelby. He couldn't see at the time why Jake didn't just flat-out ask her to marry him, but maybe making haste slowly was wiser.

"I'd better pack up tonight," Katie said. "I plan to be in Durango for the lunch rush. Lucy's going to walk me through the morning routine for at least a couple days, but you should have your daughter back pretty soon."

Luke groaned. "There goes peace and quiet." And he'd have mighty few chances to see Katie since he couldn't drive. Maybe it was just as well—otherwise he'd be hanging around the

Queen, pesky as a mosquito, and neglecting his work here.

His dad unwittingly threw him a lifeline. "When I saw you guys come riding in this afternoon, I thought you were Jo, the way you looked in the saddle. You sure you haven't ridden much before?"

"Not since I was twelve." She smiled at Luke. "But I had a great teacher here."

"You come back on your days off if you like," Jake said. "We'll put you on a horse with a little more go. We're always happy to take advantage of guests to help move cattle."

Luke had been cudgeling his brain for a way to invite Katie to the ranch, and now his father had taken the reins from his hands.

"You should have seen her face old Buckshot down," he said. "I couldn't have done it better myself."

"How did your PT go?" Shelby asked.

Elation rose in his chest again; he cleared his throat and reached unconsciously for Katie's hand. "I could feel the e-stim," he said. "In both legs."

Shelby grasped his other hand, and Jake jumped up to pound him on the back. "You're gonna make it back, son. I know you are."

After dinner, Shelby left the kitchen to

check the horses before nightfall and Katie went with her. Jake loaded the dishwasher, and Luke wheeled into the living room to examine the box of tax records Mike had left for him.

He had an idea that having real productive work would do much to carry him through the drudgery of rehab. The numbers on the check Mike had given him made him whistle, but when he broke it down by the hour, Mike hadn't overpaid him.

He pulled the envelopes from the box and arranged them on the long table under the window where he'd worked on the first batch. Too late to start tonight, but he would dig in tomorrow once Katie left.

CHAPTER FOURTEEN

KATIE FOUND LUKE alone in the kitchen the next morning when she carried her bag downstairs. She had heard voices earlier, then silence, and wondered if he had ridden out to work somewhere on the ranch.

"Dad and Shelby are sorting the heifers we sold yesterday," Luke said, pouring coffee for her. "But I thought I'd see you off on your new job. I don't envy you—I'll bet herding cattle is way easier than wrangling customers."

"You're probably right, but the cooking part will be fun, and I love the idea of helping keep the Queen open."

"Marge has quite a local following, and tourists love the atmosphere—an authentic Wild West saloon. She stages chuckwagon barbecues, too, or did. She catered Dad and Shelby's wedding party—Tom and Jo's, too. I don't know that she'll ever start doing those again."

"I could help with that," Katie said. "I worked for a caterer in college. Catering is easier than restaurant cooking, I think—fewer choices, and you know in advance how much to prepare."

"Shelby made up a big pot of oatmeal this morning," Luke said. "Will that do you for breakfast?"

She dawdled over her oatmeal, drank an extra cup of coffee, knowing she needed to go yet hating to leave. In a few short days, she had come to feel so much a part of the ranch's rhythm that moving on was already wrenching. At the same time, she was eager to start her next adventure, one that might develop into a real career.

And Luke. Her thoughts skidded to a standstill when they reached him. Ridiculous, but her heart had leaped when he'd shared his good news about his progress, as if she had a vital stake in his future.

Luke set down his mug with a thump. "I hate to do it, but I'm chasing you out of here. You need to shop for a better pair of work shoes before you jump in. Brown's right up the street from the Queen should have what you need."

Katie put her mug down more slowly. "What

your dad said about my coming back to the ranch...you think he meant that? Or was he just being polite?"

"Yeah, he meant it, and so do I. Come anytime—we'll always be glad to see you, and put you to work, too."

"You'll keep me posted about your progress?" She found a scrap of paper by the phone and wrote. "Here's my email address, and you've already got my phone number."

"Shucks, girl—you'll probably see me come walking into the Queen before you know it. I'm no hero, but I've never been a quitter, either."

She offered her hand in farewell. Luke grasped it and pulled her into an awkward embrace that almost toppled her into his lap. They both laughed as she straightened.

"Well, that was smooth," he said. "Guess I've lost my touch."

"No complaints here," she said and brushed a light kiss on his cheek. "I'll call when I get settled in."

She replayed the leave-taking in her mind as she drove. Why had she kissed Luke—a friendly gesture, like his clumsy hug? Because she had wanted to, pure and simple.

She still felt the warmth of his grasp and the slight rasp of his beard under her lips.

The very thought of her husband's touch nauseated her, but she missed sleeping with him, the comforting warmth in the night, the delight and release of great sex. No question, Brad was good in bed, probably because he'd had so much practice. Maybe he had found her boring, a simple faithful wife who lacked his wider experience.

And hadn't Luke taken dozens of women to bed? Of course he had, a handsome cowboy traveling for years to a new city every weekend. But he hadn't been cheating on an unsuspecting wife.

She wondered about the extent of his disability but suspected he would be a tender and ardent lover regardless. Better an honest man than one who would betray her with such cold calculation.

Definitely time to leave the ranch—she wasn't ready to chance another mistake like Brad, the picture-perfect husband with rot at his core.

She had put her speculations aside by the time she reached Durango. She had a job and a place to live, a ledge on which to perch while she recovered her wits and took a good look around.

She parked in the space Lucy had shown her behind the Queen and then bought a sturdy pair of black leather sneakers at Brown's Shoe Fit before reporting for duty. A few customers sat at tables or at the long bar with mugs and small plates in front of them—obviously the coffee-break crowd.

A thirty-something woman with honey-colored hair in a long braid greeted her and asked if she preferred a table or a booth. Lucy emerged from the kitchen before Katie could answer.

"Katie, you did come. I was half afraid you'd change your mind. Sue Cabot serves at lunchtime weekdays. Sue, Katie's going to help us save the Queen."

Lucy hustled Katie to the kitchen and handed her an apron. "With Sue minding the front, I can get you oriented better to this part of the operation, although you did great yesterday."

She gave Katie a whirlwind tour of the walk-in pantry, the commercial freezer-refrigerator, and the dungeon-like cellar with canned and dry ingredients on shelves built against a natural rock wall.

Lucy glanced at her watch. "We'd better get upstairs and start grabbing orders off the carousel."

The rest of the day went smoothly, with Sue handling most of the waitressing while Lucy and Katie cooked and Roger kept the tables cleared. Sue turned the sign on the door to Closed at three and hung up her apron.

"Gotta get home before the brats take the house apart," she said. "See you tomorrow."

"Her kids are angels," Lucy said as the door closed behind Sue, "and she adores them. Her daughter is only twelve, but she's already a talented painter. Sue's earnings here pay for Becky's lessons with a local artist."

"Could we sit down with the menu?" Katie said. "I haven't had a chance to look at it."

Lucy made them both chicken-salad sandwiches and joined Katie at one of the tables. "I've tried to keep it simple," she said. "I've brought a few items from the dinner menu over to lunch as specials so people can still order their favorites."

Katie studied the menu. She already had a good idea of what it offered from filling orders—standard diner fare, with regional twists like the green chili, bison burgers and Marge's famous dried-peach pie.

"Marge baked up a couple dozen pies before her surgery," Lucy said. "It's the one thing people expect here. We're down to six in the freezer."

She gave Katie a hopeful look. "I don't suppose you're a baker."

"Not fancy baking, but I can make piecrusts in my sleep."

Lucy rolled her eyes heavenward and fluttered both hands in the air. "Hallelujah, we're saved. I know how to make the filling, but I couldn't make a piecrust if you put a gun to my head."

Katie laughed. "I guess we won't have to go to that extreme. Speaking of pies, how do you feel about chicken pot pie?"

"I remember my mom making that—it was wonderful."

"Of course it was—my mom sent her the recipe. And pork pie—that's breakfast food in northern New England, along with baked beans, but you could serve it for lunch, too."

Lucy stood and hugged her. "I'll almost hate to leave—this is going to be fun." She pushed her chair in. "Let's get you moved in so you can relax before we get up at dawn for the breakfast crowd."

Lucy stopped to thank Roger, still cleaning up the kitchen.

"You gals go on upstairs," he said. "I'll lock up when I finish."

Lucy led Katie up a steep flight of stairs behind a door opening onto the street to a three-room apartment. Sunlight shone at an oblique angle through a north-facing window; a cool breeze scented with pine and snow puffed café curtains with a red pom-pom fringe. An enameled steel-top table sat in the tiny dining nook opposite a green, four-burner gas stove on curved legs. Furniture and accessories in the open sitting room matched the vintage kitchen; the whole setting harked back to the 1930s.

"All this was here when Marge bought the building," Lucy said. "She lived here at first because she couldn't afford any place else. I don't think she changed a thing. She bought a little house a few years later a couple blocks from here so she wouldn't have to climb the stairs. Now this is kind of a guest suite."

"I'm glad she didn't redecorate—this is like being in my grandmother's house." Katie ran her hand over the red-and-white table-top. "Vintage pieces like this are worth big money now."

Lucy showed her the tiny bathroom with its pedestal sink and claw-foot tub and a bedroom with a brass double bed and painted bureau. "No closet, but there's a rod to hang your clothes behind that curtain," she said. "I don't know what you're used to, but this is clean and quiet—no noisy neighbors like bars next door or auto-body shops across the alley."

Katie loved it, although the whole apartment would fit into her kitchen in Connecticut with space left over. "It looks wonderful to me—I don't need fancy."

Lucy sighed in relief. "I was afraid you'd take one look and head back East. I'll help you carry your gear up, then my fiancé is taking us out to dinner."

"You don't have to—"

"Don't worry. We'll take off afterward and find someplace to make out."

"Look, I'll go to a movie—"

"I'm kidding—Mike has an office here in town where we can have some privacy. You can unpack while I'm gone. Hope you don't mind sharing the bed for a couple nights. I don't snore."

"MY TREAT," MIKE told Katie when the check arrived after their dinner at a restaurant across the street from the Queen. "A thank-you for coming to Lucy's rescue."

"I wouldn't have eaten like a pig if I'd known you were picking up the tab," Katie said after polishing off a plate of chiles rellenos with refried beans and rice, followed by flan. "I've eaten at Mexican restaurants in Connecticut, but nothing as good as this."

"Let's walk dinner off," Lucy said. "I'll show you the downtown while there's still daylight."

They ambled along Main Avenue with its cafés and craft shops, coffee houses and boutiques, shoe and hardware stores, to the Strater Hotel at the head of the street.

"You should check out their historical exhibits," Mike said. "A lot of famous guests stayed here, all the way back to 1887."

"And you have to ride the narrow gauge railroad up to Silverton," Lucy said as they paused at the Victorian train station with its antique steam locomotive. "It goes through the high country you can't see any other way."

"I doubt I'll have time for sightseeing," Katie said. "At least until Marge comes back to work."

They parted at the Queen, and Katie watched Lucy and Mike walk away hand in hand through the soft spring twilight. She and Brad had walked like that during their college days, inseparable and confident of happily-ever-after. She tried to recall just when the magic had faded and died—about the time his construction business had shifted into high gear, she thought. He had put her aside for the job; she had become a habit and a convenience, maybe even a nuisance.

Some shift had occurred between her impulsive dash to Colorado and this moment, beginning with the touch of Luke's hand over hers on the reins. She wasn't willing to spend the rest of her life only half-alive, waiting on the sidelines at Brad's convenience when he had time for her between meetings and affairs.

She squared her shoulders and climbed the stairs to her new home.

CHAPTER FIFTEEN

LUKE PUSHED BACK from the table and rubbed his eyes. He'd have to get reading glasses if he wanted to go on with this kind of work—that would really add to his macho image. Still, he had spent several satisfying hours bringing order to the receipts and notes Mike left. Now he was ready to sort them into yes, no and maybe piles so Mike could calculate the deductions.

The house was quiet except for the shushing of the breeze in the cottonwoods and an occasional distant lowing of the cows along the creek. He checked his watch—well past noon, so his dad and Shelby must have carried their lunches with them. They'd be moving the yearlings to a loading ramp close to the main road. He should ride out and help— Dude was a pretty good cow pony.

He ate a quick sandwich of roast beef from last night's supper and wheeled out the back door. The first thing that struck him was the absence of Katie's vehicle. She was gone, with no good reason to return.

He could wangle a ride to the Queen after his next PT session, but she'd be too busy to give him more than a smile and an order of pie. And there was no way he could get up to her apartment, even if she invited him. Hell, why should she? Reeling from one bad relationship, why would she consider getting involved before the previous one was resolved?

Why was he obsessing about Katie? Okay, at first she had summoned up his teenage passion for a pretty teacher, and then she had greeted him as if she just saw a man, not a man in a wheelchair. She didn't ignore his disability but she didn't hover, either, accepting its reality as part of who he was.

Why did she have to be married? He had never gotten involved with married women, not wanting to be used as a weapon in a private war with messy rules of engagement. After the rawness of her hurt wore off, Katie would probably go back to her husband. More than likely, the Jerk would trace her whereabouts and show up filled with remorse and flashing a fancy piece of jewelry by way of apology.

Luke slammed his hand down on the wheel

of his chair. He needed to get a horse between his knees, do a man's work for the day, try and get back to normal.

He whistled for Dude and saddled in lightning time, letting the horse stretch out for a short while in a full gallop that blew the demons out of his mind. Soon he heard the bawling of cattle and his father's voice shouting instructions—the trucks must have arrived to pick up the yearlings.

He rode over a rise just as the last animal clattered up the ramp into the double-deck cattle hauler. Two men slammed the wide door shut. The driver handed Jake a clipboard for his signature and climbed into the cab. The smaller herd of yearling heifers left behind answered the mournful voices of their buddies as the massive truck lurched into gear and pulled away.

"Just in time," his father said as Luke rode up. "You and Shelby can push this bunch into the upper pasture—I'll ride ahead and open the gate." He reined Blackjack in a tight circle and set off at a lope.

"Where are the yearlings headed?" Luke asked.

"They'll summer on grass in Wyoming before going to a feedlot," Shelby said. "This means a nice check in the bank for us and less stress on our summer pasture—we didn't have a lot of snow this spring." She followed her husband with her eyes until he disappeared over a rise.

"You still worry about Dad, don't you?"

"Every minute he's out of my sight." She sighed. "I know I'm being foolish—he's gotten nothing but good reports from his doctor, but I'll never forget finding him face down in the snow. If he'd been dead, I might have laid down and died with him, just let the storm take us together."

She laughed. "How melodramatic is that? But I say a thank-you prayer every morning we wake up together."

She lifted her reins. "We'd better get these cows moving or your dad will think they've scattered on us."

They rode at a walk toward the dozen or so yearlings and got them moving in the right direction without inciting them to rebellion. Too great a distance separated Luke from Shelby to allow conversation, but he resolved to speak privately with her before the day was over. The heartbreak she had suffered early in her life hadn't hardened her. Instead, she had developed a deep compassion for others, making her the perfect listener and counselor.

Jake met them before they reached the gate, and the three of them walked the yearlings into their new pasture with none making a break for distant corners of the ranch. He climbed down to refasten the wire gate and looked at Luke.

"Something on your mind, son?"

Luke shrugged. "It'll keep."

Jake slapped his knee. "Okay, I'll take a shortcut back. I want to get that check from Art in the bank today." He turned to Shelby. "Anything I can bring you from town?"

She bent down and touched his check. "Just your own sweet self."

"You got it, darlin'." He held her hand against his face for a moment before mounting in a fluid motion to jog down the wagon track they had just taken.

Luke and Shelby followed at a walk, letting their horses pick their way homeward without guidance. The sun hung halfway down in the western sky, gilding the spring grass with a golden glow. They rode in silence while Luke tried to frame his questions for Shelby.

"What did you want to talk about, Luke?"

"You always know, don't you?"

"You're pretty easy to read even if you try to cover up your feelings with jokes."

"I want what you and Dad have," he said. "Tom and Jo, too."

"Anyone special in mind?"

He whipped off his hat and ran his hand through his hair, letting the wind cool his face. "No. Maybe. But what do I have to offer any woman?"

Shelby didn't answer at once—she never did. They rode maybe a quarter of a mile before she looped her reins around her saddle horn and ticked off points on her fingers.

"You're strong and good-looking. You've got a sharp mind and caring heart, and you're funny as hell. You're carrying more work here every day, and you might move into a new career that will put more money in your pocket than ranching ever will. Plus you'll never lack a place to live."

"And I'm stuck in a wheelchair, maybe for the rest of my life." He looked away. "I don't even know if I'll be able to…" He cleared his throat. "To satisfy a woman."

Shelby reined in her horse. "Luke, look at me."

He signaled Dude to halt and turned to face her.

"In the years I've known you, I've never

seen you be even remotely underhanded or mean-spirited. For the right woman, honesty and devotion will carry a lot more weight than how athletic a man might be in bed. And you've been around enough to know lots of ways to give pleasure."

He stared at her for a long moment, wanting to believe, afraid to hope. He shrugged. "If you say so."

She picked up her reins. "Come on. I'll make dirty rice for supper if you'll chop the onions and peppers."

AFTER SUPPER LUKE loaded the dishwasher while his father put away the leftovers and Shelby visited the horses. He almost dropped a heavy casserole dish when his phone played a few bars of "Friends in Low Places." Katie had said she would call, but he hadn't hoped to hear from her this soon.

"Hey," he said, his heart lifting.

"Hey, yourself. How's the tax prep going?"

They chatted for a few minutes about how they'd spent their day, and then she asked, "Did you really like the chicken pie as much as you said? I thought I might try it on the menu here."

"Not a good idea. Once word gets around,

you'll have people lined up out the door causing traffic jams."

She laughed. "I'll take that as a yes."

She spent a few more minutes describing the museum-like apartment. "Early to bed for me," she said. "I'll be up doing breakfast prep at five thirty. Sleep easy, cowboy."

"You, too, city girl."

His father closed the refrigerator. "Was that Katie? She all settled in?"

"Yeah," Luke said. "Sounds like she plans to stay for a while."

CHAPTER SIXTEEN

KATIE LAID HER phone down, still smiling over Luke's joke about the chicken pie. He had tasted it in the past when his mother used the same recipe, but most men didn't remember a meal even as long as it took to digest.

She looked around the cozy apartment. She had explored the kitchen cabinets, which held only basic cooking utensils. She'd have to buy a few tools to prepare her own meals here. The notion of going down to the Queen's kitchen after spending so many hours there held little appeal.

A glass-fronted bookcase beside the green brocade sofa held a few paperbacks—plenty of room for her cookbooks and the few novels she'd brought from her mother's house. The floor lamp with its fringed silk shade cast a peachy glow over the mahogany coffee table and the Brussels carpet, whose rose-and-green pattern had faded to a soft sepia. The furnishings were worn but clean and had been good quality when new; the atmosphere was one of carefully preserved gentility rather than shabbiness.

Katie started water running in the tub while she undressed and hung her grooming kit on a hook in the bathroom.

She tipped a few drops of lavender oil into the hot water—she would never again use the woodsy scent she'd loved before her husband's perfidy.

Footsteps echoed on the stairs as she was slipping into her pink terry robe after her soak. Lucy hung her purse on a mirrored coatrack by the door and dropped on the sofa with a sigh.

Katie joined her. "Good sigh or bad sigh?"

"Frustrated sigh," Lucy said and sighed again. "Mike and I just went another few rounds about my acting career."

"Have you been engaged long?"

"Too long, according to Mike. And he's right, but I hate to give it up just when I'm starting to get more than walk-ons." She sat straighter with a sparkle in her eyes. "You can't imagine the high of going into character just before you step on stage."

"You're right, I can't," Katie said. "I blew

my lines in the senior play—that was the beginning and end of my acting career."

"I can't ask Mike to relocate to New York. His family has been ranching the same land almost as long as ours, and his accounting business here is starting to take off."

She jumped to her feet and began pacing the cramped space. "He gets to New York when he can, and I come home between productions, but he wants to get married so we can start a family." She waved her arms. "Other actresses have kids—what's so bad about that?"

Katie shook her head in silent sympathy. She would have been thrilled to have half a dozen children and stay home with them, maybe homeschooling as Jo Cameron was doing.

Lucy flopped on the sofa again. "I just hope he doesn't ruin the rest of my time here before I leave for New Hampshire."

Katie stood—time to cut this off before saying something she might regret. "I brought a couple of sweet rolls up from the kitchen. I think we could both use some carbs."

They shared the pastries and hot chocolate before Lucy took her turn in the bathroom. Katie barely registered the creak of the springs when Lucy climbed into the far side of the bed.

THE BREAKFAST SHIFT went smoothly, with Katie and Lucy swapping cooking and serving as needed. Marge had always baked fresh bread and pastries for the early risers, but customers seemed satisfied with the offerings from a bakery down the street.

"You think you can handle breakfast now?" Lucy asked. "I can ask Sue if she'd like to come in earlier, as soon as she gets her kids off to school. She'd probably be glad of the extra hours."

She scrubbed at a spot on the stainless steel prep table. "To tell the truth, I'll be glad to get to the ranch. I need to do some thinking without spending every evening with Mike."

Katie pitied Lucy's dilemma. She had suffered no doubts about marrying Brad. They were in love, they would live happily ever after while he worked and she stayed home raising their children. What could go wrong?

For a moment she saw herself back in the spacious home Brad had built, with every convenience and luxury at her fingertips. And look where she was now, living alone in a tiny apartment and working her buns off in a small-town café.

And loving it.

When Sue arrived, she agreed with enthusiasm to start coming in at nine, and the lunch shift passed without incident. Katie was becoming more familiar with the menu and where to find utensils and ingredients. She could handle the job as long as she had good help like Sue and Roger.

After closing at three, Katie sat at her own kitchen table making a shopping list while Lucy packed her belongings.

"I need a few things for the kitchen," Katie said. "Any good thrift shops in town?"

Lucy's expression said she was too polite to ask if Katie couldn't afford to buy what she needed new.

"I like to browse shops like that," Katie said. "I've found really good stuff from time to time, better quality than the new crap at big box stores. And I'm helping local charities."

Lucy's face cleared. "Well, the Methodist church has one, and the local humane society sells donations, too." She wrote several addresses on the notepad by the phone. "And there's always Walmart if you strike out with these."

She zipped her weekender, carried it to the door and then turned back. "I can't tell you how much this means to me. To all of us, really. We'd wade through fire for Marge just like she would for us, but she needs more than part-time piecemeal help. I couldn't go East and leave the Queen drifting."

She flung her arms around Katie. "I declare you officially a Cameron."

The apartment seemed very quiet after Lucy clattered down the stairs. Katie had never lived alone. She had gone from her childhood home to live with Brad's parents after their wedding and then to the elegant house from which she had fled. Now the mundane task of shopping for her own apartment assumed the excitement of an adventure.

She opened the window over the kitchen sink and drank in the rustle of new leaves on the big tree behind the building. She couldn't see the Animas River, but she could hear its voice, rushing in spring spate.

Enough daydreaming—finding what she needed might take several stops, and she needed to buy groceries, as well. She'd have plenty of time to explore every corner of her new domain after she finished her errands.

Her phone rang as she gathered her shopping list and street map. She recognized Aunt Joan's number on the caller ID. She had called her aunt while on the road and again to let her know she would be staying put for a while without revealing her location. Now her heart thudded with apprehension—what emergency has prompted this call?

"Are you all right?" Aunt Joan said without a greeting. "Brad was here looking for you. He said he's sure something terrible has happened to you and begged me to tell him where you are."

"He was trying to play you. I hope you didn't fall for it." Relief made Katie's response sharper than she intended. She softened her voice. "I was afraid he'd contact you. Honestly, I'm fine, Aunt Joan. I have a job and a nice apartment and wonderful new friends."

"So if he asks me again…"

"Tell him nothing. He's lost the right to know anything about me. And don't let him bully you. I wish I could tell you where I am and what I'm doing—"

"I get it," Aunt Joan said. "If I don't know, he can't trick me into telling. Just be careful, sweetie. I'm your substitute mom now, your designated worrier."

"I'll tell you everything when I come back to settle things with Brad. Give Blondie a hug and a biscuit from me."

Ending the call with her aunt, Katie descended to Main Avenue, locking the door behind her with an ornate brass key that matched the age of the building.

At the church thrift shop, she bought a pink English teapot with four matching cups and saucers—early twentieth century—plus a silver-plated casserole spoon and three brand-new red-and-green-striped dish towels. The humane society's shop also had kitchen wares. She was mulling the choice between a red or a silver blender when she heard a familiar voice.

"Just bring a cart out to my car and load it up. I'm dumping twenty years of excess baggage."

Katie peeked over the top of the display shelf. Marge Bowman, now using only one crutch, was deep in conversation with the blond hiker-type woman behind the counter. "If I can't work," Marge said, "at least I can clear out my house. I haven't had this much fun since Hector was a pup. I'm finding things I never knew I had, stuff the last owner left behind."

Katie came out from her covert and greeted Marge.

"Here's my rescuer, Liz," Marge told clerk. "If she hasn't decided to hightail it."

"Far from it," Katie said. "I am glad to see

you out and about. Lucy left for the ranch after we closed, and I just realized we didn't talk about money." She held up a hand. "The Queen's money, not mine."

"And tomorrow's Friday, so Sue and Roger need paychecks." Marge looked at her watch. "It's nearly supper time. Come home with me—I made a big pot of soup this morning, more than I can eat in a week. You can tell me how things are going and we'll talk money. Tomorrow I'll park myself in the office at lunchtime and write out checks."

Katie helped Liz empty the back of Marge's SUV, items ranging from faded towels for the kennels to bed linens and a box of Fiesta dishes in vintage colors.

"We'll probably have a special-event sale for some of this," Liz said, squinting at the stitching on an embroidered tablecloth. "Maybe an auction. I've never known Marge to own a pet, but she's always been generous to us."

She narrowed her eyes at Katie. "I don't suppose I can interest you in adopting."

"Not right now—I've got all I can handle taking care of the Queen."

Liz sighed. "Can't blame me for trying."

Katie followed Liz inside and paid for the

red blender while Marge collected a receipt for her donations.

Katie drove behind Marge's vehicle to a Victorian cottage painted in shades of lime green and salmon. A twin to the tree behind her apartment shaded the postage-stamp front veranda; a rambling rose still in bud sprawled under the bay window.

She opened Marge's car door and offered her hand to help her step out. Marge glared at her for a moment and then accepted.

"I hate needing help, so excuse me if I act cranky," she said. She cleared her throat. "Thank you."

Katie just smiled and followed Marge's halting progress to the back stoop, a worn slab of sandstone. Inside, Katie exclaimed with pleasure—she was back in her grandmother's kitchen in Marblehead, Massachusetts. The furnishings were even older than those in the apartment. A black iron range, converted from wood to gas, dominated the space. Hand-painted stoneware dishes stood on the shelves of a white Hoosier cabinet complete with flour sifter. A round oak table with matching pressed-back chairs sat under a window overlooking the backyard.

"You like antiques?" Marge asked.

"I grew up with them, but they were just beautiful things we used every day."

"I'll give you the whole tour another day, but right now I feel like I've been rode hard and put away wet." Marge sat at the table with a soft groan. "Maybe I overdid it today just a hair. You can put supper on. I left the soup to warm—salad fixings are in the icebox and bread in the bread box. Pour us some wine if you've a mind to."

Katie accepted her new role as Marge's kitchen maid as a sign of acceptance. She lifted the lid on the big soup kettle and stirred the simmering contents, pale beans and thick broth with fragments of pork swimming to the surface.

"Senate bean soup," she said. "I've died and gone to heaven."

She turned the flame up and stirred again, her mouth watering with anticipation. She found a bottle of red wine, assembled a chopped salad and cut crusty French bread into thick slices. The soup was bubbling by the time she had set the table and poured the wine into glasses etched with the name of a Napa Valley winery.

Only after they had eaten for a few minutes in silence did Marge launch her interrogation. "What in the name of all that's unholy is wrong with Lucy? She stopped in to see me a few days ago practically in tears. I haven't seen her this done up since her mother died."

Katie rolled a mouthful of bean soup over her tongue, the best she'd ever tasted.

"Well? You've spent close time with her, and Lucy isn't the silent type."

"I really shouldn't say..." She didn't want to breach any confidences; neither did she want to offend her new boss.

"Of course you should. I've known Lucy since she was seven years old—I'm the closest thing to a grandmother she has in these parts." Marge banged her fist on the table, making the cutlery and Katie jump. "It's Mike, isn't it? Drat that girl—she's going to throw away a man in a million for some foolish notion about being an actress."

"I saw her in a play in Connecticut, Marge. If I had that kind of talent, I might have a hard time walking away."

"If she wants to act, we have a theater company right here in Durango. They'd probably be thrilled to have someone with her talent and experience."

Katie shook her head. How could she explain to Marge the difference between making it in New York, even off Broadway, and performing in local theater productions?

"Mike seems like a sweet guy," she said. "I hope they work it out, especially since Luke's sort of working for him now."

"Luke's working for Mike? What could Luke possibly do for an accountant?"

Katie explained the screening tasks Luke had taken on. "He really seemed to get a kick out of it," she said. "I guess he did a good job, because Mike brought him a second batch a couple days ago."

"Sometimes I didn't think that boy would survive to his twenty-first birthday. What he put Jake and Annie through." Marge shook her head. "Never any meanness, just stunts that could have gotten him killed. He and Tom may look like twins, but they're as different as chalk from cheese."

Watching the bull-riding videos with Luke, Katie hadn't noticed the resemblance between the brothers, but Tom had been wearing a helmet with a face shield.

"At least his parents got a little break with Tom," Marge said. "Seems like he was born grown-up. He never gave them a minute's worry until he started riding bulls. Now he and Luke are both out of the arena, so Jake and Shelby can breathe a little easier."

Except Luke might never walk again.

She glanced sideways at Katie. "What do you think of Luke?"

The question caught Katie by surprise. "I think he's...remarkable," she said. "He goes at everything full-out, doesn't he? Win or lose. I think he sees being in a wheelchair as just another challenge."

"I don't believe for a minute he's going to stay in that wheelchair. So you like him?"

"Of course I like him—I like all the Camerons I've met." Was Marge trying to play matchmaker?

"Even if he never walks again?"

"Marge, I haven't meant to be secretive—I just didn't feel like burdening people with my troubles." For the second time since arriving in Colorado, Katie told her story.

"So you ran away," Marge said with a note of disapproval in her voice.

"I left," Katie said. "I couldn't stand the sight of Brad or even the sound of his voice. But I left on my own terms." She described the measures she had taken for her own security and the parting gift she had left for him.

Marge laughed and slapped the table.

"Dang, girl. You're bad. Don't you wish you could have seen his face when he found that in his bed?"

Katie grinned in spite of herself. "And I talked to my lawyer before I left. I'll never be able to trust Brad again, and I don't intend to try."

Marge sighed. "So you're married."

"At the moment. But even if I weren't, Luke being in a wheelchair wouldn't be a deal breaker for me. I can barely remember a time when my dad didn't walk with a cane, sometimes crutches, after a construction accident. And then Mom developed lupus—up and down, mostly down. Maybe they had physical limitations, but they were my heroes."

Her voice had risen in her vehemence. She took a deep breath. "Sorry, I got carried away. My husband is a fitness freak—he plays tennis and golf and works out at the gym, but he's got a damaged soul."

"My goodness," Marge said.

They finished the meal with coffee and a bourbon-sauced bread pudding that made Katie's taste buds swoon.

"Give me a list of what you need for the apartment," Marge said as Katie began washing the dishes in the big cast-iron sink. "I'm still mucking out cupboards and drawers."

Katie left with a quart container of the soup—and the recipe—and a plastic bowl of the bread pudding, which she doubted would survive until morning.

There was still considerable foot traffic on Main Avenue from the restaurants and pubs. A middle-aged couple offered to hold Katie's leftovers and purchases while she unlocked the door. Her door, leading to her new home. She thanked them and climbed the stairs to survey her little kingdom. Loneliness, even heartbreak, might visit her in these rooms, but in this moment she was content.

She slept that night lulled by the river's song.

CHAPTER SEVENTEEN

"AND DONE!" LUKE looked over the neat stacks of paper with pride. It had taken him three days, but he was pleased with how he'd completed his latest assignment for Mike. He had asked his dad to look over some of the items he didn't recognize, products they didn't use at Cameron's Pride. Jake had also noticed omissions Mike's clients hadn't included, deductions they would have missed.

The ranchers' accounts were considerably more complicated than those for the bull riders, but his knowledge of cattle operations helped. He'd never taken much interest in Cameron's Pride's finances other than knowing there was never quite enough ready cash; debt left by his mother's illness had strained their resources even after her death. Just as they'd moved into the black, his father's heart attack and losses from a freak spring blizzard had dumped them into a sea of red ink, but the last few years they had climbed back into the black.

"I didn't think you had this in you," Jake said. "Not that you weren't smart enough," he added in haste. "I'm just surprised you'd like this kind of persnickety work."

"I guess I never sat still long enough to do something like this. And thanks for your help—I'll have to give you a cut of my paycheck."

"I'll settle for a piece of pie at the Queen after we both get done at the hospital," Jake said. "We can see how Katie's getting along."

Luke heart leaped at the thought of seeing Katie. He wouldn't have suggested it, not wanting to be a nuisance, but since it was his father's idea… And the Queen would be wrapping up the lunch service about the time he finished with his physical therapy.

Luke swung himself into the passenger seat of his father's truck and folded his wheelchair to slide behind the seat.

"I hate needing people to drive me into town," he said as his father climbed behind the wheel. "Maybe I should get my rig fitted with hand controls…" But that would be admitting he'd never be able to drive using the pedals. Maybe he was kidding himself, but he still believed he would walk again. His brain acknowledged the possibility, even the probability, he'd be in a wheelchair the rest of his life, but his heart refused to accept the verdict.

"I told you before it's no bother," Jake said. "I promised Shelby I'd get the blood work the doctor ordered, and I've got a shopping list for the Ranchers Exchange."

Jake dropped Luke off at the hospital entrance. "You mind if I watch you work out? I won't be at the lab more than a few minutes."

"Sure, maybe I'll get some new exercises you can help me with at home."

Jake nodded and pulled away to park while Luke rode the elevator up to PT.

"I've got a surprise for you, buddy," Doug said. "You're going to walk today."

Luke snorted. "What's the punch line?"

"No joke." Doug beckoned to a young woman wearing pants and a polo shirt, her long, dark hair in a ponytail. "Meet Dr. Anita Alvarez from Denver. She's brought a new toy for you to try out." He stepped back. "All yours, Dr. A."

"Anita will do," she said. "Your Dr. Barnett must have friends in high places. We don't usually make house calls, but he said you'd be the perfect subject to try our newest model. You're healthy, you've completely healed from your surgery and he says you're probably the finest athlete he's ever treated."

"Is this one of those—" he searched his mind for the term he'd seen on the internet "—exoskeletons?"

"Far from it," Anita said. "It's a computerized brace system that stabilizes your knees and ankles and tells them how to move. We prefer to create a custom fit using our own measurements, but Dr. Barnett sent us detailed information, so the ones I brought should fit you. Want to give it a try?"

Excitement clogged his throat; he nodded and transferred to the exercise platform before stripping down to his gym shorts. "Okay," he said in a hoarse voice. "I'm ready."

He closed his eyes as Anita and Doug strapped the elaborate system of pads and braces along the back of his thighs, calves and ankles. The devices were cumbersome, especially to someone whose specialty in the arena had been the ability to leap and spin on a dime. Still, they were much less confining than the heavy rig he had seen on the internet.

"Now back in your chair," Doug said.

"Hey, I thought you said I'd be walking."

"Not on your own, not just yet," Anita said. "Using these will take some practice."

Doug parked Luke's chair at the end of the parallel bars and helped him up to support himself on stiffened arms. Luke had regained some sensation as well as the ability to swing his legs from the hip in a crude walking motion, but he collapsed when he tried to walk. He had the bruises to prove that.

"Okay," Anita said. "Right foot forward."

Luke took a deep breath and swung his right leg as hard as he could, pitching forward from the momentum. Doug and Anita caught him before he fell on his face.

"Not so much," Anita said. "Just like you'd take a normal step."

Luke tried again. To his amazement and joy, his knee bent, his ankle flexed and the braces supported his joints.

"Now bring the left foot forward." Anita's voice was soft, almost a whisper.

Luke nodded and matched the right leg's movement with his left to stand squarely on both feet. He blinked away tears. His first step! He teetered like a drunk and would have fallen except for Doug and Anita supporting him.

"Deep breaths," Anita said. "Get your balance."

Luke obeyed, waiting until his pounding heart steadied, and then looked at her. "Another?"

"Okay. Right foot first."

He managed five more steps to the end of the bars and then let them lower him into his wheelchair, as weak as if he were recovering from a long illness. Doug wiped the sweat from Luke's face with a damp towel.

"Dr. Barnett was right about you, Luke," Anita said. "I've never seen anyone pick that up the first try."

Luke grabbed her hand, too moved to speak. At last he said, "I don't suppose you'll let me take this rig home."

"Not yet," she said. "I'm guessing you'd push way too hard unsupervised and do more harm than good. I'll stay in Durango a couple days to make sure Doug can take over. Meanwhile, you can start some new exercises to rebuild your leg muscles."

Luke felt a hand on his shoulder, squeezing hard.

"I wouldn't have missed seeing that for a brand-new baler," Jake said. "Up on your feet and walking…" He cleared his throat. "I'm sure ready for that pie at the Queen. How about you?"

Luke almost backed out. He was still shaking with emotion and fatigue, sweating like a racehorse, but his dad wanted to celebrate. And so did he, but...

"Don't mention this at the Queen, okay? Not till I get better at it."

"Want to surprise everybody, right? Okay, I'll keep my mouth shut, but I'm sure proud of you. I'll just grab a magazine and wait for you to finish."

"Why don't I show you Luke's new exercises, Mr. Cameron?" Doug said. "He'll need help doing them at home."

Doug led them through a few new maneuvers to stretch and strengthen Luke's leg and back muscles. "Okay, that's it for today," he said. "Same time tomorrow?"

"Yes, but let me show you something I've been doing at home. Got a resistance band?"

Luke wheeled to a sink at the far side of the room and wrapped the wide red elastic band just above his knees. Bracing his feet against the cabinet, he grasped the edge of the sink and pulled himself to his feet. His legs shook, but he was able to remain upright for a good thirty seconds before collapsing into his chair.

"So that's why you did so well your first time with the braces," Anita said.

"My brother used to be a bull rider," Luke said. "He used that exercise after a bull fractured his pelvis. I figured it couldn't hurt for me to try the same thing."

Luke and his father left the hospital and arrived at the Silver Queen in time for a late lunch. Marge sat in a booth near the kitchen with papers spread across the table.

"Well, look what the cat drug in—my two favorite cowboys. Two chicken-fried steaks, Katie," she yelled over her shoulder. "Rush order—these guys look hungry."

Luke couldn't see Katie, but her voice floated through the pass-through. "I can put them in the microwave to make it faster."

Marge rolled her eyes. "You're fired!"

"That's how many times?"

"That girl has a sassy mouth," Marge said. "Who would have guessed—she looks so sweet. So what brings you to town?"

"Luke's physical therapy," Jake said. "He… he's doing real well."

Marge leaned forward and patted Luke's cheek. "Of course he is. Just a matter of time and hard work—I'm finding that out. I'm glad I got both knees fixed at the same time. I'd never have the nerve to go through this again."

"Rehab sucks, sure enough," Luke said.

"Now, tell me what's going on with Lucy," Marge said, leaning forward. "She hasn't been back to town in a week, not that I know of."

Jake rubbed his hand over his face. "You probably know as much as I do. Mike comes over about every evening and they sit in his rig till all hours. She's talking about leaving early for New York so she can 'relax'—" he sketched quotation marks in the air "—before she goes up to New Hampshire. I guess she feels like you and the Queen are in good hands now."

"You must be plenty glad she has such a nice, safe place to live in New York. Jo's mom is pretty brave to take her in as a tenant, swapping one daughter for another. Lucy's quite a change after a sensible girl like Jo."

A few minutes later, Katie pushed through the kitchen door with two platters of chicken-fried steak. She stopped short.

"Luke! And Jake. Marge didn't say you were the hungry guys."

She stopped close to Luke. In a previous life, he would have put his arm around a pretty girl's waist and launched into his usual flirtation, but that didn't feel right with Katie.

She set the plates in front of him and Jake. "Gym clothes—you must have gone to PT. How's that progressing?"

He wanted to tell her, to share the rush of standing and moving upright under his own power. But not here, not in public.

"One step at a time," he said.

Her eyes widened. "Really? Oh, Luke."

"Hey, still early days, but maybe one of these days I can get a late-afternoon PT slot so you can come and cheerlead."

"I'd be honored," she said, and he thought maybe she understood.

"Meanwhile, their food is getting cold," Marge said. "You have got to be the dimmest waitress I ever tried to train."

Katie gave her a sweet smile. "I'm a cook, not a waitress. And you're lucky to have me." She set Jake's plate on the table.

Marge turned to Jake. "Look what you've stuck me with. I shouldn't have to put up with such abuse at my age."

"Coffee for the gentlemen, right? And I'll get your tea, Marge." Katie turned on her heel with a saucy flip of her apron.

Marge waited until the kitchen door swung shut behind Katie before turning to Jake. "Having that girl show up is enough to make me believe in God. I'm scared every day she'll get tired of this lark and go back where she came from."

"I don't think it's a lark for her," Luke said. "She told me she wanted to make a fresh start, there was nothing she wanted to go back to."

"I sure hope you're right. I might even consider—"

Katie returned balancing a heavy tray—coffee for Jake and Luke, a pink teapot with a matching cup for Marge, and two slices of peach pie. She set everything on the table and pulled up a chair. She and Marge exchanged grins as they waited for the men to finish their steaks and start on the pie.

Jake took a bite and sighed with satisfaction. "I'm sure glad you're up to making this pie again, Marge."

"Katie's making them now," Marge said. "And we're adding chicken pie to the menu next week."

"And then maybe pork pie," Katie said.

"Pushy little twerp," Marge said and struggled to her feet using a cane. "Better change the sign, Katie—it's closing time."

"I'll do it," Jake said. "I have to pull the truck up out front." He flipped the sign to Closed on his way out.

"Ladies' room for me," Marge said and thumped her way toward the back of the restaurant, leaving Luke and Katie alone.

"Truly, Luke," Katie said. "Rehab is going well? You really want me to watch?"

"Not just yet," he said. "I'll tell you when." He took her hand. "So you're staying around awhile?"

"Until Marge kicks me out. She loves to snipe at me, but just in fun, of course."

"Of course." Marge sometimes had trouble keeping help.

He heard the thump of Marge's cane. "If you're not busy on Sunday, how about coming out to the ranch for dinner?" he said. "Around noon or earlier if you like. We could ride out afterward and check the new calves."

"I'd love to," she said.

A horn honked outside the Queen.

CHAPTER EIGHTEEN

KATIE STOOD AT the door and waved to Jake as Luke opened the truck's door and swung into the passenger's seat using the overhead grab bar. He gave her a thumbs-up as Jake pulled away from the curb.

Marge was gathering her papers together when Katie went back inside. "Roger brought me the cash," she said. "I'll drop the deposit off on my way home." She stuck the bank bag into her purse, a rumpled black leather satchel the size of a trekker's backpack. "If you don't have plans on Sunday, would you like to go through some trunks in my attic? I've got no idea what we might find. They were up there when I bought the house, and I've never taken time to root through them."

"Sounds like fun, but Luke just invited me to the ranch for Sunday dinner and riding. Could we do it another time?"

"I don't reckon it's urgent, considering they've been up there at least twenty years.

Go to the ranch and help Luke to take his mind off his problems. We'll rummage on another day."

A decision Katie had been incubating since she first met the Camerons hardened into resolve. She had postponed action long enough. She climbed the stairs to her apartment, scrolled through the directory on her phone and hit Send.

When she got through to her attorney, she said without preamble, "Mr. Foster, those papers I signed? Start the process."

He didn't respond for a moment, and then he said, "You sound different, Kathryn. I didn't recognize your voice."

"I am different, Mr. Foster. I've got a job I love and new friends who've never heard of Brad and his fancy connections. How quickly can you file the papers and what else do I have to do? Will I need to come back to Connecticut to finalize the divorce?"

"It depends," he said and went on to spell out a confusing muddle of options and conditions. One fact came through loud and clear— she'd been smart to withdraw money when she had. She hadn't known what regulations might apply, but once Mr. Foster filed on her behalf, neither she nor Brad could withdraw from an account as she had done. She'd spent almost none of the money, but she had no intention of returning it.

"Just make it quick and clean," she said. "I don't want anything from him, not alimony or the house."

"He's a wealthy man, Kathryn—you're entitled to a generous settlement."

"He worked hard for what he's got—let him keep it. I'm doing fine on my own."

She could hear his sigh. "If you say so. I'll have more documents for you to sign. Where can I send them?"

She thought for a moment. "Would a post office box do?"

"Of course. Do you have one?"

"Not yet, but I'll take care of that tomorrow and get back to you."

"You've made a good start, so we should be able to settle this quickly," he said. "You left the marital home nearly a month ago, and that will be considered part of the separation period."

Only a month? Driving away from Brad's house seemed a lifetime ago. She had a hard time even picturing it, as if she had never lived there. She hadn't been allowed to put her stamp on it; even the plantings had been designed by a landscape architect to complement the elegant facade. She would have loved a vegetable garden, but those were frowned upon by the neighborhood association.

"I'll call you tomorrow with the address," she said.

She spent the rest of the afternoon baking a pie to take to Cameron's Pride, using a recipe her mother had found in an old *Yankee* magazine. Even though Sunday was a few days off, the pie would keep.

She probably should have gone to rent a post office box and set up a bank account this afternoon, but baking soothed her nerves after her call to Mr. Foster. She hadn't understood half of what he told her but came away with the impression that the divorce should go smoothly if Brad didn't contest it. Until she blocked them, his emails had begged, then demanded she return. She had no idea what his current state of mind might be. Over the past few years he had become a stranger to her.

When Katie left work Friday afternoon, the wind was gusting down from the mountains, still one moment and whipping her hair around her face the next. The temperature still felt spring-like by the time she arranged for a post office box and set up a bank account, but a milky overcast blurred the sun. People on the street scanned the sky and then shook their heads.

By nightfall the temperature had dropped and the wind had settled to a steady moan, rattling the windows.

At six she called her cousin Greg to make sure everything was running smoothly at her mother's house.

"Good timing," Greg said. "We just got the boys into bed. We're loving the house. The kids are having a great time in the yard. I put up a swing on the old apple tree. We'll hate leaving if you decide you want to move back in."

Katie made a split-second decision, burning another bridge behind her. "Would you like to buy it?"

"Whoa. You're kidding, right? It'll be quite a while before we can save up enough down payment to qualify for a mortgage."

"I'll carry the paper," Katie said and named a price a bit under the house's market value. "Figure out how much you can afford each month and send me that amount like rent." She might rue her decision, but turning her grandparents' home over to her cousin felt right. Her mother would approve.

"Your husband came by asking if I knew where you are," Greg said.

"I figured he might—that's why I didn't tell anyone."

"Okay, but I'll need to know where to send you monthly checks."

She hesitated and then gave him her post office box address.

"Colorado—that's awesome. I went skiing in Breckenridge with some buddies just before we deployed."

"I still don't want him knowing where I am. Don't let him push you into telling him."

Greg snorted. "Once you've been to Afghanistan, a pissed-off husband isn't very scary. I don't know how to thank you. Owning this house…" He whistled. "I can't wrap my mind around it. Allie's going to freak out. She's got all kinds of DIY ideas, but we didn't want to change anything without your say-so."

"Decorate away," Katie said. "Mom would be happy to see another generation of Gabriels growing up in the old homestead."

She was warming Marge's soup for her supper when her phone rang. She started, afraid for a moment she might hear Brad's voice. Instead she recognized Luke's number.

"I'm uninviting you for Sunday," he said. "Not a good time for you to visit."

The signal was poor, but she could hear the strain in his voice.

"Of course. Another time, maybe."

"Hey." His tone roughened. "I want you to come, but have you looked out the window?"

"Not in a couple hours." She drew back the kitchen curtain and looked out into swirling whiteness. "Snow this close to May?"

"We've got more than six inches here already. We've been out all afternoon bringing the cows with calves in close, just in case this turns into the kind of storm that almost wiped us out when Dad had his heart attack."

"You've been out riding in this?" Surely he was joking.

He laughed but with no humor. "I know ranching looks cool when the skies are not cloudy all day, but now is when the cattle need us most. Sitting by the fire with hot cocoa isn't an option."

She heard a deep sigh. "And we lost a horse—we found her down in the snow. Sadie was nearly thirty. We couldn't get her on her feet—Dad had to put her down where she was." His voice shook. "Tom and I saw her foaled—we grew up with her."

"You lost an old friend," Katie said, aching with pity for them.

"We knew she was failing, but it's still a shock that she's gone."

"Can I do anything? I can't ride well enough to help with the cattle, but I can make sure you guys get fed. I could babysit Missy and JJ."

"I dunno." His words were slurred. "We'll see what tomorrow looks like. I'll call you."

"Luke, take care of yourself. Please."

"Sure. Thanks."

Katie puttered around the apartment imagining conditions at the ranch. She finally went to bed listening to the wind, unable to take comfort in her snug nest while thinking of Luke and the others battling the wind and snow. What if he fell? Would Dude stay with him or drift away with the wind, unaware? Would someone find him before he froze to death?

She finally slept and awoke only when her alarm clock buzzed at six, rousing her to start prepping for breakfast.

Pure new snow blanketed the town. To the north early sunlight tinted the mountains in shades of rose and gold. What had been menacing in darkness now glowed like a Victorian Christmas card—beauty and danger, two sides of the same coin.

She longed to call Luke, to reassure herself he was safe, but he might be sleeping or saddling Dude or already out looking for the lost cattle. He had said he would call. She would wait.

CHAPTER NINETEEN

LUKE SLOUCHED IN the saddle, still weary after a short night's rest. They'd all been up before dawn and riding out looking for the missing sixteen head—thirty-two, actually, cows with their calves. Even Tom, who really shouldn't be on a horse with his back trouble, was riding.

Luke had the shortest loop to search—the lower pastures—because he had only Dude while everyone else was mounted on fresh horses. He'd had good luck, though, finding two pairs huddled under the willows. The cows were chilled and stiff, shielding their calves, but able to stagger up the creek bank when he rode at them yelling and swinging his rope. They moved ahead of him now toward the trampled-down area where other cows were chowing down on the fresh hay Jake and Shelby had put out once the snow stopped around midnight.

This storm could have been much worse.

The last late-spring blizzard had persisted for three days. He and Tom had been a thousand miles away at a bull-riding event, fuming in helpless rage that they couldn't get home to help. They'd lost more than half their herd and almost their father. Only Shelby's quick action had gotten Jake to the hospital in time.

He averted his eyes as he rode past Sadie's snow-covered body. As soon as the herd was safe, his dad would dig a grave beside her with the backhoe. If she'd been on an open range, they might have left her to the coyotes and other scavengers for natural disposal, but not this close to the barn. He blinked hard—she had almost made it to shelter.

To comfort himself, he fished out his phone and punched the speed dial for Katie's number.

"Luke, you're okay?" she asked in an eager voice.

He warmed at her concern. "Yeah, pretty much. We're all dead tired, but we're missing only a few head, and they're probably holed up safe somewhere. We had the first-year heifers close in already, and the older cows know how to ride out weather like this."

"I'm sorry about your horse—you lost a piece of your childhood."

He hadn't thought of Sadie's death like that, just that he'd be looking for her in the horse herd for a long time. "Shelby's taking it hard," he said. "Sadie was the horse she rode when she first came here, while she was schooling Ghost. She's never lost one she cared about before this."

"Almost thirty, you said. Is that really old for a horse?"

"A good long life," he said. "At least Dad didn't have to worry if it was time to put her down. She took care of it herself—she was a pushy old gal."

After a brief silence, Katie said, "So you guys are all set—you don't need me tomorrow?"

"I'd love to see you, but you'll have a better visit next Sunday. The snow will be gone and Shelby will have chance to fix something special for dinner. You like Cajun?"

"The few times I've tried it. I'm game for pretty much anything."

"I know you are, darlin'. So we'll aim for next weekend, and maybe I'll call you sooner if the PT pans out like I hope."

"Please," she said. "I'll come and shake pom-poms on the sidelines."

They ended the conversation, and Luke

rode on, warmed despite the cold wind that still whipped the fresh snow along the ground in miniature blizzards.

Tom met him at the gate. "I found three more pairs," he said. "They're hungry, but I think they'll be fine." Luke knew his brother hated admitting to weakness, but his face betrayed his pain. "I'd like to get off at my place if you'll pony my horse to the home ranch."

"You shouldn't be out here in the first place. I can't believe Jo let you out this morning."

"She wasn't too happy about it. She was right—I should have stayed home with the kids and let her go instead. Right now she'd be more use than I am." He shifted in the saddle. "Home, James."

Jo met them on the front porch of their cabin. "Thanks for dragging him home, Luke. He should be in bed, but oh, no. He's tough—he's a Cameron." She launched into a scathing description of her husband's intelligence, or lack of it, while Tom dismounted an inch at a time, groaning aloud when his right foot touched the ground.

He handed his reins to Luke. "I guess it's safe to leave me here with Nurse Meanie," he said, drawing a growl from Jo and giggles from Missy and JJ, who had joined their mother on the porch.

"I think we have a walker at the house he can use," Luke told Jo. "Left over from when he broke his pelvis."

"Use it yourself, buddy," Tom said. "You'll be up walking pretty soon."

"Hope you're right." Luke wheeled Dude away from the porch, leading the chestnut gelding while Tom limped inside with Jo still scolding.

Jake was unsaddling Blackjack when Luke rode up. "You find any?" he asked. "And how come you've got Tom's horse?"

"I found two more pairs and Tom found three," Luke said. "I dropped mine off with the bunch in the upper pasture. Tom asked me to leave him at his place—he could barely get out of the saddle." He grinned. "Jo's got a real mouth on her. She's riding him whip and spur."

Jake grunted. "Good for her. Tom doesn't know when he's had enough—none of us do. Thank God we've got women to ride herd on us."

"Speaking of which…"

"Shelby and Lucy are finishing their sweep in the south pasture," Jake said, taking the reins of Tom's horse and leading him into the barn. "We'll tally up when they get in and see how many we're still missing."

By the time Jake had unsaddled Tom's horse and turned him into the corral, Luke had almost finished with Dude. The Appaloosa raised his head and let out a piercing whinny, answered by another horse at a little distance. Lucy rode into the barn on her paint mare, followed by Shelby on Ghost. Ghost snorted loudly at the gelding but walked past without nipping at him.

"Seven pairs for the two of us," Lucy said. "All the calves seem okay—they were nursing when we dumped the moms off at the hay drop."

"And I found two. I think we might have them all," Jake said.

"Except one." Shelby fetched a rubber currycomb from the tack room and started on the ice crusting Ghost's legs.

"Let me guess—Jezebel." Jake swore with real imagination. "I should have turned her into hamburger a long time ago, but I feel guilty she's such a nutcase."

"Jake, it's a ranch. Squeeze chutes sometimes malfunction."

"I know, but the dang little heifer was stuck in there for more than an hour."

"You've made up for it by keeping her around, and she does have nice calves. She'll show up on her own, fat and happy," Luke said.

"Probably will," Jake said, and they finished tending to their horses in silence.

They returned to the kitchen for a late breakfast; they'd only been grabbing bites whenever they got a chance. Shelby put on fresh coffee while Lucy reheated the oatmeal still sitting on the stove.

"No reason Katie can't come for dinner tomorrow," Jake said.

"I've already told her next week would be better," Luke said. "She understands. She offered last night to cook for us and watch the kids if the storm held on."

"She's a good girl," Shelby said. "She just needs space to work out her problems."

Lucy stared into her coffee mug without chiming in.

"How was she to work with, Luce?" Jake asked.

"Okay, I guess." Lucy roused herself to speak with more energy. "I mean, she picked up the routine in a snap and she's not afraid of hard work, but I don't think she likes me."

"How did you manage to tick her off?" Luke asked. "She doesn't seem like the picky type."

"I made the mistake of talking to her about Mike. She didn't say much, but I could see she thought I should put on my apron and stay home like a good little wife."

Luke silently scored points for Katie. They had all resolved to stay out of Lucy's career-versus-marriage tussle, but they sympathized with Mike's position. Luke was sure he would have given up and moved on before now, but Mike had loved Lucy since he first made fun of her red hair in elementary school. She had whacked him over the head with her lunch box, apparently winning his heart forever.

"Anyway, she's taken Marge and the Queen off my conscience, so I'm grateful." Lucy pushed her coffee away. "I'm going to New York as soon as you can spare me. This summer's going to be a bear. I'd like to enjoy a little downtime before I have to leave for New Hampshire."

Jake opened his mouth, but Shelby put a hand on his arm. "Calving's over, so we should be fine," she said. "Be sure to visit Marge before you leave."

Tears filled Lucy's eyes, and she ran up the stairs. Her bedroom door banged shut.

CHAPTER TWENTY

KATIE CALLED MARGE after she finished her call with Luke. "I've been stood up," she said. "Luke uninvited me for tomorrow."

"I don't wonder," Marge said. "How did they make it through the storm?"

"He didn't think they lost many cattle, but one of their horses died, an old mare they'd had her whole life."

"Like a death in the family—I'm not surprised they don't feel like socializing. Come on over. We'll work until dark—there are no lights in the attic—and then we'll have supper."

"If you like, I'll make a chicken pot pie. You can decide if you want to put it on the menu."

"Sounds like our day is planned," Marge said.

Katie stopped at Albertson's the next day for a stewing chicken and then headed to Marge's house. Someone had shoveled the sidewalk, but Katie cleaned the front steps and back stoop with a scruffy broom she found leaning on the porch.

The perfume of sugar and spices greeted her in the kitchen as Marge pulled a pan of cinnamon buns from the oven. "We'll need fuel before we tackle this project," she said.

In her anxiety for Luke, Katie hadn't bothered with breakfast. She gobbled two buns almost without pausing, washing them down with coffee.

"I guess that hit the spot," Marge said. "You'd probably like fry bread, too."

"Fried bread? I've never heard of it."

"Ever have fried dough at a fair? Something like that but better. Have Luke take you to meet his Auntie Rose Buck. She makes the best fry bread I've ever tasted."

"As in Oscar Buck? I've already met him—I had to help Luke chase Oscar's pet bull back to his side of the fence."

"My, you have gotten around. Put your chicken on to stew and let's start on those trunks. I should have tackled them long ago, but it's a boring chore with no one to rummage with."

"I'm sure Lucy would have helped you," Katie said. "And Durango must have an historical society that would be interested."

"I don't like strangers poking through my things," Marge said with a mulish pout.

Katie filed that comment for future consideration and donned a faded work shirt over her sweater before climbing the pull-down ladder to the attic. Diamond-shaped windows at either end admitted adequate light from the sun on the new snow, but deep shadows hid the eaves and corners. Cobwebs festooned chairs with broken backs and bridge lamps with no shades. She tried not to think about spiders as she pulled a leather-bound trunk to the ladder.

"I'm going to bring this down," she said. "It's too dirty to work up here. Do you have a rope? And put some kind of mat at the bottom so we don't scratch the floors."

"I'll find something."

Marge disappeared and came back with a length of clothesline. "Will this do?" She tossed it up to Katie.

Katie wrapped the line around the trunk, not trusting the strength of the old leather handles, and eased it down the ladder. "We'll scoot it into the kitchen so we can see what we're doing."

At first they seemed doomed to failure; the

trunk wasn't locked, but the heavy latches refused to give.

"WD-40?" Katie asked.

"Under the sink."

After a liberal dose of the lubricant, the domed lid creaked open.

"This could be good," Katie said. She touched the layers of tissue paper covering the contents. "Someone packed this with care." She looked around. "We need someplace to lay things out."

Marge threw a clean sheet over the kitchen table. "Get on with it—the suspense is raising my blood pressure."

Katie laid the tissue aside to reveal long kid gloves, fine handkerchiefs monogrammed *ERJ*, lacy scarves and an evening purse beaded in an intricate floral design. The workmanship was exquisite; the condition was pristine.

Beneath the first layer they found embroidered camisoles, petticoats and nightgowns with long puffed sleeves.

"You know what this is?" Katie asked. "I'll bet this is some girl's trousseau. But it looks like nothing was ever worn."

"Maybe someone died or the engagement was broken off. My grandmother's aunt died of diphtheria on her honeymoon," Marge said. "She was just nineteen. We might find out more farther down."

They uncovered fancy aprons, good for nothing but serving afternoon tea, pillow-cases with the same scrolled monogram, blouses and long skirts, and at the bottom, careful layers with more tissue paper...

Tears pricked Katie's eyes. "It's her wedding dress, for a summer wedding."

"It can't be, it's not white."

"White wedding dresses are a twentieth-century trend," Katie said. "Mom and I went to a wedding expo..." The pain she had thought safely sleeping awoke and clawed in her heart. She took a deep breath. "A local museum loaned them a collection of gowns from the 1860s through the 1970s. Victorian and early Edwardian wedding dresses could be any color, even stripes or floral. Much prettier than the white ones, I thought."

She touched the garment lying at the bottom of the trunk. Silk organza, she thought, with pale pink rosebuds embroidered on cream-colored stripes.

She lifted the bodice with great care, but nothing more lay beneath the dress, no name or other identifying information.

"Poor girl," Marge said. "She probably never got to wear her finery."

"Maybe she was lucky," Katie said in a muffled voice.

"You're dead serious about the divorce? Luke's halfway in love with you—I've seen the way he looks at you. Just because I'm old doesn't mean I'm blind. I won't stand for him to be hurt."

Katie tried to smile. "Isn't that a bit premature?"

"Not for Luke. I've know that boy since he was a wild teenager. He'd sit here in the kitchen and tell what he'd done this time— working up his courage, I guess. Then he'd go home and face the consequences."

"I guess he's really learning about consequences now." Katie reddened. "That sounded awful. I didn't mean—"

"Some people grow up later than others. If that bull hadn't stomped Luke, he might still be a boy despite his age. And now he's had to grow up."

A hiss from the stove made Katie jump to her feet—her chicken threatening to boil over. She lowered the flame, trying to compose herself.

"To answer your question," she said, "yes,

I'm dead serious about the divorce. Whatever might happen between me and Luke, I'm not going back."

Marge smiled with satisfaction. "Lots worse places than Durango to start a new life. Let's get all this packed away again and start on another trunk. Maybe we'll find out who the bride was."

Katie moved the first trunk into a spare bedroom furnished with a painted bed, dresser and washstand before retrieving the next one from the attic. This one was larger, with a flat top and leather straps as well as latches.

"This is a piece of luggage, a steamer trunk," Marge said. "See the stickers?"

No name on the outside, but the top and sides were plastered with labels from hotels in New York City, Rome and London. And one from the White Star Line.

"I guess the owner of this one was lucky," Katie said. "He or she didn't sail on the *Titanic*."

Inside they found more women's clothing but with signs of use—day dresses, petticoats, two elaborate evening gowns, a gorgeous ruby-colored paisley shawl, a dark military-style wool coat.

"For the crossing," Katie said.

"The lady traveled in fancy circles," Marge

said. "You're right. We need an expert to look at all this. Maybe from Fort Lewis College. Tom would probably know someone—he's working on his master's."

"While he teaches high school history and works on the ranch?"

Marge laughed. "Ranch folks knew about multitasking long before everyone else."

They broke for a quick lunch of the vegetable-beef soup left from the day before. Marge pushed her chair back when they had finished. "I think we've done enough for one day—I can't take this much excitement." She fluttered her hand and rolled her eyes. "I'm supposed to be taking it easy."

"You are taking it easy," Katie said. "I'm doing all the work. Who owned this house before you?"

"The bank," Marge said. "That is, I bought it from the bank. The owner was an old woman with no heirs. Her will directed that the house be sold as is, with all the contents and the money donated to a couple of local charities. I got it for a song, although *as is* was pretty bad." She wrinkled her nose. "The lady had cats. I had to trash all the rugs and upholstered furniture. We'll work on the rest another day."

CHAPTER TWENTY-ONE

"G<small>RAB THE PHONE</small>, will you?" Jake told Tom. "You're closer."

Tom, at the home ranch to borrow the walker Luke had mentioned, picked up the phone, "Cameron's Pride."

Luke looked up from his dish of apple crisp when Tom said, "Hi, Marge."

Tom listened and then said, "Dang, that *is* interesting. I know a couple people at the college who would be all over something like that. I'll send you their names and phone numbers."

He returned to the table and his own dessert. "Marge and Katie found some old trunks in the attic—clothes from maybe 1900 or earlier. Marge wondered if someone from the college would be interested. There might be some great early Durango artifacts in those trunks."

"I guess Katie's getting along all right with Marge, spending time at her house," Lucy said. "You know how fussy Marge is about her privacy."

Luke felt like shaking his sister out of her sulk. She'd be leaving for New York before long, but meanwhile she was acting like the same moody teenager she'd been after their mother's death.

"Marge never got over the shame of her husband losing people's savings in that mining scheme," Jake said. "I doubt many even remember that now. Not her fault, but she can't forget."

"I guess you're pretty grateful for Katie showing up, Red," Luke said, mostly to rile her. "Now you're free to go."

"I guess," Lucy said.

Whoa. She didn't even tell him not to call her Red.

"Anything I can do for you, Luce? Before you leave?"

Her eyes filled with tears. "Nothing anyone can do for me."

Jake opened his mouth then jumped. Shelby must have kicked him under the table.

"If you think of anything, just holler."

"Thanks, big bro." She gave him a watery smile and put her dish with her dessert half-eaten next to the sink before going up to her room.

"Hard to watch her like this," Jake said, "but I can't think what we can do to help."

"Nothing you can do," Luke said. "Take my word."

"He's right," Tom said. "Love's like herding cats—it goes where it dang well pleases." He stood, leaning on the walker. "I'm glad you kept this around—it does help. Of course, my students are going to rag on me like the devil—bull rider to geezer in a few short years."

He left with the walker and a covered dish of dessert for Jo and the kids.

"That was me till I quit the circuit," Jake said. "I'm glad he had enough sense to hang it up when he did."

"Thank Jo," Shelby said. "She was willing for him to keep riding, but he saw what it cost her."

"Yeah," Luke said. "You never know if the next bull is going to be your last one."

SHELBY DROPPED LUKE off for his PT appointment the next afternoon and left to pick up an order at the Ranchers Exchange. Doug had taken over Luke's training with the braces from Anita Alvarez, with every session leaving Luke more confident with their use. He still felt like a robot with the stiff gait, but he was walking, actually walking, pretty much wherever he wanted in the hospital. They did stairs, although going down still scared him. Curbs in the parking lot posed no obstacle.

One of these days he was going to walk into the Queen like he'd said he would. But not just yet—he wanted to get a little better at it. He'd make a fine fool of himself if he stepped in the door and fell on his face.

Meanwhile, he could look forward to Katie's visit on Sunday. Spring had returned with a rush, as if ashamed of last weekend's tantrum. All the cow-calf pairs they'd found were doing okay, but Jezebel remained missing.

Jake had scattered grass seed and straw for mulch over Sadie's grave in the home pasture, and life went on.

Late Thursday afternoon, Luke's cell phone rang, with Tom's number appearing on the ID.

"Luke," Tom said. "You want to ride out with me? I gotta talk to you."

Luke frowned. Tom never called him by name—always *bro* or *buddy*. Foreboding perched on Luke's shoulder like a vulture.

What did Tom need to say that required the privacy of open country?

He saddled Dude and rode to meet Tom where the ranch road branched off to his and Jo's cabin. They fell in side by side, jogging until the buildings were out of sight.

"Should you be riding?" Luke said. "Monday you could barely walk."

"Riding's fine—it feels good. What did me in was all those hours in the damp and cold. And the walker really has helped. But that's what caused the trouble."

He looked down at his hands. "Man, I really don't know if I should say anything, but I still feel bad about Cherie. The way you got married, I mean. If I'd been paying more attention instead of chasing after Jo…"

What the hell was Tom talking about? Cherie was ancient history, no real harm done. Maybe they would have made it if he hadn't taken a bad hit two weeks after their spur-of-the-moment wedding in Vegas, or maybe not, but none of it was Tom's fault.

"I have no clue what you're getting at," Luke said. "I'm the big brother, remember? You don't need to ride herd on me—not then, not now."

"I guess you're right." From Tom's expression, he felt lower than a snake's belly. "But I have to tell you, now that I've started."

Luke kept silent with an effort.

"Okay." Tom heaved a giant sigh. "You heard the call I got from Marge? About the stuff in her attic?"

Luke made yeah-yeah-I'm-listening motions.

"So I got some names at the college and thought I'd drop the list off at the Queen after school let out yesterday. I haven't seen Marge in a while, and I've never met Katie."

"That's right, you haven't. You were laid up when she was first here. So you finally got to meet her?"

"I guess you could say that. I parked out front and went in using the walker."

Now Luke was getting worried and angry. "For God's sake, man—spit it out! What happened?"

"She thought I was you, walking. She came flying all the way from the kitchen, practically flattened Roger and almost knocked me over. She was calling me Luke and hugging me and kissing me all over my face." He grinned. "Say, she's pretty. You didn't tell me how good-looking she is."

Luke groaned. "So then what happened?"

"I told her she had the wrong brother and she about fainted, I think. Turned red as the tablecloths and ran back to the kitchen. I tried to follow her and tell her it was okay, but Marge said she'd take care of it."

Luke was speechless for the moment and moved by Tom's tale. Katie cared that much?

"I wouldn't have told you except the Queen was still half-full, mostly locals. Word was bound to get back to you."

"I guess I better talk to Marge," he said. "Thanks for the heads-up, bro."

Luke didn't have a chance to call Marge in private until after supper when he checked on the horses. Dude stayed beside him after his evening treat, as if he sensed his master's agitation.

"I figured I'd be hearing from you," Marge said. "Tom told you."

"In glowing detail." He grinned in spite of himself. "Has Katie come out of the kitchen yet?"

"Not until all the customers left. I told her you and Tom look like twins, but when she saw him with the walker, she just reacted."

"Wish it had been me—it would have saved a lot of confusion. She's supposed to come out to the ranch on Sunday. Should I mention it then?"

Marge was silent for a moment. "I'd say not. Katie has faced up to a lot lately. Let her bring it up. Or not."

"Sounds like you two have gotten pretty close."

"She's a good girl, Luke. Just let her pick her own pace, okay?"

CHAPTER TWENTY-TWO

MARGE STOOD IN the kitchen door without speaking while Roger busied himself loading the dishwasher. Katie turned from scrubbing the grill and faced Marge, her chin lifted in defiance.

"Well?"

Marge shrugged. "Well, what? You're not the first person to mistake Tom for Luke and vice versa. I'm sure you won't be the last. Big deal."

"Except I made a spectacle of myself in public, climbing all over Tom like some hot-pants teenager. I'm sure he'll run and tell Luke the first chance he gets."

"Again, so what? You were thrilled to see Luke walking, or so you thought. We'd all be thrilled. You just nailed the wrong Cameron. Nothing shameful in that."

"I'm supposed to go out to the ranch this weekend. What would I say?"

"Say nothing. Or tell Luke you were so

tickled thinking you saw him on his own two legs you lost your head. Your choice."

"I don't know…"

"Am I talking to the same woman who planned her getaway like the Dalton gang and rubbed her husband's nose in his mess before she left?" Marge shook her head. "I guess not. Grow up, Katie—stop acting like a silly teenager."

Marge's words, the sharpest she'd ever spoken to Katie, were like a dash of icy water in her face. Since her marriage at nineteen, she'd had few chances to behave like a grown-up woman, always following Brad's wishes—no, dictates. Her mother's final illness had forced Katie to function for the first time as an independent adult without looking to Brad for guidance or comfort.

Okay, she had acted with childish abandon today, but no real harm done.

"You're right," she said. "If anyone wants to laugh, let them."

SUNDAY MORNING DAWNED crystal clear, with the mountain snows etched sharp as a Japanese print against the impossibly blue sky. Katie had defrosted last week's pie to cement her resolve, but butterflies the size of Luna moths fluttered in her stomach, growing livelier the closer she came to Cameron's Pride.

Shelby, dressed in a maroon skirt and white silk shirt from attending church, answered the door and took the pie to set it on the stove's warming shelf.

"I thought you might bring dessert, so I didn't plan anything," she said. "Luke said you like Cajun—I made gumbo and corn bread."

"I like anything that doesn't flinch when I squirt lemon juice on it," Katie said. "Like raw clams or oysters."

Shelby laughed. "I don't enjoy those myself, and my dad was a fisherman on the Gulf. The guys are out at the barn. We got a new horse this week from the same rescue where I found Dude. You should take a look—she's a pretty thing."

"I'm sorry about the horse you lost in the storm. Luke said she was special to you."

"Sadie was my first mount when I got here—a big, bossy old girl who didn't take any nonsense from a young stud like Ghost. She was my buddy when I lived by myself at the cabin. She was eighteen then." She turned away for a moment. "She had a long life. I'm glad she went down easy."

Katie had already decided to brazen out her mistake in identity, and Shelby was the safest place to start.

"I guess you've heard about the scene I staged with Tom at the Queen."

Shelby frowned. "No, I can't say I have. Did I miss something?"

"Just that I mistook Tom for Luke with the walker and hurled myself at him like he was my sailor husband home from a six-month cruise. I almost died of mortification."

"That's right, you'd never seen Tom. They're easy to tell apart if you know what to look for. Tom has a scar on his cheek from barbed wire, but at a distance..." She laughed. "Common mistake."

"Not so common now," Katie said.

"No, not now," Shelby said with a sigh.

"I'd like to visit your new horse, unless I can help with dinner."

"Maybe in an hour—you can do the salad. Go on. This is my quiet time without the men folks."

Katie went. If Shelby didn't know about her error, maybe Tom hadn't spoken of it. She found Jake, Luke and Lucy gathered in front of a box stall.

"We need a name for this lady," Jake said.

"I'm voting for Cinderella," Lucy said. "A future princess in rags."

Katie looked over the stall door. The horse's coat was the color of honey, with a snowy mane and tail and a white stripe down her face. Only the pattern of her ribs clearly visible under her skin marred her beauty.

"What's wrong with her?" Katie asked. "Is she sick?"

"No," Luke said, "but her owner is. He got taken to the hospital with a stroke. He lost his speech and couldn't tell anyone he had a horse in the barn. She had a self-waterer but no food. She about starved to death before someone came to pick up some things for the old man and heard her calling for help."

"She looks pretty decent now," Jake said. "We saw her intake photo—every bone showing. They generally don't adopt horses out until they're in better condition, but they let us take her because they know Shelby can finish her rehab."

"Making room for them to take in another horse," Lucy said.

"She does look like something out of a fairy tale," Katie said. "Or she will when she's fat and shiny."

"Supposedly she's gentle broke," Luke said.

"Safe for a kid or an inexperienced rider. She's going to need light work as soon as we get a little more meat on her. You interested?"

The mare moved to the door and nuzzled Katie's hand. "Could I really? I'd be so careful with her."

Luke touched the horse's mane. "I dub thee Katie's horse. She'll think of a name for you."

They all returned to the house. Katie was grateful Tom and his family weren't in attendance. She'd have to face him sometime but with luck not today.

They sat down to Shelby's gumbo with good appetites and sopped up the sauce with corn bread shaped like miniature ears of corn.

"I'm stuffed," Jake said after the meal. "I'll have my pie later this afternoon." Everyone seconded his decision.

"I promised Katie some riding," Luke said. "Anyone want to go along?"

"Not me," Shelby said. "The new *Western Horseman* came in yesterday's mail. I'm going to enjoy a rare moment of leisure."

"I'll keep you company," Jake said. "Of course, I may do it with my eyes closed."

"I've got to catch up with my email," Lucy said, "but I'll saddle a horse for Katie.

Rooster's over at Tom's, but Captain's in the corral."

"He'll do," Luke said. "She's ready for something livelier."

"And I bought boots," Katie said, sticking out her foot to show off the russet leather with cherry-red uppers. "The same store where I got my work shoes. I told the clerk I'd be playing cowgirl."

"No playing about it," Luke said. "You did a good job with that bull of Oscar's. Maybe we'll ride over and visit Auntie Rose."

Lucy saddled a gray gelding for Lucy while Luke put his saddle on Dude.

"I really am glad you and Marge have gotten to be friends," she said. "She doesn't let many people get close, so I'm happy for her."

"I'm just the new kid in town," Katie said. "She considers herself your grandmother."

"Dad's parents are gone and Mom's mother lives in Georgia, so I'm grateful to have Marge. I would have been a bigger mess after Mom died except for her."

"Don't worry," Katie said. "I'm just keeping your spot warm."

Katie followed Luke away from the barn on the same track they had taken when they visited the cabin. They started at a jog and then moved into a gentle lope as she became accustomed to Captain's gaits. They passed through the steel gate onto the Bucks' ranch and soon came to a rambling house, a log cabin with a framed addition.

Oscar came out of the barn. "About time," he said. "Ma's been wondering when you'd bring your lady to visit. She's getting her feelings hurt."

"Katie works in Durango six days a week now," Luke said. "And we were a tad busy last weekend, if you recall."

"Yeah, we lost a couple head."

"Not Buckshot, I hope," Luke said with a straight face.

"Naw, we had him in the house with us," Oscar said with equal gravity.

"We're still missing one pair, but I'm not worried. She's a loner—she'll show up."

"Not Jezebel, I hope," Oscar said, and they both laughed. "I'll tell Ma you're here." Oscar disappeared into the house.

"Whatever you do, don't say you're not hungry," Luke said. "The more you turn down food, the more she'll try to feed you."

"Is that a Ute custom?"

"No, that's just Auntie Rose. She'd feed the world if she could. I'll stay mounted, but you should go inside if she invites you, which she will." He signaled Dude to lie down but remained in the saddle.

A round, brown-skinned woman with steel-gray hair bustled out and stopped at the sight of a horse lying by her door. "Luke, my favorite boy. And your trick horse."

"We're all her favorite boys," Luke told Katie as Auntie Rose gave him a hearty hug. "This is Katie Gabriel, Auntie."

"I've heard all about you and your letters," Auntie Rose said and hugged Katie, too, after she dismounted. "Come inside—we'll bring food out to share." Auntie Rose shepherded her into the house.

Inside, a kaleidoscope of brilliant colors assaulted Katie's eyes—Auntie Rose's magenta skirt and scarlet blouse, bright crocheted afghans draped over chair backs and hanks of yarn in rainbow colors hung from pegs on the rafters.

Auntie Rose turned on the burner under a huge pot on the stove. "Some fry bread first, just to keep you alive while I heat up the lamb stew." She pinched Katie's cheek with gentle fingers. "Too thin—men like a little meat on a woman's bones."

Katie laughed, despite her resolve not to insult her hostess. "Honestly, Mrs. Buck—"

"Please, you call me Auntie Rose, like Luke does." She took a ball of dough from the refrigerator and flattened it with deft strokes. She dropped it into the now simmering fat for a few seconds until it rose to the surface as a puffy golden disc. Without spattering a drop, she flung it onto a paper towel and dusted it with sugar and cinnamon before handing it to Katie.

"Take this out to Luke—he looks so thin—while I make another for you."

Katie carried the treat outside, where Luke and Oscar were deep in conversation about range conditions and beef prices.

Luke thanked her with laughter in his eyes.

"More coming, I guess," Katie said and turned as Auntie Rose appeared carrying a second piece of fry bread.

Katie bit into hers and exclaimed with surprised delight. How could mere dough cooked in fat emerge so feather-light and delicate?

"Marge said you make the best fry bread she's ever tasted," Katie said.

Auntie Rose beamed. "You keep this one, Luke," she said. "She knows how to eat. But she's too thin."

"I'd sure like to," Luke said.

Katie looked at him with startled eyes. Just teasing, or a public declaration? She couldn't guess.

"I'll put the stew on now."

"We'd love to stay," Luke said, "but I promised Dad I'd check on the cabin roof after the storm, and we want to get home before dark. We'll come again when we can stay to eat."

Her face fell then brightened. "Wait, I'll get you some cookies to eat on the ride home." She hurried into the house, returning with a paper sack, which she handed to Luke. "Pine nut cookies, your favorite." She hugged him again.

She hugged Katie, too, before waving them out of sight, her figure as bright as a tropical bird against the brown and green of the landscape.

Luke and Katie rode in silence until the house lay well behind them and then burst into laughter.

"She's wonderful," Katie said when she caught her breath. "I see why you wanted me to meet her."

"Nothing she wouldn't do for her family, and everyone's family to her."

"You think she'd teach me to make fry bread? Or give me the recipe?"

"I doubt she has a recipe, but she'll show you how to if she likes you. And she'll like anyone who's special to me."

Katie reined in her horse. "Tom told you, didn't he?"

"Whoa, Dude." He twisted in his saddle to face her. "He figured he'd better before half of Durango did. I'm honored you care so much what happens to me. And you will see me come walking in, sooner than later."

He grinned. "Then I'll have earned that kiss."

Her embarrassment blew away like a burst soap bubble. She had acted on instinct, a loving gesture that had landed on the wrong recipient, a laughable mistake, nothing more.

"Count on it," she said.

He reached across and squeezed her hand before they rode on. They passed the turnoff leading to the cabin, but Luke halted Dude before fording the creek.

"I just had a notion about our missing cow," he said and turned his horse to retrace their path. "There's a little draw near the cabin—water and good shelter. She might be hanging out there."

"Will you try to drive her back?"

"I'd like to. Jezebel shouldn't be out here all alone. Her calf would be a tempting morsel for a cat."

Katie stiffened in the saddle. "Like a wildcat?"

"More likely a mountain lion. They're around, but don't worry—they won't bother us on horseback."

She shivered and looked over her shoulder. "Do you name all your cows?"

"Not hardly. Jezebel's a special case. We really should send her to slaughter, as much trouble as she is, but Dad feels responsible for her getting scared half to death as a calf. She's plain crazy and wild as a deer."

"But you still worry about her."

"Of course. Yeah, our cattle end up as steak and handbags, but we make sure they have good lives while they're in our care."

They stopped at the mouth of a ravine choked with brush just coming into leaf. "You wait," he said. "I'm going to see if she's in here. Don't get in the way if she comes out." He rode forward and disappeared into the tangle.

Katie held Captain back when he tried to

follow. "We'll wait here," she said. "And don't play cow pony if you see something to chase."

Luke seemed gone a long time, although no more than five minutes had passed according to her watch. Just as she began to worry, she heard a yell and a crashing of brush. A reddish-brown cow followed by a calf shot past, their tails in the air.

"Luke," she called, then again louder when she heard no answer. "Luke, are you okay?"

"Sort of." His answer came faintly. "Mostly, I guess."

She kicked Captain into motion, following the trail of broken branches that marked the cows' flight. She and Captain emerged into a small clearing. Luke lay on the ground with Dude standing nearby, his saddle askew.

Katie flung herself off her horse and dropped to her knees beside Luke as he lifted his head.

"Are you hurt?" She ran her hands over his arms and legs.

He answered as he had the night he'd fallen during the nightmare. "Just my pride." He pushed himself into a sitting position. "We came on that danged old cow all of a sudden and sort of surprised each other. She knocked poor Dude sideways."

He wiped the dirt from his face. "I wouldn't mind getting that kiss right now."

She responded without a second's hesitation. The spark she had felt when they first met had glowed hotter the next day when his hand covered hers on the reins. She had tried hard to smother the growing attraction, rewarded by learning to value him first as a friend rather than a lover. Her good intentions had gone up in flames when she had rained a storm of kisses on Tom, mistaking him for Luke.

Now going into his arms was as natural as breathing.

"Wow," he said when they came up for air. "That was worth hitting the ground." He reached for her again.

"Not so fast." She brushed another light kiss on his mouth, then sat back. "I'm a sequential person—I don't even start a fresh tube of toothpaste till the old one is empty. I'm still married. I guess I'm old-fashioned that way."

She stood. "You sure you're all right?"

"I feel like a million bucks right now." He whistled for Dude, who came to stand beside him. "You think you can straighten my saddle? Just loosen the cinch a little and get it level before you tighten it again."

She followed his instructions and he nodded with approval before cuing Dude to lie down.

"Do you need any help getting on?"

"Naw, I've fallen off before." He flexed one shoulder. "Well, maybe a little help—if I could put my arms around you…"

"You phony," she said when the "help" turned into another long embrace. She helped him to sit sidesaddle and then swing one leg across Dude's neck.

"Is it my imagination, or were you able to do more of that yourself?"

"A lot of good stuff happening in PT," he said. "You want to come watch? I'll try for an afternoon appointment this week."

"Try keeping me away."

She remounted Captain as Dude regained his feet. They rode at a sedate pace to open ground.

"At least we know Jezebel and her calf made it through the storm," he said.

CHAPTER TWENTY-THREE

"WHAT THE...?" JAKE jumped to his feet, sending his copy of *Working Ranch* flying. "What have you two been up to, mud wrestling?"

"I found Jezebel," Luke said as Katie closed the kitchen door behind them. "Or rather, she found me. I thought she might be hanging out in that little draw near the cabin. She charged past me and knocked Dude clean off his feet."

"Is Dude okay?" Shelby asked, hurrying into the kitchen in response to Jake's yell.

"He's fine—the ground was soft. My saddle went sideways, but Katie got it straight again."

"We visited Auntie Rose first," Katie said. "I tasted my first fry bread."

"If I pounded on her door at midnight, she'd have fry bread ready in five minutes," Jake said. "It's her remedy for everything."

Katie laid a hand on Luke's shoulder. "You're sure you're all right?"

The glow from her kisses warmed him

again. He'd take a fall every day of the week and twice on Sundays for that kind of reward.

"I'm sure, but I'm going to grab a shower before we tackle the pie," he said. He'd pop a couple Advils in private. He was feeling a little more beat-up than he'd admitted to Katie—nothing serious, but he'd be moving a little slow the next morning.

Katie looked at the mud on her knees. "I should sponge this off."

"Nope, just let it dry—it'll come off easier," Jake said. "An old cowboy told me once, 'If someone throws mud at you, let it dry before you brush it off.'"

Luke rejoined them twenty minutes later with his damp hair slicked back. He'd changed into clean sweatpants and a black T-shirt printed with Red Pony Bar and Grill that set off his dark good looks.

"Ready for pie?" Katie asked. "It's warming in the oven."

Jake yelled up the stairs, "Pie's on, Red."

Lucy's voice floated down. "Don't call me Red." Apparently her mood had lightened a little.

They gathered around the table with coffee while Katie cut her pie and Lucy served. Everyone took a bite in silence and then another.

"What's in this apple pie, Katie?" Shelby asked. "It's almost creamy."

"Grated cheddar cheese," Katie said. "Cheese with apple pie is an old Yankee tradition."

Jake held out his empty plate. "Keep it coming."

They sat swapping tales about weather and rogue cattle, Auntie Rose and bull riding and funny anecdotes from the Silver Queen as the sun sank toward the horizon, sending long beams slantwise through the south-facing window.

Luke finally pushed away from the table. "I'm chasing Katie out of here," he said. "I don't want her driving home in the dark."

Jake and Shelby exchanged amused glances, and Lucy said, "You don't mind my coming home after dark."

"You know the road, kid," Luke said. "I'm going out to check on Dude." He turned to Katie. "Want to come with me?"

She followed him, first thanking the Camerons for their hospitality.

"We owe you," Jake said. "We likely wouldn't have found Jezebel if Luke hadn't taken you to visit the Bucks. We'll be moving the rest of the pairs over to that range next week—she'll mix in with the others then."

"I'm not sure finding her is much of a plus," Lucy said, "but at least we know her calf is okay." She gave Katie a quick hug. "Pass it on to Marge for me."

Katie followed Luke to the barn. As soon as they were deep in the shadows, he pulled her into his lap for another kiss until she beat on his shoulders in mock distress.

"Cowboy," she said in a breathless voice, "we've got to stop meeting like this."

He frowned. "How come? You're practically divorced."

"*Practically* doesn't cut it for me." She pushed her hair from her face. "Giving in before I'm free would make me no better than my soon-to-be ex."

He sighed and released her. "How soon is soon?"

"My lawyer is sending me documents to sign—they'll probably be in my post office box tomorrow. I have to send them back notarized for him to file. If Brad doesn't contest it, the divorce could be final in less than a month."

"And if he does? Contest it, I mean."

"Push harder, I guess. I have online access to all his past credit card bills—I should be able to ferret out the hotel stays for Mr. and

Mrs. Garrison while I was taking care of my mother, although maybe he just took women to our house. I wouldn't mind nailing him to the wall, but all I want is out."

"How stupid could he be to risk losing you?" He pulled her closer and kissed her forehead. "I guess I'll have to settle for waiting. And I respect that you won't pay him back in his own coin."

"That would be an insult to both of us. There's an expression…"

"Yeah, there is," he said, "but you're too ladylike to say it."

He tipped her face up for a last gentle kiss before nudging her off his lap. "Get moving, cowgirl. I'll let you know when to join me for PT."

Luke checked the horses, spending extra time with Dude, who stood with his head hanging over his master's shoulder. Luke scratched under the horse's jaw, picturing the day when he and Katie would ride out together with no more parting at the end of the day. The palomino mare would be a perfect horse for her, gentle but lively. Maybe they'd breed her to Ghost—Katie would get a huge charge out of being godmother to a foal, gold like her dam or silver like Ghost.

Katie might want to stay on running the Queen, and he could take accounting courses at the college while apprenticing in Mike's office. They could find a little house in town if she liked and be at the ranch every weekend—

"Luke." His father's voice yanked him back to the present. "You plan to spend the night out here?"

"Just chatting with Dude," Luke called. "I'll be right in." He gave his horse another treat and sent him out to graze with the others. It had been quite a day, climaxing with Katie's response and his momentous discovery that he could still respond to a woman's body warm and pliant in his arms.

Jo DROVE LUKE into Durango for his Monday PT appointment on her way to the dentist. "Tom told me what happened at the Queen," she said. "I guess Katie survived her embarrassment."

"Better than survived. We had a good talk about it. I'm going to ask Katie to marry me as soon as she's free from her creep of a husband."

Jo reached across to squeeze his hand. "I'm so happy for you. I haven't gotten a chance to know Katie very well. Bring her around so we can get better acquainted." She laughed. "Now that she can tell the difference between you and Tom. How about we go to the Queen for lunch after I pick you up?"

"Maybe not today. She's got a lot on her mind right now—I don't want to crowd her. We'll let it simmer a couple days."

"You're probably right." She pulled up in front of the hospital. "Call me when you're done."

Doug whistled when he saw the bruises on Luke's legs. "You gotta stay out of those bar fights."

"I tangled with a crazy cow yesterday. She flattened me and my horse making her getaway."

"You need to send me a photo of you with your wonder horse for the bulletin board so people can see what's possible. You too sore to use the braces today?"

"Not likely—I wouldn't miss a chance to do my laps. And I'd like an afternoon appointment sometime this week. My lady wants to see how far I've come—she gets off work at three." Pride suffused him with the knowledge he could show Katie off to his friends.

He did shorten his workout in reluctant deference to his bruises but still hiked a complete circuit of the hospital and parking lot. Returning to the PT area, he lay down on the exercise platform for Doug to remove the braces.

"Take them off yourself," Doug said. "You'll have to do it when you get them home. We're going to let you solo any day now. I've been talking to your doctor in Austin. He figures you'll be ready soon."

"He as much as told me I wouldn't walk again."

"Classic motivation. 'Don't tell me I can't.' He's got your number."

"I guess you're right. I've never been too good with taking no for an answer."

Doug folded his arms and stood back while Luke unstrapped the braces and eased out of the stirrup-like foot pieces. He was sweating again by the time he finished. "Okay? Can I take them home now?"

"Next session you can put them on yourself. Then we'll talk about turning you loose with them."

CHAPTER TWENTY-FOUR

KATIE FLOATED THROUGH the next day on a cloud as sweet and light as Auntie Rose's fry bread. Marge arrived around lunchtime, as she had been doing lately. She cornered Katie in the kitchen. "So how was the visit to Cameron's Pride?"

"Fine, except a wild cow knocked Luke's horse down." The memory of the ensuing kiss flooded her face with color. "Luke and Dude are both all right. And I tasted Auntie Rose's fry bread—heavenly."

"A little more to the day than cows and fry bread," Marge said, giving her a shrewd look.

"Lucy said to give you a hug for her." Katie matched action to words. "And the Camerons got a new mare from the same rescue as Luke's horse. A palomino, I think. I'm going to ride her when she fattens up a little more."

She couldn't quite bring herself to talk about Luke—not even with Marge—as though voicing her happiness would bring bad luck. "I had a very nice day," she said.

"Humph," Marge said and returned to the dining room to perch on a stool beside the antique brass cash register.

After work Katie checked her post office box—sure enough, it held a thick envelope from Mr. Foster. She scanned the contents and approached the clerk. "Where can I get my signature notarized?" she asked.

"Your bank will have a notary," the plump, grandmotherly woman said. "Or the UPS store."

Katie read the documents twice in her car to make sure she understood them, then drove to the First National Bank of Durango. She signed in several places before a notary and hurried to the post office in time to overnight them to Mr. Foster's office.

"That was fast," the clerk said. "Important business, I guess."

"Just the rest of my life," Katie said.

She shopped for groceries with a clear mind; she'd done all she could for the moment. That night she lay awake thinking of Luke and worrying how Brad might respond to her demand for freedom.

The next afternoon she called Mr. Foster to

make sure the documents had arrived. "Move as fast as you can," she said. "I need to get out of the marriage as quickly as possible."

After a long silence, he said, "I hate to ask, but is this divorce time critical? Do you have some sort of deadline to meet?"

His question puzzled her for a moment, and then she laughed. "I'm not pregnant, Mr. Foster. I just want the freedom to enjoy my new life here. You can't imagine the wonderful people I've met and the experiences I've had. I'm never moving back to Connecticut."

"What about your mother's house? I understand it's been in the family for several generations."

"It's still going to be. I'm selling it to my cousin who's living there."

"You can't do that. You're prohibited from disposing of any inheritance before the divorce is settled."

"My mother was smart," Katie said. "Because of her health, she put both our names on the deed after my father died. I've been co-owner for years."

They discussed a few more technicalities and then he said, "Someone will serve these papers as soon as possible, probably tomorrow. I'll let you know his response."

She worked the next day with a lighter heart.

Luke called that evening. "Want to be at the hospital tomorrow afternoon at three thirty? I want to show off for you. Come to the front entrance."

KATIE PARKED IN the visitors' lot a little before three thirty and made her way to the information desk.

"I need to find the physical therapy department," she said to the pretty Hispanic woman directing visitors and patients.

"Someone will show you the way," she said with a smile and pointed over Katie's shoulder.

"Need a guide, little lady?" Luke stood behind her.

She staggered against the desk, faint with shock. She scanned his face—no scar. This was really Luke standing on his own feet. She flung her arms around his neck, oblivious of the gathering crowd in the lobby. One person applauded; others joined in. Someone gave a shrill whistle.

"Whoa. Don't knock him over," said a muscular man in a polo shirt marked Mercy Regional Medical Center. "He still tips pretty easily."

Katie stammered half questions, unable to complete a sentence.

Luke put his arm around her shoulders. "Doug, let's get her out of the lobby before she passes out." He led her toward the elevators with Doug on his other side. His gait was stiff, punctuated with mechanical clicks and thumps, but he was walking, actually walking.

Katie had recovered her wits somewhat by the time they reached the PT department. "All right," she said. "Now that you've shocked the pants off me, tell me everything."

Luke introduced Doug Pruitt and they took turns explaining and demonstrating the braces. "The best part is that more of Luke's natural function is coming back the more he's up with the braces. These give him mobility while he's healing. Could be he'll be able to walk without them eventually."

"Count on it," Luke said.

"I knew you were holding out on me." Katie smacked Luke's chest; he caught her hand and kissed it.

"Don't say this wasn't a nice surprise." He snapped his fingers. "I almost forgot to tell you—Saturday is Auntie Rose's seventy-fifth birthday. Shelby wants to throw a surprise party for her. I doubt Marge is up to catering the whole thing, but we'd appreciate if you guys could provide the sides, like beans and corn bread. I know it's short notice, but Shelby just found out the date. We can always go to Albertson's deli—"

"Don't be ridiculous," Katie said, returning to familiar ground. "How many guests?"

"At least fifty—the Bucks have lots of relatives."

"Desserts?"

"Shelby's making red velvet cupcakes instead of a single cake. That's Auntie Rose's favorite, and they'll serve easier. But a few pies would be good if you can manage it."

"Don't worry about a thing. We'll deliver on our end."

Luke hugged her. "I told Shelby we could count on you. How about we come pick everything up Friday right at closing time so we don't interfere with the Saturday breakfast crowd?"

KATIE PUT IN long hours on the special orders, but with Marge's help they had everything ready by noon on Friday. Marge had prepared her special cowboy beans at home while Katie baked pies—three peach and three apple—as well as the corn bread in the big commercial oven after closing.

The hectic activity took Katie's mind off a call she'd received from Mr. Foster. The divorce papers had been served on Brad, who apparently had received them with surly dismissal, threatening to toss them in the trash.

"Spouses frequently react that way when reality hits them," he said, "but they usually come around in time. You're asking him for nothing, which I still think is foolish. That may make the divorce a bit more palatable. I can point out to his attorney that with your husband's assets, he'll be getting away lucky."

She hoped he was right.

The Cameron men arrived half an hour before closing Friday afternoon. Jake and Tom, now without the walker, went to the kitchen and started loading food into coolers for the trip to the ranch. Marge directed their work like a general marshaling her troops while Luke, in his wheelchair, held the door open as the containers were carried out to Tom's Expedition. Katie sat by the cash register tallying the day's receipts, and Roger refilled coffee mugs for a few lingering diners.

The last customers left, and at five minutes before three, the door opened and a man stepped inside.

"Sorry, we're closing," Katie said without looking up.

"I know. That's why I waited till now."

Katie's head jerked up. The roll of quarters in her hand hit the floor and split, sending coins rolling in all directions.

"Brad," she said in a tiny voice. "What are you doing here?"

"I've come to take you home, Kathryn. You've made your point, and I promise I'll never give you reason to leave again."

"How did you find me?" She refused to panic. "Of course, the notary stamp from the bank."

He looked around the Queen's dining room. "You weren't hard to locate in a town this size. I'm sorry to find you working in a place like this. And living upstairs over a saloon. If you're that determined to play at running a restaurant, I'll set you up with a nice café after we get home."

He shook his head with a mock look of sadness. "Running off like a spoiled child. I've been frantic with worry about your safety— you're such an innocent."

His arrogant self-assurance stiffened her

spine. She heard the soft whisper of rubber tires behind her as she slid off the stool to stand with her chin up and shoulders squared.

"I'm not going back with you—not now, not ever. You killed my trust forever. Now get out. We're closed." She felt Luke take her hand.

Brad laughed, waving a dismissive hand at Luke. "This is what you're settling for? He'll give you a fine lifestyle, won't he?"

"It doesn't matter that he's in a wheelchair. He's twice the man you'll ever be," Katie said, her voice rising. "And my lifestyle here suits me fine. I've got a job, a place to live… I've got friends here."

"You have friends in Connecticut."

"Your friends, not mine. My friends weren't fancy enough for the country club—they couldn't help you land big contracts. They're just good people I like and who like me. But you made them feel unwelcome, so they stopped calling. I'm done with you, you…" Words failed her for a moment. "You pathetic child."

She felt a hand on her shoulder and the solid wall of Luke's chest behind her. He teetered, but he was standing.

"Keep talking, darlin'," he said in her ear. "You're doing fine."

Shock and wonder struck her speechless, but she didn't dare turn her back on Brad.

Marge leaned through the pass-through with her nickel-plated revolver in her hand. "What's all this noise? Who the hell is this?"

"Meet Brad...what's his name, Katie?" Luke asked. "Carrion?"

Katie fought down hysterical laughter. "Garrison."

"Brad Garrison," Luke said. "Katie's almost ex-husband."

"I don't care if he's Brad Pitt. It's after three o'clock and we're closed. I haven't shot an intruder in a while, but I haven't forgotten how." Marge aimed the gun and cocked it. "Now git and git fast, while you still can. Katie's not going anywhere with you."

The kitchen door opened, and Tom came out to stand beside Luke. "You need help finding your way out, mister?"

Jake stepped up next to Tom. "I reckon the three of us can help you to the curb."

Bradley Garrison looked from one to another, hatred seething on his face, and backed out the door, slamming it hard enough to shiver the etched glass in its frame. Moments later tires screeched on the pavement.

"That went all Western in a hurry, didn't

it?" Luke said and collapsed into the wheel-chair. "Dang, I didn't know I could do that."

Katie wrapped her arms around him. "You stood! On your own! Can you do it again?"

Luke laughed. "I'm not even going to try. Don't wear it out, sweetheart."

Katie sagged against the bar. "I should have thought about the bank's notary seal. It never occurred to me he'd come here assuming I'd go back with him."

"It did to me," Luke said. "I'm just surprised it took him this long. I know I'd move heaven and earth to get you back."

"You might want to give the sheriff a heads-up," Tom said. "He came on like a real crazy."

Marge joined them with her finger now off the trigger. "I suspect you'll get your divorce pretty quick." She blew imaginary smoke from the barrel of her revolver. "He won't want to go up against the Cameron gang again."

Jake threw back his head and howled with laughter. "Marge, you're a pistol."

CHAPTER TWENTY-FIVE

"IF I WAS a drinking man," Jake said, "which I'm not, I'd say we should all raise a glass to the lately departed Mr.—" He turned to Luke. "What did you call him?"

Luke ducked his head in pretended shame. "Sometimes my mouth runs away on me. It burns me up he thinks he can throw away a good woman, then pick her up again whenever he takes the notion."

"Men!" Marge said. "Always want the one thing they can't have. Tell you what—I'm putting a sign on the door that we're closed tomorrow. I guess we're invited to the party, Jake. Right?"

"Marge, it wouldn't be a party without you there. You want someone to drive in and fetch you tomorrow? Because I think Katie should come home with us. No telling if that so-and-so might decide to make another visit once we leave."

"I guess that's a good idea," Katie said. "He

apparently knows I'm living upstairs above the Queen."

"I've been driving for a while now," Marge said. "And I'm glad Katie's coming with you. She could stay at my house, but she'll be safer at the ranch."

Luke turned to Jake. "You guys had best get that food home so it doesn't spoil. I'll wait while Katie grabs what she needs and ride with her. I doubt we'll have any trouble this soon."

"You're right," Jake said. "Marge, please don't come armed tomorrow. We can take care of any trouble that might show up. But you were real persuasive."

He stopped to give Katie a hug. "You handled yourself like a real Cameron." He and Tom left.

"No higher praise than that from Dad," Luke said. "Run up and get your gear. I'd wait at the bottom of your steps, but your..." It galled him to call Brad Garrison Katie's husband. "That guy knows me now. Roger, you mind waiting outside for Katie?"

"My pleasure," Roger said and took off his apron. "Come on, cookie. I'll guard the gate, then the boss and I can lock up."

Luke slumped in his chair after Katie left.

To tell the truth, he was feeling a little shaky after the volcanic surge of energy that had brought him to his feet. He felt his chair rolled to a table where Marge had set coffee and two apple fritters.

Marge lowered herself into a seat. "You look a little done up," she said. "Me, too. I figured we could both use some sugar."

Luke concentrated on steadying his hand before he reached for the coffee. He took a long swallow and a bite of his fritter before speaking. "I used to feel like this back in the locker room after a bull nearly nailed me. You're a superman while the adrenaline's flowing, but afterward—"

"Like standing up when you're supposed to be paralyzed."

He laughed. "Yeah, like that. But I have been standing. Okay, with help, but it's coming back."

"Does Katie know that?"

"I asked her to meet me at PT a few days ago. I sneaked behind her in the lobby. She dang near fainted. I've been using these computerized braces that help me walk and sit, climb stairs—just about everything. And the more I walk with them, the more it feels like I can do it on my own. Like today."

He took another bite, drank and then looked Marge in the eye. "Did you know Katie's husband is rich?"

"I thought he might be, from a couple things she's let slip."

His chin dropped. "A rich man who has country club friends and can set her up with a nice café to run."

"I was hoping you didn't pick up on that."

"He's right. Even with me on my feet again, she'd be working her butt off on the ranch or here. Maybe she'll get tired of it and wish she'd gone back with him."

Marge slapped her hands on the table. "How can you be so unfair to Katie? You think that little of her, that she'd run out on you over hard work? She's seen at least a little of what ranch life is like, and she's worked here like a stevedore without a word of complaint."

He shrugged, refusing to be reassured. "Maybe it's like a wilderness trip, roughing it so you can go home with survival stories to tell at cocktail parties."

Marge rolled her eyes skyward. "You want to blow the best chance you'll ever get? Now, at your age? Don't be stupid."

The door opened, and Roger entered. "Your

lady friend's outside waiting, you lucky so-and-so. If I was twenty years younger…"

Luke got one more stern look from Marge before he wheeled himself out to climb into Katie's waiting vehicle.

Katie leaned over and kissed him, making him feel like a bigger idiot. Or a monster for luring her away from a life of security and luxury.

"I'm so happy Marge decided to close tomorrow," she said. "I didn't mind the extra last-minute baking, but I did feel a little like the one kid in the class not invited to a birthday party. Because I had to work tomorrow, I mean. Is it a surprise party?"

"It's supposed to be," he said, trying to stifle his qualms, "but Auntie Rose will probably hear about it in advance through the moccasin telegraph."

He looked out the side window as she drove, weighing what he had just learned about Katie against Marge's scolding. Marge was right. He should keep his mouth shut and take his good fortune on faith.

"I have a hard time picturing you at a country club," he said and could have torn his tongue out.

"Me, too," Katie said. "I hated tennis. Golf

was a little better—I could pretend I was just taking a nice walk in the country. But the luncheons afterward made me want to scream—all the talk about this cruise or that island vacation. And whose husband is screwing around with whose wife." She sighed. "I guess I should have paid more attention to that part."

Yep, stinking rich. "Sounds pretty lame. What do you like to do?"

"Well, cook," she said. "I read a lot. I like to hike—our house is next to a big conservation preserve, so I could get into the woods in about two minutes flat. I hiked in all kinds of weather because I didn't enjoy the house. Too big, too fancy, not my taste at all. I like my apartment much better. I'd love to buy a house like Marge's and restore it."

Good news and bad—he didn't know which way to jump.

"I've never been much for hiking. Nothing against it," he added in haste, "but I get my nature fix on horseback. I'd be willing to try it. There's a gal right now hiking the Appalachian Trail using the same kind of braces as mine."

"I'm still over the moon that you stood

today," she said. "Does that mean the nerve connections are back?"

"More like jump-starting a dead engine— a onetime jolt of energy. But yeah, seems like every day I can do a little more."

Luke's mind was still a muddled mess by the time they arrived at the ranch. He was glad to let Shelby and Lucy snatch Katie away for a recap of the action Tom and his dad had already described.

"I so wish I could have seen the whole thing," Lucy said. "What a great dramatic scene! Luke really stood up? On his own?"

Luke sneaked to his room and closed the door. He needed time alone to think. He'd been so wrapped up in relearning to walk, he hadn't given Katie's welfare a thought, selfish bastard that he was.

He stretched out on the bed, weary to his soul. He had worked like a demon in rehab, accomplishing everything the therapists asked and more. Since meeting Katie, he'd tried even harder, as if climbing toward a reward on a mountaintop. Instead he found himself on the edge of a cliff with the ground crumbling under his feet.

He'd been injured before but had always battled back, which was maybe why he hadn't fallen prey this time to the despair stalking close on his heels. Only now, with his recovery nearly assured, had the black cloud caught up with him. What good was a healthy body if he couldn't have the woman he'd waited for all his life?

Good thing he hadn't yet asked her to marry him—how soon would she tire of the hard work and rugged lifestyle compared to the luxury and ease she'd left behind? And having her stay only from a sense of duty would be worse, the ultimate humiliation.

A soft knock sounded on his door, and he heard Shelby's voice asking if she could come in. He propped himself up on his elbows and then fell back.

"Yeah, why not?"

Shelby stepped inside and closed the door behind her. "I saw you slip away. Are you all right?"

"Sure, couldn't be better."

She didn't speak for a bit and then said, "That's good. Can I do anything for you?"

He knew what she was asking, giving him a chance to open up, to throw himself on her counsel again, but he needed to put on his big-boy boots. To stand on his own, emotionally as well as physically. Katie had called her husband a pathetic child. He was no better.

"Yeah, there is," he said. "I'll go check the horses after supper. Could you make sure no one follows me?"

"Anyone?"

"Like Dad or Lucy, I mean."

"Sure," she said. "Many a time horses have been my only comfort—they set my mind straight." She looked at her watch. "Supper's in half an hour."

CHAPTER TWENTY-SIX

KATIE SAW LUKE'S door close. Was he okay? He'd been a little quiet on the ride home, not exactly frowning, but with lines of tension bracketing his mouth and furrowing his forehead. Had he injured his back in his superhuman effort to stand, to come to her aid?

She decided to check on him after she finished snapping the green beans for tonight's supper, but she relaxed when she saw Shelby knock and then step into his room.

Supper was an assortment of leftovers cleaned out of the fridge to make room for the party food. Luke seemed fine when he emerged from his room, but she caught him watching her during the meal, his gaze cutting away when it met hers.

"Thanks," he said when Lucy offered him a helping of bread pudding for dessert, "but I'll have mine after I check the horses."

Katie watched him wheel himself to the barn and disappear into the shadows. Should she follow, or did he want to be alone? She'd always tried to find the right balance between listening to Brad's problems with weather and workers and machinery while trying not to pressure him. Obviously she hadn't gotten it right. Maybe she'd do no better with Luke, but she had to try. At least he would know she cared.

Shelby had Lucy helping her to frost dozens of cupcakes, each to be decorated with a pink rosebud. Katie knew she should pitch in; instead she slipped out the back door and hurried to the barn before anyone could ask where she was going.

The interior lay mostly in darkness, but she could see Luke's silhouette against the sunset at the side door. Dude stood beside his master's wheelchair, his head lowered to enjoy Luke's caresses. The horse lifted his head with a soft snort at Katie's approach.

Luke turned his head. "Hey, girl. I hoped you'd join me." He motioned toward a tack trunk in the passageway. "Have a seat and enjoy the afterglow."

They sat without speaking while the sky faded from pink to rose and then to lavender. The first stars appeared. Katie couldn't read his expression in the gathering gloom, but she could see his hands clenched in his lap and his shoulders hunched as if expecting a blow.

At last she reached toward him and laid her hand over his. "How can I help?"

"I don't know that you can. I've got to figure this out for myself."

Feeling her way as if walking blindfolded, she said, "Marge mentioned you've been married before."

He gave a snort of laughter. "Just barely—it didn't last but two weeks. When I landed in the hospital with a broken neck and ruptured spleen five years ago, Cherie caught the next bus to Kansas City. Her dad got busted up riding broncs—she couldn't handle the idea of getting stuck with a disabled husband." He shrugged. "At least we didn't do each other any harm."

He looked at their joined hands. "I wouldn't get off that easy the next time."

Katie was torn between longing to comfort him and wanting to slap some sense into him. Keeping her voice soft, she said, "Trying again isn't easy for anyone. It takes courage to stick your head up over the barricade."

"I don't know if I have the guts for it. Maybe I never did."

"Luke," she said, "is bullfighting dangerous?"

"You're kidding, right? Besides my neck broken twice, I've had both shoulders rebuilt, torn ligaments in both knees. Plus little stuff like concussions, broken ribs." He snorted. "More stitches than I can count. And now it's put me in a wheelchair. Yeah, it's dangerous."

"Then why did you do it?"

"Truth?"

"And nothing but the truth."

"It felt good. No, it felt over-the-top fabulous. Okay, I took pride in protecting the riders, but I wouldn't have kept at it so long if I wasn't having fun. I'd go back to it if I could."

"So it was worth the risk."

He was silent; she could almost hear the wheels turning.

"I wouldn't worry if you were a ranch girl," he said at last, "but I'm scared you don't know what you're getting into. I grew up working dawn till nightfall—that's what ranching is like. We've been beat up and knocked down—rebuilding is worse than starting from scratch because of new debt. You're not used to living like that. It could get old real fast."

She leaned against the wall, cocking her boot heels in the dirt. "You've got the wrong idea about me. We lived with my grandparents because of Mom's health and my dad being on partial disability. I held jobs after school and summers from fourteen straight through college. I worked in Brad's company office until he went upscale and kicked me out of the office. He said I should concentrate on establishing social contacts and I hated it. I didn't know how miserable I was till I started at the Queen."

She reached forward to pat his knee. "Maybe I don't know about blizzards and losing cattle, but hard work doesn't scare me. I languish without it."

She stood and bent to kiss him, a soft loving kiss without the heat of passion. "I'm going to the house to help ice Auntie Rose's cupcakes."

"You go ahead," he said. He grabbed her hand and kissed her palm, molding her hand around his cheek. "I think I'll sit out here with Dude a little longer."

Jo had arrived to help while Katie had been talking with Luke. She handed Katie a cupcake with white frosting and something pink and green on top. The shape could have been a snail or a seashell or a piglet eating lettuce. "Do you think Auntie Rose will know it's a rosebud?"

"How many have you done?" Katie asked.

"Four," Lucy said. "Ninety-six to go."

"Stop the production line." She went to her vehicle and returned with a box. "Lucky I haven't finished unloading my car." She opened the box, revealing a set of cake-decorating tools. "I took a course thinking I might start a specialty cake business." She fitted a tip on one of the tools and reached for the bowl of green frosting. "And we're up and running."

She had leaves on nearly half the cupcakes by the time Luke returned to the kitchen.

"Make yourself useful," she said and set a tray on his lap. "Carry those to the far end of the counter so the leaves can set before I start on the rosebuds."

"Yes, ma'am," he said and did as he was told.

She smiled at him with love and trust before turning back to her task. In another hour all the cupcakes were done.

Shelby awarded two of the first four to Luke for his help and gave the other two to Katie. "Take these to Jake," she said. "He's tending the barbecue pit out back."

"I'll take them," Lucy said.

"No, let Katie go." Shelby gave Lucy and

Jo each a tray. "These should go down to the cellar where it's cool."

Katie made her way through the spring darkness toward the glow of coals in an open pit. A side of beef turned slowly on a spit while Jake used a cotton mop to slather an aromatic sauce on the meat.

"Shelby sent out a treat for you," she said, handing him one of the cupcakes.

Jake examined it by the light of the fire. "What's that on top, a pig?"

"That was my guess, too," Katie said. "The rest have rosebuds—I had my cake-decorating kit in my car."

Jake bit into the cake and sighed with pleasure. "My sweetheart sure makes a mean red velvet cake. Go ahead, eat—I don't want but one."

Katie tasted the second cupcake. "Is there anything Shelby can't do?"

"She sure makes my world go round. I'd pretty much given up on life after Annie died—crawled headfirst into a bottle of Beam to get away from all the sadness. The boys had their careers and Marge took Lucy under her wing. Me, seemed like I had nothing and nobody till Shelby happened along."

"I know she feels the same way about you, especially since your heart attack."

He laughed. "That woman is likely to drive me back to drink with her coddling, but I love it." He pointed a finger at her. "Don't you tell her that."

She mimed zipping her lips shut. "It took a lot of courage to risk loving someone again."

"Are we talking about me and Shelby or you and Luke?"

She tried to laugh but didn't quite pull it off. "Wow, are all Westerners this direct?"

"I'd say mostly yes. We deal with some pretty big stuff out here, life and death that's not on TV or stuck away in hospitals. We don't waste time—we just get on with living. So what about you and Luke?"

She finished eating her cupcake and licked frosting off her fingers before answering. "Before today, I'd have said we were on the same course, until my husband—"

"Soon-to-be ex." Jake chuckled. "Luke's always had a mouth on him. But go on."

"Something's changed—I don't know what."

"Times when he was growing up I wanted to drown him in the rain barrel, but you can count on him to his last breath. He'll stew over whatever's bothering him till he sorts it out and then do the right thing. Just have faith in him."

On impulse, Katie leaned over and kissed Jake's cheek.

He laughed. "There you go, sugar—done like a real ranch gal."

"Can't trust you out of my sight for a minute." Luke's voice came out of the darkness. "Getting cute with my old man."

"Old man yourself," Jake said. He handed Luke the mop and bucket with the sauce. "Tend to this cow while I take a break inside."

Luke slopped sauce on the beef as it turned and then set the bucket on the ground. He rolled his chair out of the firelight and held out his hand. "Come here, darlin'."

Katie went without hesitation and let him pull her into his lap. They sat in silence with his arms around her waist and her face tucked into the hollow of his neck. She breathed in the mingled scents of smoke from the fire, the cotton of his shirt and Luke's own clean musky tang. She wished she could sit like this all night, but after a peaceful interval she raised her head.

"I've been here almost a month," she said, "in your town and your home with your friends and family. I've learned a lot about

HELEN DEPRIMA   301

you, but you know almost nothing about me. Doesn't that scare you?"

"I know more than I did yesterday. I know your husband's rich and he wants you back."

"Too bad—I don't want him or his fancy lifestyle, never mind his screwing around."

"I'm still worried you'll get tired of the hard work. Maybe the country club would start looking good to you again."

"And maybe you'll get itchy to start chasing girls around bull-riding events again. So I shouldn't take a chance on you?"

He didn't answer. At last she took his face between her hands. "We both know life doesn't come with any warranty—you buy it as is. I'm not too scared to try. Are you?"

"I'm scared, all right, but I want you anyway," he said.

She stuck out her hand. "Deal," she said and they shook as if sealing a solemn pact. She snuggled into his arms. "Does someone have to stay up all night with the barbecue?"

She heard the back door slam and then Jake's voice. "You guys all straightened out? I sure hope so, because the beef needs painting again."

Katie scrambled to her feet and grabbed the mop and bucket. "I'm on it," she said, smearing sauce on the meat with more enthusiasm than expertise.

Jake took the bucket out of her hand. "I'm relieving you of duty," he said. "Get back inside."

She kissed his cheek a second time. "Thanks, Jake."

"My pleasure, sugar."

Luke laughed. "There she goes getting cute again."

CHAPTER TWENTY-SEVEN

LUKE SLEPT BETTER that night than he had since his wreck. His last waking thought was that he still faced a long, hard trail to get back on his feet, but Katie's sweet sanity had calmed his heart. They would have to deal with the Jerk—maybe that would also be a rough ride—but they'd do it side by side.

Bustle in the kitchen woke him at dawn. He lay awake listening to the women's voices— Katie's weaving in and out with Lucy's chatter and Shelby's quieter tones. He smiled. Now he was truly home.

He jumped at a bang on his door. "Get out here, you lazy bum!" Lucy, of course. "We need you to take ice out to the barn."

"In five, Red."

"Don't call me Red!"

He pulled on his best shirt and Wranglers in honor of Auntie Rose and joined the uproar in the kitchen. Katie shot him a smile that started his day in fine style before running down the cellar steps. She returned with a bag of ice in her arms and plopped it in his lap. "To the barn, cowboy."

"And don't ask her to come with you," Lucy said. "We need her here."

Katie shrugged. "Later," she said.

Luke carried the ice to the barn where his father was draining water from a galvanized watering trough.

"Dump it on," Jake said, pointing to the side of beef wrapped in heavy plastic. "You can help me stick it back on the spit about an hour before we eat."

"How are you going to get Auntie Rose here for the surprise?" Luke asked, emptying the ice over the meat.

"We're taking your lady's name in vain. We told Auntie Rose today is Katie's birthday, so teaching her to make fry bread would be a nice gift. All we could think of—she has everybody else's birthdays memorized."

"Sneaky. Did you have this all cooked up in advance with Marge?"

"I asked her about closing the Queen when we got there yesterday. She was going to tell Katie, but the details kind of went south when Katie's—"

"Call him the Jerk, like I do."

"I'll never understand how your mouth never got the crap beat out of you," Jake said.

"I always talked my way out of any outright ruckus. I'm a lover, not a fighter."

"Anyway, Oscar's bringing Auntie Rose over around eleven for Katie's fry bread lesson. Everyone else is slated to arrive around noon."

Luke wheeled to the barn door and scanned pink-and-gold clouds heralding the sunrise. "We couldn't have a better day for it. Maybe some nasty weather day after tomorrow, but we're good till then."

"We could hide out here all morning, but I guess we'd better get to the house and get our orders," Jake said. "Good thing all the calves are on the ground—the cows can take care of themselves for one day."

Shelby kept everyone busy all morning setting up tables and dragging hay bales for seats to a level meadow behind the old bunkhouse. With luck, Auntie Rose wouldn't see the preparations when she arrived with Oscar. Luke stowed boxes of plastic plates and utensils under the tables and carried six-packs of soft drinks to the barn, ready to replace the beef in the ice-filled watering trough.

When he rolled through the kitchen, he noticed Shelby and Lucy had deferred to Katie's catering experience, turning command over to her.

A last flurry of activity cleared the kitchen a few minutes before eleven, and they all sat around the table when the rattle of the cattle guard announced Oscar and Auntie Rose's arrival.

"How do you plan to keep Auntie Rose from hearing all the vehicles arriving?" Luke asked. "That cattle guard is better than a burglar alarm."

"No problem." Shelby turned on the vent fan over the range; its soft roar drowned out all sound from outside. "And we'll keep her away from the window."

The kitchen door opened and Auntie Rose entered, resplendent in a purple paisley skirt topped by a turquoise velveteen tunic. An elaborate beaded necklace completed the ensemble. She reached into a shopping bag and handed Shelby a round tin decorated with a star and a picture of the Alamo. "Cookies for my favorite boys," she said. "I'll take them out to the barn."

"I'll take them, Ma," Oscar said, following her into the kitchen.

"I'll go with him," Luke said. "To make sure Dad gets some."

Auntie Rose patted his cheek. "You go ahead. I'll have your young lady making fry bread as good as mine in two shakes of a lamb's tail."

She pulled a voluminous green apron from the same bag and a second one for Katie. "Happy birthday," she said and smothered her in a hug. "It's my birthday, too—seventy-five."

"Really?" Katie avoided Luke's eyes. "Happy birthday."

Auntie Rose waited until the door closed behind Oscar. "The family is setting up a surprise party for me at home." She winked. "Don't tell Oscar I know."

Katie shot Luke a look of comic dismay as he left the kitchen.

"Your mom just told Katie there's a surprise party planned at your ranch," Luke told Oscar. "I had to get out before I cracked up."

Oscar snorted. "Pretty hard to sneak anything past Ma. She'll still get her surprise unless she comes trotting out to the barn when people start arriving."

Oscar and Jake hoisted the side of beef from its ice bath and skewered it on the spit to finish over fresh coals. Jake cut a long sliver of meat from the last rib and tore it in half for Luke and Oscar to sample. "Another hour should do it, don't you think?"

Oscar downed his in two bites. "Tastes fine to me now, but it's your cow and your party."

"Any idea when Marge is coming?" Luke asked. "You think she's okay to drive this far with her new knees?"

"You know Marge," Jake said. "She'll get here if she has to hitchhike."

The first guests arrived on horseback. Mike's parents from the neighboring ranch rode up to the barn and dismounted.

"I told Bob we could ease the parking by riding over," Donna Farley said, handing the reins of her sorrel mare to her husband. "What can I do to help?"

"I'm about ready set out plates and such," Luke said and led the way to the impromptu picnic area. "Katie said to make stacks of plates and napkins but leave the knives and forks in their boxes." He handed Donna two horseshoes he had hung over the back of his wheelchair. "You can weigh them down with these."

"Did you wash them?" She examined one and rolled her eyes. "Of course not." She spread a paper napkin on top of the plates before anchoring them with the horseshoe and did the same with the napkins. "Cleaner than picking everything up off the ground after the wind blows them around, I suppose."

She stood back with her hands on her hips. "Now that I've got you cornered, will you please tell me why your sister is torturing my son?"

Luke threw up both hands. "The last I heard from Mike, they agreed to hold off on any decision till after this summer, so I'm staying out of it. I've got my own problems."

She sighed. "I suppose you do. Bob and I met Katie last week when we stopped for lunch at the Queen. She and Marge are pretty funny, like an old-time vaudeville team. So this is a certain thing for you?"

"Certain as death except for one problem— she's still married. Her lawyer back East is doing his best to hurry up the divorce, but Katie's an old-fashioned girl. Until she's single…"

"No hanky-panky. And meanwhile, you burn."

He wagged his head. "With a blue flame."

She patted his hand. "You play it her way. Sounds like she's worth the wait."

Ghost neighed in his corral as Jo rode up

on her bay mare. "Tom sent me over to help,"
she said. "He's doing his part by keeping the
kids away—they'd run right in and yell, 'Surprise!'"

Luke checked his watch. "You could wait
near the road and show people where to park.
Send them around the front of the house so
Auntie Rose won't see them out the kitchen
window. As soon as we get a good crowd,
Oscar can go fetch her."

Jo nodded and kicked her horse into a
quick jog toward the main gate. Soon Luke
heard vehicles arriving, and the Buck clan
plus more of Auntie Rose's friends began to
gather behind the bunkhouse. Donna helped
Luke keep them herded away from the back
door, no small chore considering the number
of children from toddlers to teens.

A few minutes before noon, a La Plata
County Sheriff's Department SUV rolled
up to the barn. A lanky man with salt-and-
pepper sideburns climbed out and opened the
passenger door. Marge Bowman accepted
his hand and stepped down with the air of a
queen descending from her coach.

"Hope you don't mind an extra guest," she
said. "I caught Sheriff Tate trying to break

into the Queen this morning for his breakfast burrito, so I invited him to drive me out here."

Jake shook the sheriff's hand. "You're always welcome, Ben. Party's just about to start."

He looked at his watch. "Luke, you and Donna round everybody up outside the back door."

"How many guests did you plan for?" Donna asked.

"Shelby told me around fifty," Luke said.

"You've got way more than that here already," she said.

"No problem," Jake said. "Shelby bought plenty of plates and the like. And you can bet people brought food to share, like the loaves and fishes—just you watch."

Tom rode up with JJ in front of him on the saddle and Missy behind with her arms around his waist. "Where's Jo?" he asked.

"Directing traffic at the front gate," Luke said.

Tom lowered JJ to the ground before sliding down after him. "Missy, go fetch your mom."

Missy scrambled forward into the saddle and kicked Tom's gelding into a run, her red curls flying as she galloped up the lane.

Tom shook his head. "If I didn't know better, I'd swear she's Lucy's kid."

A few minutes later, Missy returned at a more sedate pace beside her mother.

"Any idea how many folks came in at the gate?" he asked Jo.

"A hundred and sixteen, and I saw a few more coming across country on horseback."

"Sounds about right," Jake said. "Okay, Oscar, time to spring the trap."

Oscar entered the back door and the crowd fell silent; even the children were quiet and no restive babies fretted.

Auntie Rose stepped out onto the porch, and "Happy birthday!" exploded into the air in the best surprise party tradition. She clapped her hands over her mouth, and then a smile wreathed her face like a rising sun. She hugged Oscar, grinning at her side, then Shelby and Lucy and Katie.

"Oh, you are all so bad to fool an old lady." She trotted down the steps, her lively steps belying her words, and started hugging everyone within reach.

Lines formed for strips of barbecued beef while Oscar helped the women carry pans of beans and trays of cornbread to the long serving tables. As Jake had predicted, guests had brought posole and succotash, elk stew and chili, salads and cakes and pies and cookies. Someone had set up a deep fryer and was handing out fry bread. Drumming began at the far edge of the meadow.

Auntie Rose sat enthroned under a cotton-wood in a chair carried from the tack room and covered with an almost-new saddle blanket. An old TV tray served for a table, although she was too busy receiving birthday wishes to eat more than occasional bites. Children ran shrieking in play with Missy's bright curls weaving in and out among the darker hair of her Ute cousins.

Luke saw Katie return to the house carrying a big coffee urn to be refilled. He followed, overcome by the need for a few moments alone with her.

No one at the party commented on his wheelchair—the Animas Valley was a small community in population—but he felt conspicuous making his way up the ramp. He paused for a moment and peered through the glass in the door.

Katie sat in a kitchen chair holding a baby, bending over it like a Madonna in a Renaissance painting. One chubby fist reached for a lock of hair escaping from her ponytail. The absorption on her face kindled a fierce desire in Luke to see her holding their child.

She looked up and beckoned. "I'm babysitting one of Auntie Rose's grandchildren—I think." She bounced the baby on her knee. "This is Caleb, June Black Horse's youngest. June's in the powder room."

Luke tickled the baby's chin. "Not Auntie Rose's blood kin. June was married to Sam Buck before he got killed in a construction accident. Auntie Rose still considers June a daughter, so Caleb here is sort of a foster grandson."

Katie hoisted Caleb over one shoulder and patted his back until he rewarded her with a loud burp. They both laughed.

"You look like you know what you're doing," Luke said.

"I should. I started babysitting when I was fifteen, and I spent a whole summer on the Maine coast as the nanny for three-month-old twins."

"I've been thinking about your name," Luke said. "Gabriel, I mean. Sounds like a good name. Gabe Cameron—what do you think?"

June Black Horse entered the kitchen before Katie could answer, flicking her long braid over her shoulder. "You want to keep him? He's been cross as two sticks since he got his immunizations yesterday. You've got him charmed."

"I'd love to," Katie said as she handed Caleb to his mother, "but you'd want him back."

"I reckon we'll have to rustle up some of our own," Luke said.

"More babies for Ma to spoil," June said. "Nothing would make her happier."

"I'd better start carrying cupcakes up from the cellar while the coffee brews," Katie said and disappeared down the cellar steps.

Luke glanced out the kitchen window and saw a second sheriff's department vehicle pull up behind the house. Deputy Bud Seaver drove; a second man sat in the front passenger seat. A quiver of apprehension ran up Luke's spine, and he shot out the door before Katie returned from the cellar. Jake, Sheriff Tate and Luke converged on the car as it rolled to a stop, with Oscar a few steps behind.

"What's the problem, Bud?" Sheriff Tate asked.

"Sorry to bother you at the party," Seaver said, "but we've got a complaint somebody's holding a woman out here against her will."

"Exerting undue influence," Brad Garrison said as he climbed out of the car.

Luke was pretty sure he could launch out of the wheelchair and beat the crap out of the Jerk, but that would only make matters worse for Katie.

He gritted his teeth, but Jake smiled. "Feel free to look for the lady." He waved his arm in an inclusive gesture. "We've got over a hundred folks here by last count. How would you like to start? Want me to line everybody up?"

A few more men drifted over: June's husband, Del Black Horse; Auntie Rose's tall grandsons, Sammie and Brian; Bob Farley and Mike with Lucy at his heels. The drumming sounded suddenly louder.

Garrison cast a look around the circle. "What is this, some kind of cult?"

Oscar's grin held the charm of a shark about to snack on an unwary swimmer. "We call it a tribe, mister."

"No call to get all Western," Jake said. "Let's satisfy Mr. Garrison so he can be on his way. Unless he'd like to stay for dessert. How about we search the house first?"

Luke spun his chair in a tight circle and was up the ramp before Jake, Sheriff Tate and Garrison could reach the door. First into the kitchen, he saw no sign of Katie, but four trays of cupcakes sat on the table. He heard steps coming up from the cellar.

To give her at least a moment's warning, he raised his voice. "We've got company, Kathryn."

Her footsteps halted and then resumed. "We've got lots of company." Katie's voice was steady. "Can you take this tray when I get to the top? I've got three more to bring up."

CHAPTER TWENTY-EIGHT

KATIE BENT ALL her concentration on ascending the stairs without dropping the cupcakes. At the top, she handed the tray to Luke, lowering one eyelid in the tiniest wink to reassure him. Then she turned to face Brad.

"I didn't know you'd been invited," she said, trying to keep the anger out of her voice. She would not let him spoil Auntie Rose's big day.

Garrison spoke to Sheriff Tate. "This is my wife, Kathryn Garrison. I believe she's under undue—"

"I heard you the first time," Tate said. Katie couldn't tell if he was ready to laugh or swear. "What about it, Katie? You married to this—" his mouth twitched "—person lodging the complaint?"

"Guilty as charged," she said. "But only for the time being. How long have you known me, Sheriff?"

He pondered. "A month? Six weeks? Long

enough to put on five pounds from your cooking."

"Do I seem brainwashed?"

"Marge rags on you pretty hard," he said. "But I notice you give it right back to her."

The door opened, and Marge stumped into the kitchen with the aid of her cane. "I saw another cop car pull in. What in blazes is going on?" She spotted Brad. "Oh my God, it's Carrion," she said in disgust. "I knew I should have brought my .38."

Garrison pointed his finger, his face dark with anger. "That woman threatened me with a gun."

"Which she is properly permitted to own and carry," Tate said. "Marge, is this the yahoo you called me about yesterday? You want to press charges?"

Katie laid a hand on the sheriff's sleeve. "I'd like a few minutes with this gentleman." She refused to call Brad her husband; he had ceased to deserve that title. "In the barn." Like Luke, she had come to take strength from the company of horses.

"Not out of sight," Luke said with a scowl.

"Of course not. Oscar, would you please make sure the party keeps rolling? Don't let Auntie Rose get involved."

"About time to sing 'Happy Birthday,' right?"

"Perfect. Jake, if you could start carrying out the cupcakes..."

"Yes, ma'am," he said. "Whatever you say, ma'am."

"Pretty clear who's in charge here," Tate said. "Okay, out to the barn. But I'll be watching the whole time, Garrison."

Oscar and Jake left first and cleared the crowd away from the door. Marge followed, giving Garrison an evil glare over her shoulder.

"If we go out the front door and around the far side of the house, no one will notice us," Katie said. She looked at Luke. "See you outside."

"Whatever you say, ma'am," he said, echoing his father.

Luke had the big sliding barn door pushed back by the time the others appeared. He set the brakes on his wheelchair. "I'm staying right here," he said.

The sheriff patted his shoulder. "We'll keep you company, son."

Katie walked ahead of Brad halfway down the long center aisle and stopped in front of a box stall. The palomino mare stuck her head over the door with a soft snort.

"This is Dawn," Katie said, the name jumping into her mind unbidden—a golden new beginning for her and the horse. "She belongs to the Camerons, but I'm going to help with her rehab."

"You can't be serious." Brad flung up his hands, making the mare shy back into her stall. "This is a fling, a fantasy. I don't blame you—I drove you to it. But this has got to be a passing whim."

"Maybe, but it's better than just existing at the edge of your life the way I've obviously been doing." She led him to the side door opening to the horse pasture. The snowy peaks of the San Juans loomed beyond the level creek bottom with its fringe of willows.

"This is my world now," she said. "This is my life. Durango is a nice town. I have friends here, people who come into the Queen every day and enjoy my cooking. Marge and I work well together—I'd love to buy in as a partner."

"With the money you cleaned out of our account, I suppose."

"No more than I deserved for fifteen years of faithful service." She came down hard on *faithful*. "Katie the Irish maid, almost like one of the family. And I took much less than a good divorce lawyer could get for me. All I want from you is my freedom."

"I see you're screwing around already," he said with a sneer.

"Don't try to judge me by your standards. Luke and I have too much respect for each other to behave the way you've done."

He seemed to shrink under her unrelenting gaze. "You won't give me another chance?"

"You're kidding, right?" She turned and strode ahead of him toward the sunlight, leaving him to follow. "We're done, Sheriff," she said. "I'll have your burrito with green chili ready for you on Monday morning."

Brad climbed into the deputy's car without another word.

The party began to wind down, with parents carting exhausted children and cranky babies home. Auntie Rose left with Oscar, unaware of the near meltdown at her party. She had thanked Katie repeatedly for the rosebud-decorated cupcakes. "Every one like a little birthday cake," she said. "So much work, so much love. I'm so happy for my favorite boy." She kissed Katie's cheek.

The last guests left before sunset and the leftovers were parceled out between Marge,

Tom's family and the home ranch. Katie and Luke went together to check the horses.

"I've thought of a name for my horse," she said, fondling the mare's ears and straightening her creamy forelock. "Dawn."

"Couldn't be better," Luke said. "I knew you'd come up with something."

They moved to the door overlooking the horse pasture and watched in comfortable silence while light faded from the sky and the first stars appeared.

At last he said, "So what happens next?"

"I truly can't say. Maybe he'll fight me over the divorce, maybe not. I'm not going to think about it right now."

"Good plan," he said.

KATIE DROVE TO Durango the next afternoon. Heeding Jake's advice, seconded by Luke and Shelby, she planned to spend the night at Marge's instead of returning to her apartment. She didn't think Brad would try accosting her again, but he knew where she lived. Better to wait until she was sure he had left town.

Marge had carried home leftovers guests had brought to the feast. "I'd kill for the recipe of that pumpkin succotash June Black

Horse makes. And her chili-chocolate cake. Did you get a taste of the beef?"

"I'm afraid not. There was none left by the time I got a chance to eat. And after I helped tend it the night before."

"Never mind," Marge said. "There'll be other parties." She winked. "Maybe even a wedding. Which reminds me, a history grad student at Fort Lewis found out about our mystery bride. We missed some letters in a separate compartment. No tragedy, just a heck of a romantic tale."

"I'm glad," Katie said. "I don't need any sad tales. So why didn't she use her pretty clothes?"

"The bride's name was Emily Ruston. Her father was upstart rich from silver and arranged for his daughter to marry into a local family with roots almost as deep as the Camerons'. Her parents took her to Europe to buy her trousseau, but on the return sailing, she fell in love with a young journalist from New York. They eloped the minute the boat docked."

Katie took a second helping of elk stew. "So how did everything end up in your attic?"

"Emily and her husband lived in the East for a while, but she was homesick, so they moved back to Durango. Her parents welcomed her and bought her this house, and guess what? Her husband made his own silver strike and did very well for himself. She lived in this house the rest of her life."

"I guess she never got to wear her wedding finery," Katie said. "What are you going to do with the clothes?"

"Why? You want them?"

"Not really. What would I do with them? But I wonder if I could fit into that wedding gown." Maybe Emily's good luck in love still clung to the dress.

Marge rose from her seat and gave Katie a peck on the cheek. "I suspect Emily would smile down to see it finally put to use. You'll get your own happy ending—I feel it in my witch's bones."

BUSINESS WAS BRISK as usual the next morning at the Queen. Sue Cabot kept the carousel spinning with orders, and Roger moved almost at a trot clearing tables and resetting them as customers arrived hungry and left well fed.

"Breakfast burrito with green chili," Sue said through the pass-through. "Extra cheese."

"Sounds like Sheriff Tate's here," Katie said.

"And someone asked for a bagel with light cream cheese. I told him he might have better luck at the café down the street, but he changed his order to coffee, whole wheat toast, dry, and orange juice."

The hairs on the back of Katie's neck prickled. "Where's Marge?"

"She ran to the bank—we're out of ones. Something wrong?"

"Probably not. Where's Mr. Wheat Toast sitting?"

"The small table by the window. You want me to give the sheriff a heads-up?"

Katie peered into the dining room and sighed. "No, I'll take care of it."

She left the kitchen, stopping for a moment by Sheriff Tate's table to tap his shoulder. He followed her glance and started to stand.

"Not yet," she said and moved toward the table Sue had pointed out.

"Good morning, Brad. Your orange juice okay?"

"I'm sorry to bother you at work," he said, half rising. "I'm leaving today to catch a flight from Albuquerque. Could you spare me a few minutes in private?"

She considered his plea. What harm could

it do? She glanced over her shoulder. "Just a second," she said.

She crossed to Sheriff Tate's booth. "I'm going to talk with…" Again the word *husband* stuck in her throat.

"Garrison," Tate said. "You okay with it?"

She nodded. "We'll go into Marge's office and leave the door open. If you could just enjoy another cup of coffee…"

"I've got your back," he said, "and I won't let Marge barge in. I hope I don't have to draw my weapon on her—too much paperwork." He stood and switched to a seat facing the rear of the restaurant.

She beckoned to Brad, who followed her to Marge's small office. She sat in the swivel chair at the roll-top desk and waved Brad to a battered Windsor chair.

She looked at her watch. "I have maybe ten minutes before the customers start getting restless," she said. "Pretend you're pitching a big project to a new client."

"You know me pretty well."

"Not as well as I thought. What happened, Brad? We started out so well. We wanted the same things. At least I thought we did."

"I thought so, too, until the business took

off," he said. "I guess I fell in love with the success and prestige."

"I tried to go along on the ride," Katie said, "I really did. But I need to create something of my own. I'd never have left if we'd had children—"

Brad grunted as if in pain. "Yeah, about that. When I was twelve, I got mumps. I'd had my baby shots, but somehow I got sick anyway. I didn't think about it till we'd been married awhile and you didn't get pregnant. I got checked out—the doctor said our chances were slim to none."

She stared at him, finally managing to say, "Why didn't you tell me?"

His failure to confide in her hurt almost as much as his infidelity.

"We could have worked something out," she said. "Some procedure, or adoption."

He looked down at his hands. "I was ashamed. Like I was less of a man. Things got weird at home…"

"About five years ago." She recalled he hadn't touched her for nearly six months. "That's when you really started burying yourself in your work."

"And the other, too." He turned away with

a grimace. "First I went to a prostitute, but that was…"

"Please. I don't need all the details."

He shrugged "After that there was a sales rep at a conference in New York—"

"So you had to prove to yourself what a stud you were." Bitterness welled up in her. "But you didn't turn to me."

"I didn't think…you'd understand how worthless I felt. After a while it got to be a game with two prizes, talking women into bed and getting away with it."

"Okay, I get it," she said, sadness mingling with disgust. "I guess it won't be as much fun now without the intrigue."

"What if I sold out and moved here? There's always work for a good contractor, and you're right—Durango is a nice town."

He shocked her into silence. Give up what he'd worked so hard to build in Connecticut? Just to win her back? For a moment she almost said yes, if only to honor the magnitude of his offer.

"I could build you another house, better than the first one."

She regained her footing. "That was never my house. Your partner designed it, and his decorator furnished it. You let me choose the interior paint and the countertops, then changed the colors on me."

"Vanessa thought the softer tones would be more modern."

"Guess what? I'm not modern—I'm old-fashioned. If you'd cared what I wanted, we'd have bought an old farmhouse to restore, not an Ethan Allen showroom. Did you have sex with Vanessa, too?"

His face told her the random shot had struck home. "I'll sell the house and buy whatever suits you," he said. "We'll do anything it takes if you want a baby. I never realized how important that was to you, because it didn't matter much to me until I found out I couldn't."

"And it still doesn't matter. I'm done with settling for second best," she said, her voice rising. "I'm holding out for a man who wants children as much as I do, who'll be a full-time father. Not someone who thinks a baby would be a nice little project to keep me occupied."

"Everything okay?" Sheriff Tate stuck his head around the doorjamb.

"We're fine, almost finished," she said. "Let me go, Brad. Go home to Britt Cavendish. She looks like she would appreciate your house and your ambitions."

"She's gone—she meant nothing to me."

Somehow she wasn't shocked by his casual dismissal. "I'm sure you can find someone to take her place. Take up sailing—that should get you in with the silver-spoon crowd."

She stood. "Have a safe trip back. Maybe I can forgive you someday, but I'll never trust you again. We're done."

CHAPTER TWENTY-NINE

"JUST LET ME off out front while you park," Luke said. "I'll wait for you."

Shelby didn't ask if he needed help, only braked in front of the Silver Queen. He pulled forearm crutches from behind the seat and slid down from the truck an inch at a time until he was standing square on the pavement. He waited a few seconds to be sure of his balance then stepped away to slam the door, giving Shelby a thumbs-up.

He made the two steps to the curb and then onto the sidewalk. He looked up just as Brad Garrison left the Queen. They saw each other at the same instant, their eyes locking like a clash of sabers.

With intense concentration, Luke moved forward until he stood only an arm's length from Garrison.

"Enjoy your breakfast?" he asked.

"No, not that it's any of your business. And stay away from my wife."

"That's her call, I reckon. Seems like she'd rather you stay away. Far away."

"You feel pretty safe, don't you?" Garrison's fists balled at his sides. "You know I won't hit someone who can't defend himself."

Luke lunged forward, almost falling, and Garrison took a quick step backward, livid with fury.

"Well, look at you! I told Katie you wouldn't stay in that wheelchair long." Marge stepped between the two men as if Garrison didn't exist. "Let me open the door for you, Luke. I want to see her face when you walk in."

Luke held his ground long enough to show he was willing to play this out before walking ahead of Marge into the restaurant. The door swung shut behind them.

Katie stood stone-like, both her hands covering her mouth. Then she ran to Luke, almost knocking him over when she flung her arms around him.

"I'm so glad you're here! Did you see Brad outside?"

He steadied himself against the door frame and smoothed her hair back from her flushed face. "Yeah, we passed the time of day."

Marge snorted. "Like two bull elk about

to lock antlers. You're dang lucky I showed up when I did. You want to wreck your new toys—" she pointed at his braces "—scrapping with someone six inches taller and fifty pounds heavier?"

"He'd be no bigger than me once I got him on the ground," Luke said, knowing she was right. He'd been a breath away from making a damn fool of himself. "Why was he here?"

"Sit and let me catch up on orders," Katie said. "Then I'll tell you all about it."

Sheriff Tate appeared beside them. "Too bad I didn't walk the gent out, but I guess I can go make La Plata County safe now. If you'll give me my check…"

"On the house," Marge said. "I'm grateful you were here to back Katie up."

Katie darted to the pastry case and came back carrying a paper bag. "To hold you till lunch," she said.

"Just don't tell my wife," he said, accepting the bag. "She'll make me start eating breakfast at home."

Shelby came through the door. "Did I just see—"

"Yes," they all said, and she laughed.

Katie and Marge headed for the kitchen while Luke and Shelby chose a table in a quiet corner. Sue and Roger stopped to exclaim over Luke's braces and congratulate him on being upright again.

Twenty minutes later Katie came to their table, bringing three pieces of apple pie to go with the coffee Sue had poured.

"Brad was on his way out of town," she said, taking a seat. "He stopped to let me know he was leaving." She traced the pattern on the oilcloth table covering with her finger. "He offered to sell out in Connecticut and move here if Colorado suits me better."

"The hell you say!" Luke's resolve to keep his mouth shut vanished like smoke in a strong breeze.

"And he was willing to do whatever it takes to start a family if that would make me happy."

Luke laid his fork down before he dropped it, his fingers as clumsy as a two-year-old's. He'd done his best, he'd played fair. Now he saw his hopes receding like taillights on a dark desert two-lane.

"I told him to go home and find someone who likes his lifestyle better than I ever would," Katie said.

Luke looked down to hide tears stinging his eyes.

The counter bell on the kitchen pass-through dinged in triple time. Katie jumped to her feet. "Enjoy your pie," she said. "Marge never rings the bell like that unless she's about ready to blow."

Shelby laid her hand on Luke's as Katie disappeared into the kitchen. "You've never done things the easy way, have you?"

He shook his head like a punch-drunk fighter, his emotions wrung dry between anger and despair and now hope again. "There's got to be some reason why Katie's the only woman for me. I guess love really is like herding cats."

Marge joined them, taking Katie's seat. "Luke, what do you think—should I ask Katie if she'd like to buy into the Queen? There's only two people in the world I'd consider asking, and it doesn't look like Lucy will be around much. Katie has a sassy mouth, but I couldn't abide some meek little mouse I'd always worry about offending."

"Why ask me? I've got no say in it."

Marge heaved an exaggerated sigh. "I'm soliciting your opinion and preference as a courtesy, assuming you plan on becoming her husband. Maybe you don't want her tied up with that kind of responsibility."

"Do I look stupid?" he said. "Like Doc Barnett told Dad and Shelby, the bull stomped on my back, not on my head. You really think I'd try to steer Katie off something she'd like to do? She wants to help run the Queen, we'll make it work."

Marge turned to Shelby. "I've always said this boy is a lot smarter than he looks. Okay, I'll get her out here…"

"Whoa!" Luke struggled to his feet. "I don't want to be anywhere around when you talk to Katie. She has to decide for her own self with no pressure from me or anyone else."

He dropped a ten-dollar bill on the table. "Let's blow this joint, Shelby."

Shelby didn't break into his silence on the drive home. "Did I do the right thing?" he said at last. "Not sitting in with Katie and Marge?"

"If it felt right to you, then it was. And I agree—Katie has a lot of heavy decisions to make right now. She doesn't need to worry about what you might think."

Luke fiddled with the fastening on his right brace. "Hey, she could change her mind and go back to her husband. I mean, the guy really upped the ante. How can I compete with that kind of offer?"

Shelby cast an exasperated glance at him as she steered under the Cameron's Pride sign. "This isn't a cattle auction, Luke, Lot number forty-three to the highest bidder. If you trust Katie that little, you'd be better off without her."

He flung his head back and squeezed his eyes shut. "God, you're right and I'm an idiot."

"She told me while we were decorating Auntie Rose's cupcakes she loves being on her own for the first time in her life. She needs this time to herself."

Gloom settled in his mind like smoke from a prairie fire. "Maybe she'll find out she doesn't want to get married again."

"Didn't you tell me she wants kids? Can you picture her doing that outside of marriage?"

She braked in front of the barn. "Get on your horse and ride the south fence line. Visit Auntie Rose and let her talk about her party. Stop fretting about Katie—she won't let you down."

CHAPTER THIRTY

MARGE TURNED THE Closed sign outward at exactly three o'clock and summoned Katie to her office.

"Would you like to buy into the Queen as my partner?" she asked with no lead-in.

Katie was dumbstruck. She had thought about the possibility but only as a far-fetched dream. "I don't know what to say."

"That'll be a first. I know I'm not easy to get along with, but we've done pretty well so far. You don't argue with the way I've always done things, but your new ideas are good. Things keep going like this, we'll be able to start opening for dinner again."

"Maybe on Friday and Saturday nights when folks come into town for shopping or a movie," Katie said, excitement bubbling in her chest. "Nothing fancy, just our lunch menu expanded a little. And we could offer small plates of new items so people can sample and let us know what they like. Have special tasting events, maybe even music on the weekends."

Her heart fell. "How much of an investment would you need?" Living rent-free and eating mostly on the job, she still had most of the money she'd brought from Connecticut, but a big expenditure could wipe that out. She could apply for a loan...

"I've got no clue," Marge said. "I just wanted to float the idea past you to see if you'd strike at it. I'll have to sit down with my accountant to come up with a figure."

"Besides..." Katie hated to seem ungrateful for this dream opportunity. As different from Elizabeth Gabriel as an irascible alley cat from a cozy tabby, Marge had come to fill the hollow in Katie's heart left by her mother's death. "I shouldn't take such a big step until I get settled with Brad."

"Maybe you'll decide to take the hubby up on his offer."

"You know better, but I can't focus on any new commitment with the divorce hanging over me."

"Including Luke?"

"Especially Luke. He already knows I can't give him what he wants until I'm free of Brad. Not that he's pressuring me."

"He wouldn't," Marge said. "Under that wild, good-ol'-boy front, he's a real gentleman—all the Cameron men are."

"Can we go on with our present arrangement awhile longer? I hope you know how much I want to accept your offer."

Marge leaned forward and patted her knee. "Don't fret—I'm not planning to sell the Queen out from under you. Any notion how we can light a fire under your soon-to-be ex, as Luke calls him?"

"I do have an idea. Brad probably figures I'm not smart enough to track his screwing around, but I know someone who is—my cousin Greg, who's buying my mother's house."

"He's a private detective?"

"No, but he was an MP in the Marines, and he's a whiz with computers. All I need is a record of few overnight stays at a hotel for Mr. and Mrs. Garrison while I was taking care of my mother 24/7." Bitter reality struck again. "Of course, he probably just took women to our house the last few months, since he knew I wouldn't walk in on him."

"Until you did. Too big for his britches, so to speak."

"I'm hoping I won't have to get hateful—

better to end a fifteen-year marriage with a little dignity. But I will take him to court if he forces me to."

"You're better hearted than I would be." Marge said. "Rub his nose in his dirty business, I say."

"If Greg can get me hard evidence, my attorney can send it to Brad's and let him point out the consequences. Right now I'm being reasonable, but if Brad wants to play rough, I'm up for that, too."

"So THAT'S THE STORY," she told Greg that evening. "I'm sorry to drag you into this mess, but you're my best resource. I don't have the money to hire a PI, but I'll bet you can find out what I need."

Her cousin had listened to her tale without comment. Now she heard a deep sigh. "The kids are right here," he said, "or I'd tell you what I think of that—" he cleared his throat "—that rotten so-and-so. Give me his credit card info and which hotels he'd be likely to pick. I'll start there."

"I really don't want this to get around. I just want to pressure him into agreeing to the divorce quickly. I've wasted enough of my life on him."

"Not to worry, I'll dig up the dirt on Mr. Can't Keep It Zipped. It's the least I can do to thank you for everything you're doing for us."

"I'll probably have to make a flying trip back once Brad agrees to the divorce. We'll finalize the sale then."

She had called Greg first because of the time difference; now she could talk to Luke at her leisure.

"Hey, cowgirl," he said when he answered. "Your horse is looking for you. Another hundred pounds and she'll be ready for some light work."

"I'll be ready when she is. And Luke, I have incredible news."

"From Brad?"

What else could he think? "I'm afraid not," she said, her elation dimming a little. "Marge asked if I'd like to buy into the Queen as a partner. I've wanted something like this for years. We work well together, and it would take a big load off her shoulders. What do you think?"

"Something that makes you sound this happy, I say go for it."

"You wouldn't mind?"

"I've got no right to mind." His voice held an edge. "And I don't. You've been bossed and held back long enough." His tone softened. "You want this, girl, we'll make it work."

Tears stung her eyes. What had she ever done to deserve this luck, this kindness? Loving Luke, being the woman he needed would be her joy.

"Got a plan how to pry yourself loose from what's-his-name?"

She told him about her call to her cousin. "I'm hoping that waving embarrassing evidence in his face will make him fold. But I will go after him if I have to—no more Ms. Nice."

He laughed. "I'm not surprised, the way you backed down Oscar's bull. Which reminds me, Tom and Jo are taking the kids to Pueblo next weekend for a bull-riding event. They asked if we'd like to go along. We could pick you up right at noon—then we'd make it in time to watch on Saturday night and stay over for the final rounds on Sunday."

She thought she caught a note of pleading in his voice. "It's important to you, isn't it?"

"Sort of, I guess," he said. "Maybe I'll never go back into the arena, but I still need to face the bulls down. Better men than me have been hurt as bad without shying off."

"Will my going along help?"

She could almost see his shrug. "You watched those videos with me—that was my first step."

"I'll talk to Marge tomorrow. She's almost a hundred percent now—she and Roger can probably finish up lunch if I leave at noon."

"Maybe this isn't a good idea," Luke said. "You may change your mind about having kids after five hours in the car with JJ."

CHAPTER THIRTY-ONE

AT TEN MINUTES before noon on Saturday, Katie swapped her black work shoes for her cowboy boots and placed a sack of cookies beside her overnight bag in Marge's office. She had just set an order of the meatloaf special and a garden salad on the pass-through counter when she heard Missy's voice.

"Mama said to come get Miss Katie. We're outside waiting."

Marge bustled into the kitchen. "Get moving, girl. Sue's here to work till we close, so you have a good time. You'll understand Luke better after seeing real bull riding."

"I hate to leave early…"

"You're fired if you're not out of here in one minute flat. They're probably double-parked."

Katie hugged her and grabbed her gear, following Missy, who wore pink cowboy boots matching her pink plaid shirt.

Tom sat at the wheel of a Ford Expedition

with Luke in the front passenger seat. "Sorry we have to stick you in the back seat," he said, "but Luke needs the leg room in front. You and Jo can take turns swatting the kids."

"Just JJ," Missy said. "I'm too big to swat."

Jo rolled her eyes at Katie. "Welcome to the Cameron traveling circus. You'll probably be ready to jump ship by the time we get to the top of Wolf Creek Pass."

"I imagine you guys have had lunch," Katie said, "but I brought dessert. Okay if the kids have cookies? I made them this morning."

Missy and JJ quieted for the moment as everyone accepted the saucer-size disks, aromatic as a spice cabinet. Jo took a bite. "Gingersnaps?"

"They're called Joe Froggers, a local specialty in Marblehead, Massachusetts, where my grandmother grew up."

"Frog cookies!" JJ made croaking sounds, and Missy answered with her own rendition. "I want another frog cookie."

"Half," Katie said. "If your mother says okay."

"And after you say please," Jo said.

Peace reigned again, and Katie watched the scenery flow by. Had she really driven down this road tight jawed with fear little more than a month ago? Then she had been fleeing from her ruined marriage in shock and heartbreak. And in guilty shame that she hadn't been able to keep her husband faithful, neglecting him to care for her mother. Now she knew Brad's behavior had already been an established pattern; her mother's illness had simply made his betrayal easier to continue.

On impulse, she leaned forward and laid her hand on Luke's shoulder; he turned with a smile and covered it with his.

"Enjoying the ride? A little different than coming down off the pass in a snowstorm."

"Everything's changed since then."

"For the better, I hope."

"In so many ways," she said and sat back to enjoy the ride.

THEY ARRIVED IN Pueblo just before the event started. JJ and Missy, after making the long drive with relative good behavior, began bouncing around in their seat belts demanding food and souvenirs.

"What you get tomorrow depends on your behavior tonight," Tom said. "You don't want Miss Katie to think you're little animals, do you?"

Tom dropped Luke and Katie off at a rear

entrance before parking closer to the main doors.

"They've got second-row tickets," Luke said, "but I figured we'd watch from the chutes."

He led Katie past the locker room, stopped every few steps by well-wishers pleased to see him walking and amazed at his high-tech braces. Katie couldn't keep track of the introductions, although she understood that bull riders wore thick vests and brightly colored leather chaps while the other men—and a few women—wearing simple jeans and plaid shirts were bull owners or other Professional Bull Riders functionaries.

"Time to put these babies to the test," Luke said and pointed to a steep metal stairway leading to a walkway behind the bucking chutes.

"You can't possibly be serious. What if you catch a toe in the open gaps?"

"Then you'll have to catch me before I hit the dirt," he said with a grin and started up the steps.

Katie shook her head in disbelief and followed, keeping one hand on his back, just in case.

Luke hung on to the hand rails and made it to the platform. "You mind standing to watch?" he asked. "There are seats the next level up, but maybe I shouldn't push my luck." He led her to a corner just beyond the chutes and waved to the rest of the family. Missy and JJ jumped up and down and waved their arms.

"Is this their first event?" Katie asked.

"Heck, no. Missy's been coming since she was two and JJ since before he could walk. Look at all the kids here."

Katie scanned the sold-out crowd. Fans ranged from babies in arms to silver-haired women wearing fringed jackets and weathered men in hats that had seen hard usage.

The lights went down, Klaxons sounded and *Warning!* flashed on the message boards. Men ran into the arena splashing liquid from fuel cans onto the dirt.

"Cover your ears, darlin'," Luke said. "It's about to get noisy."

Explosions accompanied jets of fire and letters spelled out in flames as the announcer yelled, "Welcome to the one and only PBR!"

"This is crazy!" Katie said, giddy with excitement.

"You got that right, even before the bucking starts."

Luke gave her quick thumbnail bios on the

cowboys parading into the arena. Three men followed the riders, their loose-fitting jerseys, shorts and gym shoes in odd contrast with their cowboy hats.

"Those are my partners, Wes Jenkins and Billy Daws," Luke said, "plus the new bull-fighter who took my place."

Katie turned to study his face. "How are you doing?"

He gave her a crooked smile. "Fine so far, but I might get the screaming heebie-jeebies in the middle of the night." He turned away and removed his hat as a mahogany-skinned girl with lustrous black hair delivered a country-style rendition of the national anthem.

The lights came up, and bulls filled the chutes. A huge brindled beast with sweeping horns kicked the gate directly below them, shuddering the steel floor where they stood.

Luke tightened his hands on the railing.

"Will the bull that hurt you be here?" she asked.

Luke reached into his hip pocket for the day sheet he'd picked up on the way in and ran his finger down the list of riders and bulls. "Yep, he's here, ol' Sidewinder himself. Toby Wallace should get a good score on him. He's not a mean bull—I just got between him and the exit."

Cowboys began lining up behind the chutes, some performing elaborate warm-up routines before their rides while others chatted apparently without care. Katie had an unobstructed view as a young man who looked no more than fourteen eased onto the bull's back below them. He settled his mouth-piece in place, wrapped the thick rope around the bull's chest into his hand and nodded his head. The gate swung open.

The next eight seconds looked to Katie like a carnival ride gone berserk as the bull jerked the rider back and forth like a dog's toy. When the buzzer sounded, the cowboy flew off, arms and legs windmilling. He landed hard and crawled to the fence while the bullfighters danced around the huge beast as if performing some primitive rite.

Defeated, the bull snorted and trotted out of the arena while the announcer gave the rider's score.

"A little different than watching those videos, right?" Luke's face was alight with excitement.

"It's..." Katie tried to come up with some-thing positive to say but couldn't. "It's completely useless. What earthly good is riding a bull? Risking your life like that?"

"I'd say you've got bull riding pegged. Of course it's useless, but so is mountain climbing and racing cars and sailing little boats across the ocean alone. Talk to Jo about it. Her dad died in a stock car race. She almost refused to marry Tom because of the risks."

He slung an arm around her shoulders. "Now we've got that settled, let's enjoy the show."

She couldn't imagine enjoying this kind of mayhem, but with Luke's running commentary and a flow of well-wishers congratulating Luke on his recovery, she did. His fellow bullfighters approached during a lull while girls in tight jeans and skimpy tops tossed a sponsor's T-shirts into the crowd.

The taller man, leathery as an old saddle, grinned up at them. "So I says, that looks like Luke, and Billy says no, can't be—he's still lazing around home milking that stomping for all it's worth."

"Looks like I told Wes wrong," Billy said. "There you stand, big as life and twice as homely. When do you plan on coming back to work?"

"You can't see the rest of me," Luke said.

"From the waist down, I'm rigged up like a dang robot. Believe me, you don't want me in the arena with you. Not yet."

"We'll save your spot in the locker room," Billy said. He and Wes trotted away as the next rider climbed into the chute.

A slight gray-haired man in a denim shirt marked Sports Medicine tapped Katie's arm. "Excuse me, miss. Are you with this sorry specimen of a cowboy?"

Luke turned so quickly he almost over-balanced, a big grin lighting his face. "I wondered when you'd show up. Tell me I'll never walk again, will you?" He took a few steps back and forth on the narrow walkway. "Guess I made you a liar. Katie, this is Doc Barnett. He patches up all the riders and bull-fighters."

"Orthopedic surgeon and master of reverse psychology," Barnett said, taking the hand Katie offered. "The best way to get Luke off his butt was tell him he'd never make it. But I'm guessing you might have had a hand in motivating him."

"He was still in a wheelchair when I met him," Katie said, "so I'm thrilled with his progress."

A muted groan went up from the crowd.

"Gotta get back to work," Barnett said. "Keep me posted."

The cowboy in the dirt got up without help, and the event continued. Sidewinder was one of the last bulls to buck, by chance from a chute almost below where they stood. To Katie, he looked as big as—or bigger than—Oscar's bull Buckshot.

"And that monster's hooves came down on your spine?" she asked in horror. "How did you even survive?"

"Just one hoof, and he was moving right along, so it was more a glancing blow."

Katie saw that the bullfighters were all looking up at Luke while Toby Wallace performed the ritual of pulling his hat down tight and settling his mouthpiece in place. Luke gave them a quick wave, and his hand tightened on hers as the gate swung open.

Sidewinder shot out of the chute in a single long leap then began to spin like a whirligig. Toby hung on for almost five seconds before being flung away by centrifugal force. Billy and the other bullfighters leaped in front of Sidewinder as the bull bore down on the rider, who was slow getting to his feet.

Toby scrambled to safety on all fours, but a sweep of one horn caught Wes Jenkins under

the chin and lifted him off his feet. He collapsed facedown as his partners closed over
him and a man on horseback sped in to rope
Sidewinder.

Dr. Barnett and two helpers ran into the
arena, but Wes was sitting up by the time
they reached him. One of the medics held a
dressing over the gash on his jaw while they
helped him to the sidelines.

"He'll be fine," Luke said. A fine sheen of
sweat covered his face. "Just two more rides.
We'd better get down those steps before it
gets crowded."

Katie insisted on going down backward
ahead of Luke, not that she could have done
more than slow his fall. Luke continued to
the rear door without stopping to chat, and
they waited outside for Tom to pick them up.

Missy and JJ fell asleep before Tom had
inched his way out of the parking lot, and
Luke rode in silence.

"What did you think of bull riding?" Jo
asked. "You had a close-up look from where
you were."

Katie didn't want to offend. "I had no idea
how intense it would be. And I'm really, really glad Luke's not involved anymore, except
as a spectator."

HELEN DEPRIMA   357

"Bad luck that Sidewinder clipped Wes, but a couple of stitches and he'll be working tomorrow's rounds."

"Surely you're joking."

Jo laughed. "I said the same thing the first time I saw Tom ride at Madison Square Garden. He got thrown hard against the fence and had to be helped out. I was sure he would be on his way to the emergency room. These guys take tough to a level mere mortals can't comprehend."

Tom pulled off I-25 onto a two-lane road then onto an unpaved driveway. "We always stay at the Foothills Lodge," he said. "You and Luke have a two-bedroom suite—number six."

He stopped outside a rambling two-story log building and went inside. He emerged in a few minutes with keys and handed one to Luke. Parking outside a long L-shaped section attached to a larger log building, he picked up Missy, who mumbled a sleepy good-night. "See you guys at breakfast," he said while Jo carried JJ to one of the doors farther down the covered veranda.

"Home, sweet overnight home," Luke said, handing Katie the key before he picked up his bag.

The door opened into a sitting room with a bathroom separating the two bedrooms.

"I'm a little wound up," he said. "I need coffee. Join me?"

"Too funny—you drink coffee to calm down. Like the British with their tea, I suppose. Sure, I'll have a cup. Want a cookie? There's a couple left in the car."

"Bring my crutches, would you? Behind the seat."

Luke was seated on the small sofa when she returned; his braces lay on the floor.

"I didn't know you could walk without those," she said, handing him the crutches.

"I've been practicing around the house with no one watching. Yeah, I've taken a few tumbles, but I'm getting better at it. Coffee's ready if you'll pour."

They sipped in silence until Luke set his mug on the coffee table. "Did you mean what you said, that you're glad I'm not involved with bull riding?"

"Are you planning go back?"

"No—yes. If I'm able. I need to prove…"

"That you're not scared?"

"Hell, I know I'm scared. I need to prove I'm not scared *off.* I'm thirty-six—there are older guys, like Wes, still working—but I'm about ready to quit. Would my working a little longer be a deal breaker?"

She wanted to say, "Even once could leave you disabled for good," but didn't. "I'll hate it, but do what you have to. I'll be there peeking between my fingers."

"Bless you, girl. I figured you'd understand."

"I don't, except it's important to you. As long as there's an end in sight."

He pulled her into his arms. "Dang, I've got me a good one." A light kiss became deeper until he released her before she could pull away.

"Go to bed, Katie, before I lose it," he said. "We've come this far—we can wait and do it right."

CHAPTER THIRTY-TWO

LUKE WAS GONE when Katie woke the next morning. A note written across last night's day sheet sat propped in the bathroom sink.

Breakfast in the lodge. Hope you slept better than I did.

She smiled and dressed hurriedly to join him. In the spacious common room, sofas and chairs upholstered in Pendleton blanket fabric faced a sandstone fireplace with a chimney soaring two stories to a cathedral ceiling. Mounted elk, pronghorn and mountain sheep trophies on the walls stared past a chandelier fashioned from intertwined antlers.

Twenty or so guests sat on benches at a long table in the dining room. A second table held chafing dishes of eggs, hash browns, bacon, sausage, pancakes, flour tortillas and green chili. Fresh fruit and biscuits and breads rounded out the array; servers with coffee and juices circulated around the table.

She filled her plate and slid into the space Luke had saved for her. "Morning, darlin'," he said. "I thought you might like to sleep late."

She blushed, wondering if everyone assumed they had spent the night in each other's arms.

"Today's event starts at noon," Tom said. "We promised the kids we'd hit the concourse beforehand, so the bus leaves here at eleven."

Missy and JJ grinned at her over their plates of pancakes and bacon. "Daddy wants to see his friends at the booths," Missy said.

"And we've been awful good." JJ gave his mother a pleading look. "Haven't we?"

"Pretty darn good," Jo said. "You each get to choose one souvenir."

JJ started bouncing in his seat, and his father frowned at him. "Don't blow it now."

"We'll sit with you today," Luke said. "Katie got the backstage tour last night."

After a leisurely breakfast, they returned to their suite to gather their belongings. Luke checked his watch. "Fifteen minutes to lift-off. Come here."

Katie went into his arms. "Not long enough to get into real trouble," she said.

"Don't throw down a challenge like that. Now where were we?"

Small fists banging on the door broke them apart. "I may have to go back East and persuade ol' Brad with Marge's .38." He held up both hands. "Just fooling."

Katie tucked her shirt into her jeans with shaking hands. At that moment, Luke's joke seemed to have real merit.

Today's competition was less shocking to Katie after her introduction the night before. As Jo had predicted, Wes Jenkins worked the arena with his fellow bullfighters, apparently unhindered by the row of stitches along his jaw. The event ended with no one carried out of the arena. Missy and JJ counted themselves the biggest winners, taking home a sparkly pink cowgirl hat and a miniature bull rider's vest signed by the cowboys.

"What do you say, Katie?" Tom loaded their bags into the van. "Would you go to another event?"

"On my own, maybe not. With family, absolutely. Thanks for including me."

"You're as close to family now as not—just a matter of time," Jo said.

"From your mouth to God's ear," Luke said, and they all laughed.

KATIE'S PHONE RANG the next morning a few minutes before she was ready to flip the sign on the Queen's door to Open. Her heart began to pound when she recognized her cousin's number.

"You want the good news or the bad news?" Greg asked.

"Bad—let's get it out of the way."

"Your husband bounced on more beds than the test pilot for a mattress factory. The good news is that you've got enough evidence to make him beg for an uncontested divorce."

She should be delighted, but all she felt was shame and sadness that she had been so oblivious.

"Katie? You there?"

"Of course. Could you deliver a hard copy to my lawyer?" She gave him Mr. Foster's office address. "And send one by registered mail to my post office box. I don't want any chance of this leaking out."

"I don't know why not. He sure doesn't deserve any breaks."

"You're right, but he'll be more reasonable if I show I'm not out to humiliate him. And a million thanks—I knew I could count on you."

"My pleasure, cuz."

Katie went through the rest of the day on autopilot, jerked into reality only when Mr. Foster called shortly after two o'clock.

"Your cousin delivered the documents, Kathryn—pretty damning. How do you want me to proceed?"

"You're the professional—just get me out of the marriage."

"You won't let me go for a settlement? You're entitled—"

"I've got everything I need right here. Tell his lawyer how lucky Brad is I'm not trying to nail his hide to the barn door."

Foster laughed. "I believe you've learned a new language out there."

"I've learned a lot out here. Now get me cut loose."

Marge entered the kitchen. "You don't get many phone calls. That one sure put stars in your eyes."

"My cousin came through for me and took what he found to my lawyer. Could you get by if I have to make a fast trip to Connecticut?"

"Of course I can, and if I can't I'll put a Closed for Vacation sign on the door. Go do what you have to."

"Right now I have to call Luke." She punched

in his cell number. "I need to see you," she said without preamble.

"Is ten minutes soon enough? I'm at Mike's office. He's orienting me to some of the work I could do for him."

"Ten seconds would suit me better, but I'll try to be patient."

"Maybe these braces can be programmed for running."

Seven minutes later Luke stepped through the door. "Spit it out, girl. This better be good."

She did an impromptu war dance around him. "Greg got what I need to pressure Brad. My lawyer's going to talk to his lawyer. With luck, I should be Katie Gabriel again in two shakes of a lamb's tail, as Auntie Rose says. But I'll have to fly to Connecticut."

"You want me to go with you?"

"Yes, but no. Your being there would just confuse the issue. I have to do this on my own."

He studied the fake Persian rug in front of the door. "You'll come back?"

She took his face between her hands. "I'll come back."

THE PROCESS TOOK a bit longer than two shakes of a lamb's tail, but two weeks later Katie spotted Greg waiting for her at Hartford's Bradley International Airport.

He took her small suitcase. "You packed light."

"I'm staying only long enough for the hearing tomorrow and to turn the house over to you. I'll show you a few things I'd like shipped to Colorado if you can do that for me. I'm glad my plane was on time so we can take care of the deed with Mr. Foster this afternoon."

Katie studied the thirty miles from the airport to her mother's house as if viewing a foreign landscape—the traffic, the endless succession of mini malls and chain restaurants, the close horizons hemming in a sky dull with early summer humidity and exhaust fumes. The serene blue of Colorado skies and the endless vistas had spoiled her for the East. Her home now lay a day's drive west of I-25.

At least the tree-shaded road leading to her mother's house harkened back to happy childhood memories. Bikes with training wheels now sat beside the back door, and a rope swing hung from a branch of the apple tree. The perennial border had doubled in size—Greg's wife must like flowers—and a plot planted with young tomatoes and peppers made a brave showing in the sunny spot next to the carriage house.

Allie greeted them at the back door. "The kids are with my mom while we take care of business," she said. "Our appointment is in an hour, so you have time to powder your nose and have a cup of tea. I made blueberry muffins."

The Mercedes crept up the driveway so softly that Katie didn't notice it until the door slammed. Brad approached with his hands held palms outward to show he meant no harm.

"With the hearing tomorrow morning, I knew you'd be flying in today. Please, could we talk a few minutes? And I need to show you something."

The sadness in his face made Katie bite back bitter words begging for release. "There's nothing left to say, Brad. We'll tidy up the loose ends tomorrow and move on."

"Please," he said again. "An hour of your time."

"We have an appointment in an hour."

"Half an hour, then. A short ride with me."

Greg stepped forward, every inch a Marine. "I don't think so."

"Believe me, I mean Kathryn no harm."

"Mister, I was an MP—you wouldn't believe the things I've seen. It takes just a second..." He aimed a phantom gun.

"Search me." Brad held his arms out. "Search my car—no weapons."

Greg did and then came back. "Tell you what—Allie and I can follow in our car. Once he gets this out of his system, you ride to Mr. Foster's office with us."

Katie walked to Brad's car before the discussion got heated; Brad nodded and followed her. If this last act would help end the connection between them, she would humor him. She wasn't exactly afraid, but a trickle of apprehension crawled between her shoulder blades. He'd never raised his hand to her, although she had seen him grab tools from workers' hands for sloppy work and push dozer operators out of their seats to do the job himself. What if he—

He climbed behind the wheel and turned to her with a strained smile. "Half an hour, I promise." He started the engine and drove away at a crawl with Greg's Wagoneer close behind.

"I've put the house on the market," he said.

She stifled a dozen stinging comments that

leaped to mind. "You should get a good price for it," she said.

Brad drove through the village center and out toward what remained of farmland beyond, now carved into mini estates with a few colonial and nineteenth-century farmhouses on greatly reduced acreages. He pulled into an unpaved lane and braked beside a Federal home with peeling white paint set in a grove of hardwoods. A massive red barn loomed behind the house, and a stone springhouse crouched beside a pond dimpling in the summer sunlight.

"Built in 1814, with eighteen acres left of the original farm," he said. "The barn needs a little work—you could keep horses here if you like. And there's an old herb garden in back. The house is a little rough on the outside, but the architectural details haven't been touched. All it needs is some TLC to bring it back."

The house of her dreams, once.

"Would you like to see the interior? I have the key."

Alarm bells clanged in her mind. "No, thanks."

"I was afraid you'd say that." He reached across her, and she resisted the impulse to shrink away.

"I took some photos, if you'd like to look." He pulled a manila envelope from the glove box and held it out to her.

"I'm sorry, Brad. It's too late. If you put this kind of effort into a new relationship, you'll do fine."

He pitched the envelope into the backseat. "I should have known better. Get out. Go back to your new ragtag friends and family."

The last shreds of regret fell away. "I believe I will," she said. She left his car, closing the door with a gentle touch, and climbed into Greg's vehicle. "You guys ready to buy a house?"

CHAPTER THIRTY-THREE

LUKE STOOD AT the airport perimeter fence and watched the tiny speck become a toy plane which quickly grew to full size as it floated over the end of the runway. He'd spent a couple bad nights during Katie's absence, still unable to believe she would return until he saw her walk through the security portal.

She had called after Garrison's last-ditch effort and again after the divorce had been finalized the next day. Even with her reassurances, Luke had prepared himself to accept that, surrounded by childhood memories, she might decide there was no place like home.

He turned and set a good pace toward the terminal—a fine welcome if she didn't see him waiting for her. He reached the lobby just as she came hurrying down the concourse trailing her rolling bag behind her. For a moment he reveled in watching her unaware, her head held high and her eyes scanning right and left. Then she saw him, and a smile lit her face and his heart like sunrise after a dark night.

She dropped the handle of her bag and ran to him, giving him the kiss he'd been waiting for, free and unafraid.

"Oh, it's so good to be home," she said when they broke apart.

She retrieved her bag and linked her arm in his, snuggling against him like a giddy teenager. Truth was, he felt about seventeen himself.

"I gotta take care of something before we go any farther," he said, pulling a small box from his pocket. Steadying himself with a hand against the wall, he dropped to one knee and opened the box. "Katie Gabriel, will you marry me?"

She looked into his face, tears shimmering in her eyes. "You know I will."

He slipped the modest diamond solitaire on her finger. "Marge loaned me this so I could do it right. We can pick out whatever suits you together."

"Nothing expensive," she said. "I don't need flashy jewelry." She helped him to his feet and into her arms.

"My car's here," she said after a kiss to seal their promise. "I suppose I should go to work."

"Shelby's helping Marge today. She dropped me off to meet you. The day is ours to spend any way we want."

She giggled.

"Okay, maybe not any way we want, but you can take time to catch up with yourself. What's your second choice?"

"You're really okay with my buying into the Queen?"

"Please don't ask me that again. I'm Luke, not Brad."

The brightness on her face faded a little. "He seemed so sad I almost felt sorry for him. Until he turned ugly."

"No 1814 houses in Durango," Luke said, throttling both anger and relief. "But how about we look at some properties I scoped out while you were gone? If you're going to run a business here, you can't commute from the ranch, especially in winter."

"You wouldn't mind living in town? Won't your dad need you?"

"Once you and Marge get everything organized, you'll be able to take a couple days off at a time, and I can stay at the ranch during the busy times like calving season. Maybe we'll board Dude and Dawn closer to town so we can ride out for an evening."

"And if you're going to take accounting classes and work for Mike..." She clicked open her car doors. "I'll drive, you navigate. Where to, boss?"

He directed her to several addresses in and near Durango. Each had points to recommend it, but none seemed to click with her. "I don't mean to be fussy," she said, "but I grew up in a house with history. These newer ones leave me cold."

"One more to look at." He gave directions to the older part of town then onto a street she knew well. "Pull over here," he said. "What do you think?"

"I think I'm dreaming—that's Marge's house."

"By golly, you're right. Could you stand to live there?"

"With Marge? I guess we could make that work," she said after a moment's hesitation.

"Well, I don't—I want you all to myself. Marge says she's tired of keeping up a house. She's talking about moving into the apartment. She checked into putting a mini elevator from the cellar up through the kitchen to the second floor—not as expensive as you'd think. Easier to bring supplies up from the storeroom, too."

"If we can swing it..."

"How about the payments from your mother's house?" He took her hand. "Living here would mean a lot to me, too. I spent many an evening in that kitchen when I was a wild young buck, whipping up the nerve to go home."

"Do you think Marge would mind if we went in? There's a key in the garden shed."

"Like this one?" He dangled it in front of her eyes.

"You planned this all along."

"Just saving the best till last," he said.

ON A GOLDEN day in early September, Luke stood under the giant cottonwood at Cameron's Pride with his father and brother beside him, letting his eyes range over the crowd gathered for the wedding.

Most of the guests had been here for Auntie Rose's birthday, plus townspeople from Durango who were now Katie's friends.

Luke's fellow bullfighters had made a flying trip from this weekend's PBR event, along with Doc Barnett, who stood chatting with Luke's physical therapist. Jake and Shelby had welcomed members of Katie's family, including her cousin Greg and his wife with their two small boys, who stood goggle-eyed at the sight of real-life cowboys as well as the Camerons' Ute relatives.

Since Katie's return from Connecticut, buying Marge's house, setting up the partnership in the Silver Queen and his rehab had run parallel courses at breakneck speed. The wheelchair was now being used by a teenager in Hesperus recovering from a tractor rollover. The braces had been returned to Denver, and Luke was managing well with a cane.

A murmur swept through the crowd as Katie came toward Luke on her cousin's arm, as beautiful as a dream in Emily Ruston's wedding dress. Although they had met less than six months ago, each had traveled many miles in pain and joy to reach this moment.

If Brad Garrison's faithlessness hadn't driven her from their marriage, she would likely have lived out her days more or less content but never knowing real fulfillment.

Except for his fateful encounter with Side-winder, he would have been working an event somewhere across the country when she arrived carrying her mother's letters.

He'd still been a kid despite his hard years on the road; now he understood what it took to be a man. He stepped forward and joined hands with Katie as they faced the minister together.

* * * * *

Be sure to check out the rest of the
CAMERON'S PRIDE *books by*
Helen DePrima: INTO THE STORM
and THE BULL RIDER.

Available at Harlequin.com.

Get 2 Free Books,

Plus 2 Free Gifts— just for trying the Reader Service!

LI17R